Laura and the Enchanted Forest

P.A. Jackson

Second Edition

June 2020

For Linda

lily of the valley

&

Emilia

Table of Contents

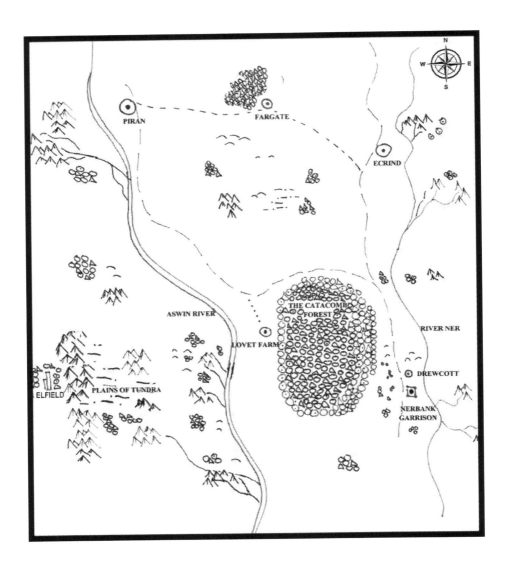

Chapter 1

Laura and the wolves.

In an isolated farmhouse, next to an enchanted forest, Laura hurries from her bedroom into the family room to greet her parents. Today, the twenty-first of March is her eleventh birthday. Laura enters the family room, which is next to the kitchen. She is looking forward to seeing what her parents have made for her. They always present her with beautiful gifts.

Her mother Martha was preparing breakfast, a short slender woman with soft cool hands, 'good for making pastry' she always says. Her long wavy hair, like golden honey, flowed around her shoulders. She is thirty-six years of age. She has laid out four bowls of steaming hot oatmeal, and one bowl of gruel for Casper, Morgan's faithful dog. After eating, Martha took Laura's hand and led her into the great room.

The room, a little shabby, was seldom used. In the centre stood a long and ancient table, surrounded by eight time-worn chairs. On this table, Laura's presents were laid out. Raoul, her father, presented her with a new pair of leather boots. They were tan coloured with fleece inners; he had created them himself. A skilled tanner, his hands seasoned and lined from years of farming.

Martha gave her a gold dyed tunic with yellow crisscross stitching across the centre. "It's a little large, but you will grow into it. You are growing so fast; you're are almost as tall as me; you take after your father."

She tied a matching headband across her forehead, pulling around her light auburn, shoulder-length hair. "To keep your hair nice and tidy."

1

Like Raoul, she had made these items herself.

Hugging both parents, with a sparkle of appreciation in her eyes, she smiled, "thanks—they're beautiful."

The other person living on the farm was Morgan, her uncle; six foot six inches tall, lean, and intelligent. He was Laura's teacher. Every day, from early morning until noon, he taught Laura. After lessons, he helped his brother working the land. Morgan told Laura he had a special gift, but she would have to wait until midday when her lessons finished.

Its early spring and the sun had started to warm the soil. Today's lesson is outside, Morgan and Laura leave the farmhouse, watched by Martha and Raoul. Laura ran ahead, weaving down the unhurried slope, her arms outstretched like a swift on the wind.

Martha smiled, "our daughter is growing into a young woman. Remember the time Morgan gave her a wooden doll he had carved from a piece of timber?"

"Yes, it was five years ago; even at that age she was tactful, telling Morgan it was too intricate to play with, and she would keep it as a decoration on her cabinet. She always favours and appreciates practical gifts."

"I wish I had been able to bear more children; she would have loved a brother or sister."

"She will make friends when we eventually move, the farmhouse is almost beyond repair."

Martha sighed, "It's so idyllic here. Laura loves the countryside; I don't think she would enjoy living in a town."

‡

With Casper at their heels, they make for the open field that drops to the great Aswin river. Here they sit, next to a Willow tree; so, Casper, a small bristly haired caramel coloured dog who looked like an old man, with his catlike whiskers could lie in its shade. Today she learned about flora and fauna. Laura absorbed everything Morgan had to teach. She studied diligently, but today was different. Morgan sat and talked about the flora in the surrounding fields, but Laura couldn't contain her excitement. She knew he had something special, his gifts were always unusual and useful. The pain of waiting all morning became unbearable. The sun had now reached its peak.

"Morgan, it must be midday now, what is my birthday gift?" asked Laura.

"It's near enough," said Morgan, reaching into his black leather pouch he had around his neck. "I've been making this for six weeks; you will never see another one like it."

He pulled out a rope, a thin strong rope.

"Put it around your shoulder, how does it sit?" he asked.

Laura's eyes glowed, "It's incredibly light, like gossamer, I don't know it's there. Thank you, it should be useful."

"Take care of it, a rope is an essential item to have. I see you climbing trees and small cliffs, you have learnt well, and you know all your knots. Take this for safety and use it wisely."

Laura gave Morgan a hug, "your gifts are always useful, thank you."

Laura was allowed to play where she liked, except the Catacomb forest, which ran alongside the farm. 'It's enchanted, there are many dangerous and mystical beasts inside' they told her. The roar of a mighty beast echoed in her room at night. Recently she had heard the cackle of a strange ghoulish cry.

When Laura wasn't being taught, she usually played by the great Aswin river that flowed by the lower meadow. She skimmed flat stones across to reach the opposite bank. Laura was an exceptional swimmer. From the age of nine, she had been swimming to the large flat rock that protruded in the middle of the river, like a giant lily pad. She would often sit on the rock; she named the yearning edge and wonder what life was like on the unknown land. What animals lived there, trees to climb.

Laura decided she was now old enough to explore the other side of the river. She placed her clothes into a bag made from tanned rabbit hides she carried on her back and swam to the flat rock. Pausing for a moment, she warily studied the opposite bank. She slid off the lily pad rock into the cool water and swam to the opposite bank.

She climbed out of the river, sat and dressed.

The land, not unlike Laura's side of the river, the flora wild and verdant. Clumps of dense sedges bordered the water's edge; wild ryegrass covered the ground. The air carried the scent of camellia and primroses. Her heart pounded with a mixture of trepidation, excitement and fear. She ventured around the cluster of birch trees, always keeping the river in sight. At first, she never ventured far into this country, after a few days, she moved further inland making sure she could still hear the roar of the water as it swirled around the yearning edge rock. As the days passed Laura ventured deeper and deeper into this new landscape. She saw the overgrown grasslands, small woodlands and a mountainous region. There were different types of animals living on this side of the river that Laura liked to watch. Hares with their leverets, she even spotted an elk grazing in a field near the river.

Laura had scrambled up a common ash. She loved being at the top of trees, viewing the landscape. At the base of an old crab apple tree, she spotted a pack of weasels playing with their young. A yelp came from above, the weasels scattered. Laura looked up and saw, on a crag beside the tree, a young white animal on a narrow ledge. A tree sapling had rooted on this ledge, this must have

4

broken the animal's fall, from there he managed to crawl onto the ledge.

Higher up Laura saw a much wider trail, with a cave, and a path leading around the edge. She scratched her chin. *The whelp must have ventured too near the brink, lost its footing and fell. If the young animal slipped from the narrow ledge, it wouldn't survive such a fall. How can I help?*

Laura wanted to help the baby animal; he wouldn't be able to survive on that ledge, before long he'd tire and fall. She always carried the birthday rope coiled around her shoulder and waist. With the aid of the rope, she would save the small animal. The tree she had climbed grew adjacent to the crag.

Nearby she saw a shrub clinging to the crag. She tied the rope around the trunk of the tree and twisted it around a branch, the other end wrapped around her waist. Balancing on a thick branch, she inched herself along until the branch started to sag. From that point, Laura made a flying leap, her left hand wrapped around the shrub, her right hand slides into a nearby crack. Her feet scramble around trying to find two footholds. She hung there for a few moments, taking in deep breaths. Loosening the rope, Laura began climbing up, by sliding her slender fingers into crevices and gripping shelves.

It didn't take long to reach the ledge. She swung around and sat a little way from the animal, which she now recognised as a white wolf pup. Sitting on the algae-covered ledge, Laura looked down with no fear.

The pup, shivering with apprehension, edged away from Laura.

She spoke softly, "don't be scared little one, I've come to help you!"

Gradually reaching her arm out, Laura gently stroked the back of his shiny body. His fur, which was pure white, felt as soft as a feather. He scampered towards Laura, dipping his head into her hand. Now he wasn't so agitated, she picked him up and held him tenderly against her body. The pup became tranquil. He looked up at her with his bright blue eyes.

Laura was unaware there were two pairs of eyes blazing down from the wolfs cave above, watching her every move.

She tucked the cub inside her new tunic, his paws stretched around her body. He could feel her heartbeat, and she his.

Laura realised the downward climb would prove to be more difficult, especially with the wolf pup inside her tunic. As she envisaged, the journey down proved to be much harder. Carefully stretching to each foothold, step by step, she eventually reached the part where her rope bridged the tree and the crag. From this point, she easily lowered herself to the ground.

Exhaling a sigh of relief and satisfaction, she falls to her knees, throwing both hands out onto the ground, gasping air into her lungs. A rasping sound filled her ears. She raised her eyes and jerked backwards, falling onto her rear. Two large white wolves were waiting at the foot of the tree. As she grasped the size of these wolves, she realised the dangerous situation she was in. They stood the size of a small horse, towering above her. Squatting on the floor, looking up at the teeth of these animals made her body tremble.

The largest wolf, named Baron, was getting agitated and wanted to strike Laura to get his pup back. He started scraping his paws into the earth, snarling, baring his fangs, blood dripping from his teeth from the morning's kill. The hairs on his back raised, getting ready to spring. He was heavily built, mostly white but with black ears. His eyes were grey, he was a strong aggressive wolf. He stared intensely through the slits of his eyes at Laura, who, with trembling hands, was undoing her tunic.

Sheena, the other wolf, pushed hard against Baron's side and nipped his ear; with a husky deep-throated murmur said, "wait! This child has a kindly heart, Kylo would have died if this human hadn't got him down, we couldn't have saved him. If you kill this child, others will come looking."

To Laura, it sounded like a series of growls.

Sheena, an impressive-looking wolf, pure white fur, and sharp icy blue eyes, just like her pup. With the gift of insight, she had an excellent scent awareness. She could also sense feelings and traverse her mind across distances. She was descended from the Longclaw white clan.

They both stood towering above Laura, as they communicated, all she heard were barks.

Laura was looking for branches to grab and wondering how fast she could get up the tree but realised with the cub in her tunic they would certainly attack. Reaching inside her tunic to release the cub, her hands shaking like an unset jelly, she took the cub and placed it onto the ground. The pup looked back at her with his lively blue eyes. She was breathing rapidly now. Although terrified of these enormous wolves, she gave the pup a gentle prod to encourage him to return to his parents.

"Take our baby home," Sheena bayed.

Baron picked up his cub between his teeth, with a sideward scowl at Laura, walked away.

Sheena moved closer to Laura's face, almost touching her nose. She bore into her eyes, emitted a low guttural sound, then followed Baron. Had she been able to understand, Sheena was telling her to leave, and never return. She watched the wolves walking away, leaving her alive. Laura had never been so frightened in all her life.

Slowly getting to her feet, she pushed both trembling hands against a tree, trying to calm herself. She gritted her teeth to stop her jawbone from having spasms. Walking back to the river with a knotted stomach, she was startled when a woodpecker started drilling a tree. She dashed for the safety of the river, expecting to feel those large teeth around her body.

Will they tear at my body; fight over my bones? terrible thoughts entered her mind.

Reaching the riverbank, without a pause, she silently plunged into the river. The current dragged her downstream, taking in a lungful of air as she sank below the surface; swimming underwater, she steadily reached the opposite bank in one go. Her head shot out of the water, gulping air into her lungs. Climbing out of the river, with heart-pounding as if to burst out of her chest, she collapsed onto the grassy bank. There she lay, on her back, in sodden clothes, glancing across the river. Breaking out into a cold sweat, deciding to never again cross the river.

‡

After several weeks Morgan asked Laura, "where's your rope? I haven't seen you with it recently, have you lost it?"

"No, it's safe, I know exactly where it is," replied Laura.

It was still attached to the common ash tree when she rescued the wolf pup, but retrieving it would be another dilemma. It's dangerous and foolhardy to go back where two fiercely huge wolves lived. She knew Morgan wondered why she hadn't got the rope, but shivered at the idea of crossing the river again.

Every afternoon Laura continued to wander around the meadow and woods, watching the foxes at play, or studying the small insects in the surrounding fields. Often, she would creep along the riverbank, spying on the small animals, shrews, voles and toads. Laura's eyes were constantly drawn to the opposite bank. She would often peer across the river, into the distant forest, eager to catch sight of the wolf cub, hoping he was safe and in good health.

Another few days passed, Laura experienced a desire inside her head, pulling her to the opposite side of the river. Against her better judgement, Laura decided to try to recover her rope. She set about making a craft to aid crossing the river and ensure a speedier return. With vines and logs she collected from a nearby woodland, she constructed a simple craft that would carry her across the river. With a strip of wood from the farm, she crafted a paddle. After two days, everything was ready.

She launched the raft into the river. She climbed in, it uneasily bobbed on the water as she paddled across. On reaching the other bank, she moved silently and furtively to the tree and her rope. She scrambled up, removed the rope, and slung it around her shoulder and slithered back down to the solid ground. With the rope safely back in her possession, she breathed a little easier, making her way back to the river, running as fast and as stealthily as possible.

When she was halfway between the river and the tree, a white wolf bounded out of the bushes, hitting her chest, knocking her to the ground. Alarm bolted through her bones. Half sitting up she tried to scuttle backwards, slipping onto her back. Far from attacking Laura, he was frolicking around her; then he jumped onto her lap. She realised it was the pup she had saved from the ledge.

"Goodness you have grown, you're much heavier now."

He sat on Laura, looking into her eyes. He remembers me; she hugged him.

"This could be dangerous, perhaps we can play by the great river, I would feel safer there," she muttered to herself, and the pup.

The wolf pup jumped up and ran towards the river. A surprised Laura followed him across the countryside to the river bank. He jumped into the river, Laura followed, they splashed and frolicked together in the water. Afterwards, they played fetch, Laura throwing sticks for the wolf to retrieve; she made a fuss of him, caressing his back and stomach.

"I must go home now."

As Laura crossed the river, the pup gave a plaintive howl.

Laura looked back, "I'll come back tomorrow, at the same time, if you're here we can play again." She looked on, stunned the pup became excited. *He appeared to understand every word I said.*

The next day after her lessons with Morgan, she raced to the river and her craft. There, standing on the opposite bank, stood the wolf pup.

After playing for a while, Laura said, "I need to call you something, you're as white as snow, so I will name you Snowy."

Although his wolf name was Kylo, he readily accepted Laura calling him Snowy. He always came running to Laura when she called him.

A week passed by and Laura sharp understanding perceived Snowy was intelligent and quick at learning. She also found him following her words with awareness.

Whilst playing she looked him in the eye, "can you understand me? no, you can't—can you?"

She cocked her head as he softly whined.

Deciding to test Snowy, she walked him further downstream, to a bend in the river and said, "meet me here tomorrow."

The next day, as Laura approached the bend, Snowy was waiting to greet her.

Laura queried, "can you understand what I'm saying?"

He responded by kneeling and stretching his front legs out.

"Are we friends?" asked Laura.

Snowy started yelping.

"This is extraordinary, I hope your parents won't attack me if they find us playing together."

Snowy looked at Laura plaintively, then jumped up, resting his paws on her shoulders.

During the following days and weeks, Laura and Snowy continued to meet and play by the river bank. Their bond got stronger by the day. This was Laura's first friend and the first mate for Snowy.

As she looked back one day, she realised that Snowy had matured into a young and large wolf.

Chapter 2

Zee, the sorceress.

In a village called Fargate, twelve days walk, north-west of Ecrind lives a seventeen-year-old girl called Zee. Tall and majestic, she had long black woollen hair cascading past her hips, wine red lips, and orb-like hazel eyes. Her complexion was a soft blushing pink, she wore on each finger a bright blueberry glass coloured ring.

For two years Zee had visited Maya the witch who lived in the woods, called Fargate forest.

She pounded on her door late one night, begging the witch to teach her how to mix potions and teach her spell-casting. "I want to learn for the good of my village, and to help people the best I can," said Zee.

Maya answered the door dressed in a long loose-fitting dress. It hung like a black wave with a bleeding water snake around the hem. "Go away, the village will defile me if I teach a child."

Zee persisted, "I will be discreet, no one will follow me, it will be our secret."

Maya, with a rusty voice, said, "no," and slammed the door.

Every day Zee hammered on the witch's door, "let me in, I want to learn."

After twenty days Maya, exasperated, opened the door, "knowledge does not come cheap, there is a price to pay."

"I have no coins, isn't there another way?"

"You will be my maid; you will be bonded to me."

"Yes, anything."

"You will gather my ingredients, herds and such like from the forest."

"Yes."

"You will clean for me, be my cook."

Zee cautiously agreed to all of Maya's demands.

Maya, in return, reluctantly agreed to teach Zee to be a sorceress. "You must come here cloaked, undercover of the twilight shadows and always enter by the back door."

At every opportunity, she stole away at dusk, stopping until dawn. Maya often retired to bed early, but Zee stayed up, examining the potions, reading Maya's books, and finding out where the ingredients for potions grew.

It was late evening, Maya had retired for the night, Zee was busy mixing potions in the cabin. Maya was awakened by the jangle of a ladle stirring liquid in a beaker, and Zee chanting.

Maya crept into the room, "I could hear you mixing potions, what are you doing?"

Looking around, Maya saw with horror the various herbs and vegetation Zee was using, hemlock, bloodroot, John's wort, sulphur, and many more. "Zee, what are you doing? Those are dangerous ingredients when mixed." Her raven eyes widened. "You're making a transformation and an obedience potion." She pointed a bony finger at the vials, "and a shrinking potion within, why; what's going to happen with three different enchantments mixed?"

"I don't care what materialises, I'm getting my revenge," cried out Zee.

Her real reason for learning sorcery was her plan to exact revenge upon those that had mocked and taunted her since she was a child. Zee let all her misery pour out, the years of name calling, cruelty, tears and loneliness.

From an early age, they ridiculed her for her attractiveness. The children in the village were jealous of her good looks and always called her names like skinny Zee a walking skeleton and goblin face. She always feared going out, no assurances from her parents could help, she always ran away in tears when the name calling started. This only made them do it more, shouting more vicious, hateful and revolting names, whenever she ventured out.

She turned on Maya, "they would spit and call me names. They told me to leave the village because they said I had dragon breath and it makes them ill! They once tried to drown me! I was alone, walking by a river when five appeared, they beat me, grabbed my arms and legs and then threw me into the river, I couldn't swim! I was washed towards some reeds where I was able to crawl out. They would slap and beat me whenever they could." Zee pounding the tabletop declaring, "they're bullies and deserve my revenge, they act like monsters so I'm going to turn them all into little slimy bugs. Now go back to bed, you're not stopping me!"

"No," Maya replied sharply, "I will get the blame, I forbid it, leave now, and don't return."

"Not without my revenge potions," shouted Zee.

Maya gripped Zee's sylphlike arm and tried to throw her out of the cabin. Zee smashed her fist into Maya's cushiony stomach, forcing her to release her arm. Maya tried to wrap her hands around Zee's neck, but Zee, with the palms of her hands, pushed Maya's face back, almost snapping her neck. Zee stepped forward, swung her fist hard into Maya's face, breaking one of her glass rings. Maya fell back onto the table containing the potions. Several vials

14

containing her revenge potions fell onto the stone floor and smashed, spilling the contents over the flagstones. Zee grabbed another vial of processed moonflower and hollyhock seed and threw it at Maya. The vial smashed on Maya's weather-worn face, cutting into her skin. The liquid ran down the gullies of her wrinkles and seeped into the scratches the vial had caused.

Maya screamed as she fell to the floor, with blood trickling from her cheeks and nose, "you fool, idiot—crazy stupid girl."

Zee stood shaking, her face red, eyes bulging, grabbed the remaining vessels containing her revenge potions.

Maya, with hand raised, swirled her fingers gesturing towards Zee, ranting, "uoy ot esrever."

"What are you mumbling? You silly old hag; you've broken my vials; I've only got three left!"

Tumbling out of the cabin she shouts back, "hateful old crone, I will get my revenge against the three ringleaders."

Running into the woods, Zee found a clearing just inside Fargate forest that was surrounded by seven hazel trees. She prepared the grassy clearing by delicately placing tiny stones in circles. The three vials containing the potions for each of her guests were hidden behind a tree root that was protruding from the forest floor. A fourth vial containing only water was placed apart from the others. This was for herself.

Returning to the village, she tentatively approached her worst three enemies.

Smiling sweetly, "you keep asking me where I go each day, well I will tell you; I visit my fairy friends."

They started laughing, "you are a silly hideous girl," as they pointed fingers and distorted their faces.

"Look at this," she said, holding out her hand, disclosing the tiny gemstones she had stolen from Maya's collection.

"They gave me these gems, the last time I saw them!"

One night in Maya's cabin, Zee discovered a secret compartment in the storeroom. Inside were several tiny gemstones. She grabbed a few, intending to entice the tormentors to her snare.

Lily tried to snatch one, but Zee closed her hand saying, "if you want one, you will have to meet the fairies yourself."

Lily, fidgeting, looked at the other two, "shall we go?"

"It won't hurt to look," said Liz, nodding at Rowan. "If she's lying, we can beat her with sticks and roll her in the mud."

Zee led the way, leading the three victims to her carefully staged spot inside Fargate forest.

"This is where I meet the fairies," beckoned Zee, "look they always leave watermelon to drink, it tastes amazing."

Zee picked the vial containing plain water and handed the three revenge potions to her victims.

She drank the plain water in one gulp, saying, "that tasted delicious."

As Liz, Rowan and Lily drank the potion, Zee jumps upon a fallen tree trunk and recites her curse.

"Stone and bone,

Ugly and foul,

You will be,

Servants to me."

"Now vengeance is mine," she shouted in joyful delight.

"W—what's happening to us," stammered the three wide-eyed victims, as they felt the effects of Zee's spell.

A blinding blue light emitted from the revenge vials, and shot into Zee's body, sending her tumbling back behind the tree trunk.

uoy ot esrever suddenly became clear to Zee, *reverse to you, the hag has hexed the potions back to me.*

Grabbing the trunk, she tried to scramble back up, her head just peering over the tree trunk. The three victims watched Zee's transformation, as her eyes turned from hazel to dark brown, to jet black. They screamed and tried to run, they all fell to the ground, unable to move.

"Help, help, someone—please help me," begged Liz, putting her hands over her face as tears filled her eyes.

A cold sweat ran through Lily. She pleaded, "I'm sorry, I won't say nasty things anymore, please stop. Let me go home."

Terror crept over Rowan's face. He cried and called for his mom. Lily put her arms around him as they all crumbled to the floor, and one by one they fell unconscious, including Zee.

‡

Something prodding her sharply in the back awakened Zee. She rolled over; the dawn sun broke through the canopy, casting smoky shadows in the clearing. Putting her hand to her face, she saw, not her slender fingers and pink nails, but twisted bony storks with green fingernails.

Her heart shuddered. *So, the hag hexed my potions.* She sobbed.

"What shall we do for you mistress?"

Zee sat up, "who said that?" she asked swirling her head.

There stood three stone-like scrawny creatures with thin bony arms and legs. They had shrunken and were no taller than Zee's knees.

"Is that you Liz, Lily, Rowan?" asked Zee, gingerly touching one of the creatures with her long green nail.

There was no response. They looked blankly at Zee, who unsteadily got to her feet.

"Go home," snapped Zee, pointing in the direction of the village.

"We are your servants," they answered, "we follow you."

Zee, hoping to get help, walked towards Maya's cabin, with the three creatures scampering along.

They looked a sinister group walking through Fargate forest, led by Zee. She was still tall, but now she had a scrawny misshapen body. Her hair was white and dishevelled, with a few black streaks, a reminder of its former colour. Her skin, lemon-like was covered in grey flecks. During the transformation she had clawed at her clothes, they now hung torn and shredded. Unlike her three victims, the hex had only taken her body, not her mind, it had become weaker bouncing from her three victims.

When they reached Maya's dwelling, the door swayed loosely on its hinges. Stepping into the cabin, Zee saw it was empty, Maya had fled in terror, believing she would be blamed for Zee's actions. Zee, knowing she could never return home, decided to empty the cabin of anything useful Maya had left.

"You two imps," she yelled, "collect those books, you!" pointing at the third, "collect those potions."

Whilst the imps were doing Zee's biddings, she mixed another batch of her transformation, shrinking and obedience potion. She poured the elixir into twelve vials and placed them into her body pouch. Everything that Zee required was bagged up and carried out, Zee with most on a backpack, the imps carrying what they could.

‡

That morning, in the village, everyone was out looking for the four missing youngsters.

"I saw them heading towards Fargate forest yesterday," said Will the carter.

Everyone from the village was now heading towards the forest, making for the witch's cabin. They found the door unlocked and wide open. Inside they saw all the broken vials and liquids covering the floor. There were speckles of blood everywhere, under the broken, upturned table, shards of Zee blueberry ring.

Zee's mother knelt picking up the broken glass, trying to hold back the tears, sniffled, "they must have put up a fight, but that witch has overpowered them."

All day they searched the forest, but no clues of their whereabouts were found, so they returned to the witch's cabin. Alvin the cartwright, with a flint, started the fire. Within minutes the witch's home was ablaze. The next day nothing remained but stone and ashes.

‡

Zee and the three imps had wandered the countryside for three weeks, living off wild berries. On the twenty-second night, Zee was awakened by shouting. Following the commotion, she made her way to the noisy men. Hiding behind a spiky hawthorn bush, Zee viewed three scruffy vagabonds sitting alongside a dusty road arguing. Turning to return, she was pulled by the hair and dragged out.

A fourth, spidery, young man, with a cauliflower ear and a broken nose, had discovered Zee.

19

"Look what I have found spying on us."

Zee quickly wrapped her cloak about herself, covering her face.

"What are you doing?"

"Nothing, I'm just a poor peasant."

"Well, that's a fancy cloak—what's in that bag?"

Hugging her bag said, "nothing!"

"Hand it here."

"No—it's mine."

He gave her a violent punch in the stomach. As she keeled forward squealing, he snatched it away.

Zee, kneeling, was agitated and shaking with anger.

"What's in all these vessels; is it a drink?"

The corner of her mouth twitched into a grin, "it's a new ale my family have made, I was taking samples to an alehouse hoping to get orders."

"We'll taste it first."

The four men grabbed a vial each and took a swig.

"That's a strange taste, it's not ale."

Zee sprang to her feet as they all fell to their knees.

"You robbers at night,

Steal from me you might,

You will be,

Servants to me."

The one that had discovered Zee was trying to crawl away. Zee grabbed his hair and yanked him over. She stood over him and threw back her cloak to reveal herself.

He screamed.

Zee stood in their midst, absorbing their actual essence as they started shrinking, losing their skin and turning into bony creatures.

Spreading her skeletal arms and bony fingers out, she went into a dreamlike state, "Ahhhh! this is rejuvenating me."

They lay on the dusty road unconscious, with no soul. Zee looked across the road, up and down as far as the eye could see was a dense forest. She returned to collect her three imps.

"Drag those thugs until they recover, they have joined our company."

They had arrived at the north edge of the Catacomb forest. Fearing nothing, she ventured into the forest and came across a maze. Wandering in, Zee soon got lost.

"You two," she said pointing at two of her imps, "find the way to the centre of this labyrinth."

They had just gone around the first corner when a sound of thunder shook the ground.

"There's a huge beast running this way," hissed one of the imps running back to Zee.

Zee fumbled inside her bag as the beast came skidding around the corner on all fours. He reared up, stabbing his black double curled horns between Zee's neck; trapping her against the trees. He was squat, powerful, and covered in coarse jet-black fur. He stank of animal blood and bone.

"What's a scrawny creature like you doing in Tad's labyrinth? I shall enjoy crunching your bones."

His face was touching Zee's face, steam was pouring from his nostrils covering Zee in mucus. Zee, with a vial of her potion in each hand, pushed them up into the minotaur's nostrils.

He staggered back on one knee, "what trickery is this?"

"Tomorrow morning you shall be the servant of Zee."

He fell onto all fours. "Never, I shall kill you first."

"Stone and bone,

Minotaur's home,

You will be,

Servant to me."

He tried to stand, gurgled, and collapsed onto the floor.

The curse recited, she turned her back on the minotaur and called the imps together.

"Learn the secret of the maze, and find the creatures home, now!"

Her obedient imps scampered around on all fours, scraping the soil and sniffing the way to the centre.

Zee entered the minotaur's lair, crunching discarded bones underfoot. "This," she said spreading her scraggy arms out, "will be our hideout, until I can find a cure for this hex."

Chapter 3

Barons anxiety.

In the woodlands, May bells and bloody warriors were in bloom. Laura wanted to take them home for her mother, but Morgan told her that flowers belong where they grow.

Arriving back at the farm, Martha said, "Raoul wants to speak to you, he's in the family room."

"Laura, do you want to accompany us to Ecrind, it's time for us to trade part of our crops for tools," asked Raoul. "Your mother agrees, it's time for you to travel and see the big town."

The prospect of going to a big town thrilled Laura, "is Morgan coming?"

"Yes, I have two handcarts to take, so I will need his help. We leave tomorrow morning."

With assorted vegetables and berries loaded into the carts, and plenty of Martha's bread, pies and treats, they started the journey. Not taking the road, they took the direct footpath by cutting across fields and meadows. Taking the journey twice a year, Raoul knew the best places to bed down, and the quickest route to take.

"This will be our first stop," said Raoul, "it's an old deserted bears cave."

After eating Martha's potato and carrot pie, they sat at the entrance watching the sunset.

"Have you ever told Laura the history of the farm, and the reason for the secret passages?" asked Morgan.

"No," replied Raoul, "this is a perfect opportunity."

"I've always wanted to know why our home has a secret passage," wondered Laura as she unrolled her sleeping mat, "And the secret hiding place behind the inglenook."

"Our ancestors once lived in the village called Drewcott, but they were in a petty feud with another farmer over a piece of land. It escalated, resulting in the men fighting our forefathers. They decided to leave the village to start a new life, taking a few of the villagers. After travelling for a few days, one man found this isolated region. The soil was good and fluffy, ideal for growing crops. They settled there, next to the Catacomb forest. They built the farmhouse and cultivated the land. Afraid that the villagers would find out where they had settled and attack, they dug a tunnel from the farmhouse, so they could escape into the forest. They also created hiding places within the farmhouse. One day, four of the settlers became curious about the forest and decided to go inside to investigate. There are dangerous beasts and supernatural beings within, they were told. The four men, ignoring the warnings, walked into the enchanted forest to investigate; they were never seen again. That's when the stone wall was built around the farmyard, but that didn't stop many from being anxious. One by one everybody left, apart from our family, we have continued to farm the land."

"How did you meet mother?" asked Laura.

"I met your mother by chance, her parents performed in a travelling show. Their wagon had crashed, and one wheel had shattered. They were on the Piran road at the end of our farm lane. I offered to repair the wheel, but it took several hours, so I gave them shelter for the night. Martha sat talking throughout the night, there was an instant connection between us. With the wagon repaired, she was preparing to leave. I asked your mother to stop, she readily agreed. We married a few months later."

‡

After six days they reached Ecrind around midday.

Laura's excitement soon waned as they walked into the town, amid the bustling activity. Her head swirled around as they strode down the narrow, cobbled alleyways, she hung tightly onto Raoul's arm. Her eyes darting upwards at the towering stone buildings that were tightly knitted together. Many more were made of stone and wood, and a few entirely of wood. Laura was getting nausea from the foul odour swirling up from the gutters.

Fighting for air, she gasped, "I can't breathe!"

"We're here now," said Morgan, pushing a door open, and pulling Laura inside.

"Sit here," he suggested, finding a stool.

"Have you a jug of water for this girl," he called to the merchant.

"A country girl used to the open spaces," the merchant said, handing Laura a pitcher of water.

He was a short man, with a chubby red face that bore a friendly smile. Laura smiled back and nervously sipped the water. Laura watched as Morgan and Raoul bartered with the merchant, they shook hands and exchanged goods.

Outside Laura wrapped both arms around Raoul's arm and shut her eyes as they walked away.

Casting his eyes at Laura, Morgan said to Raoul, "instead of finding a tavern, let's find somewhere on the outskirts to sleep."

‡

It was Summertime, Laura had just returned from Ecrind; it was a sunny afternoon. The sun had bleached the grass to straw, no rain had fallen for five weeks. Laura was just finishing her outdoor lesson under the Willow tree.

As Morgan and Casper made their way to the farmhouse, Laura ran, her heart pounding with excitement. Her craft was resting in the place she had moored it, hidden amongst the tall reeds. Pulling it out of the reeds, she jumped in and paddled hard to reach the opposite bank, eager to see her friend. She hadn't seen Snowy since going to Ecrind and was excited, fourteen days was a lifetime.

As she approached the riverbank, she stopped rowing. In the distance, she saw a large white wolf; she panicked. *His parents are here*. She stood on her craft, staring at the figure, *it's Snowy*.

He came rushing out of the undergrowth. For many days he had been waiting for Laura. They ran to meet each other like two young lovers, but this was a child and a large wild wolf. Laura put her arms around his neck, but now her hands no longer met at the back. Stepping back, she saw he was now a young adult and growing into a huge wolf, just like Baron and Sheena. They ran together, sprinting through the woodlands, leaping over a fallen tree trunk. Laura soon tired, so they strolled through the woods and grasslands, glad to be in each other's company.

Sheena and Baron unexpectedly emerged from behind a hawthorn bush. Laura froze, in her joy at seeing Snowy she had forgotten about his parents and had wandered deep into the forest. Baron curled his mouth, showing his chalk-white teeth as he glared at his son. With a disgusted expression, his front paw swiped at Laura, sending her smashing against a tree; knocking her unconscious.

Baron advanced towards her listless body; a pounding stab in his side from Snowy sent him rolling over.

Baron lay on his side, momentarily dazed. He sprang to his feet, facing his son. "I have no desire to fight you," he growled, "that human child was warned to stay away, she was a danger to our existence."

Snowy stood snarling at Baron, "you have killed my sister, I will rip you up into little pieces and eat your heart while it is still beating; prepare to fight."

Baron roared, "you call that useless human scrag your kin."

"She has been coming here because I wanted her here, I called across the river to her, using my power. She is my sister; I am her brother."

The heavy pungent smell of a broken family was festering in the air, as the two wolves circled each other, baring their teeth ready to fight.

Sheena jumped in between Baron and Kylo, her front legs splayed out snarled at Baron, "stop! This ground will soon be awash with our blood, back down."

Baron clawed at the soil; an intense storm raged in his grey eyes.

Sheena's icy blue eyes pierced into Baron, "lay one claw on me and it will be the last thing you do in your life."

Baron took a step back.

"Kylo has my powers, you will beat him, but his keen senses will alert him to your moves, he will inflict terrible injuries on you."

Turning to her son she bayed, "quell your anger, the child is still alive—cannot you sense it?"

Snowy lifted his nostrils and took in Laura's inner spirit. He ran to her side, with one eye on his father.

"There's a strong bond between those two," said Sheena, "come, let's leave, we will talk to Kylo later."

Baron agreed to leave, "maybe he will come to his senses, and keep away from that wasted and insignificant human child. I have no desire to fight our firstborn."

Kylo watched his parents leave, as Laura regained consciousness, dizzy and shaking she tried to stand, but fell to her knees. Not sure what Baron would do if he returned, he gripped the back of Laura's tunic, picked her up, and carried her to the river's edge, where he placed her. With his paw, he indicated she should wash her face with water, which she did, this helped to revive her.

Snowy snuggled up to Laura, they lay there for a short time. Laura got up to leave, he tried to tell Laura to go home and return tomorrow.

Laura finally understood and said, "I will be here tomorrow."

Snowy sprayed his front legs out, *Laura understood me.*

On the way home, Laura passed Morgan working in the vegetable plot.

"Those look nice cabbages," observed Laura, trying to sound normal.

Ignoring the question, "what happened to you?" asked Morgan.

Laura was limping and holding her side where Baron's paw had struck.

"I slipped and fell against a tree; I need to rest."

Morgan looked surprised, Laura never falls, but he let it pass and said, "go and rest yourself."

That night Laura had little sleep, her body ached, and she was badly bruised on the back. She was going to ask Martha for an ointment for the bruising but was worried about the awkward questions, so bore the pain.

‡

Kylo returned to the cave, Baron was sitting high above, at the top of the crag, his lookout. Sheena was lying a little way behind Baron. Kylo climbed up and sat beside Baron.

Baron spoke, "many seasons ago, through a pass in those mountains," nodding towards the horizon, "we lived with a large pack, then humans arrived with their long spears, swords and knives. They killed us for sport, and our fur, setting traps, digging pits. It was not a noble fight, many of our kin suffered a slow death. Elfin folk of the forest lived nearby, in their magical realm, hidden in the woodlands. They could have helped if they desired, but they preferred to stay hidden in their foolish and fanciful tall towers and leave us to our fate. I have no time for elves but I despise humans, we hunt to live but they hunt for sport. They had no regard for the land, destroying everything in their way, cutting plants and trees. killing our food supply just for fun, our land was becoming barren and uninhabitable, due to mankind and their destructiveness."

Baron snorted, "we decided to disband our pack. We split up and went our separate ways, we had a better chance a survival if we spread all over the land. That's how we came to live here, and why I dislike humans."

"You mean there's more of us around?" asked Kylo.

"Yes, and soon you will leave to find your own mate, and your own district to live in, you will forget about that human child," replied Baron.

"I may leave to find a mate, but no Baron I will never forget Laura."

After a long silence Kylo, wriggled on his stomach, right to the extreme edge.

Gazing over the precipice he exclaimed, "it's a long way to the bottom."

Baron just moved his head in agreement.

"Laura risked her life to save me—a complete stranger, a wolf, a wild animal."

"That's why Sheena convinced me to let her leave that day," replied Baron.

Kylo continued, "when she carried me, I could feel something inside, I was clinging to her body, my claws were digging into her skin, she didn't complain. I sensed her kindness and caring whilst I was pressed up against her body. We have been meeting and playing for a long time, we have a bond, she's akin to a sibling."

Baron's head snapped around, "sibling!" He spat out the word with disgust. "She's a human child, a destroyer of forests"

Sheena, who had been sitting nearby, quietly spoke, "that was the first time Kylo found his perceptive ability, and it was with a human. It will be impossible to break."

"Laura isn't like those hunters, she talks to me, pointing out trees and plants like they are living. She has shown me so much when we're together, she will touch a tree and say she can feel its life force." Kylo looked Baron in the eye, "we wolves can understand the language of humans, but she cannot understand my tongue, she calls me Snowy, that's my human name."

Baron had been listening intently to Kylo, he found it so hard to understand, especially the comment sibling.

He rose and walked away, as he did, he said, "let me and Sheena meet her tomorrow, I want to look into her eyes."

He continued, "Kylo, you have inherited Sheena's gift, I have no doubt about that. From me you have inherited the fighting ability, I'm still sore from your headbutt."

‡

Laura, after a restless night, awoke the next morning. She was bruised all over her back but tried to hide her discomfort from the family. Walking the best, she could, she made her way out of the farmhouse with Morgan. The lessons went so slow as she tried to disguise her pain.

Morgan, seeing something was distressing Laura said, "let's finish early today, I need to help Raoul with his work."

He stood up and said, "take care."

Once he had gone, she sluggishly rambled across the field to the river where her craft was out of sight, behind the common reeds. Laura saw Snowy was on the opposite bank waiting. After crossing the river on her craft, she tied it up and hobbled towards Snowy. It upset him to see she was still in pain, knowing Baron had caused her injuries. He pushes his head against her body to comfort her, she brushes his back.

Hearing a noise from the undergrowth, she looked up and froze with fear, emerging was Sheena and Baron.

"Oh no," she cried out, backing away.

Snowy, seeing Laura in distress gave a soft bay, "do not fear my friend."

She couldn't understand what he had expressed, but the sight of his parents petrified her. To stop herself from crying out in terror, she gritted her teeth, and clenched her hands so tight they turned white.

Sheena and Baron stopped short of Snowy and Laura and sat, with their front paws stretched out on the ground.

It confused Laura, "what's happening?" she inquired. Snowy gave her a gentle push towards his parents.

Laura stood between the two enormous wolves, not knowing what to do.

Sheena looked at Laura and turned to Baron, "look at that child, she is petrified of us, yet she still returned to see Kylo."

Snowy scraped the ground with his paws, three lines joined together, Laura understood the meaning. Laura knelt onto her knees and placed her shaking white hands, one on Sheena's paw, the other hand on Baron's paw; Baron shuddered, he was agitated, never in his life had a human touched him. Sheena was absorbing Laura's feelings, she realised what was happening, and cautiously relaxed.

Sheena spoke to Baron, "It's as I first sensed, Kylo and this child have a connection, they're brother and sister—almost. It would break both their hearts to be kept apart, can you not sense it?"

Baron looked at Kylo, then into Laura's eyes, he knew Sheena spoke the truth. "Yes," he said.

Baron stood and relented, "make sure she tells no one or brings anyone to this place."

Kylo stretched his legs out in play stance, ran to Baron and rubbed his head against Baron's forehead. Laura knew from his actions that they had accepted her as Snowy's friend, and would no longer harm her. She breathed out a sigh and almost collapsed with relief.

Laura said to Snowy, "I need to return home and rest today, my body aches."

Giving Snowy a hug, she hobbled back to her craft.

Fighting wolves are proud and don't apologise, but Sheena walked with Laura to her craft, and before she got in Sheena lightly placed her paw on Laura's back. She said, "take care child," then walked away.

Laura wished she knew what Sheena was saying, so she turned and briefly lowered her head in acknowledgement.

As she paddled back, Laura knew that the existence of three large white wolves living across the river must never be revealed, to anyone. Hiding her craft, she watched the wolves returning to their cave. She went straight home to her bed, happy in the knowledge she had a friend. Laura slept soundly the rest of the day and throughout the night. Next morning, she awoke feeling refreshed and full of life, although still badly bruised from the tree she was thrown against.

Laura continued to meet Snowy whenever she could, they were often seen running together across the open grasslands and through the woodlands. Sheena and Baron sat atop of the crag watching them play.

Baron a little uneasily grumbled, "It's not natural."

Chapter 4

The Nash brothers.

There was a tunnel hidden in the kitchen's larder, behind the barrels of flour, it led to the edge of the enchanted forest. Laura often ran along this passage to play outside although they told her to never go into the magical forest. She couldn't resist sitting on the edge wondering what animals and plants lived and grew there. It looked dark and foreboding, the trees seemed alive with their rustling branches reeling in the wind.

One day, Laura was sprinting through the tunnel with outstretched hands, skimming the sides to guide herself through the dark. As she neared the exit, she stubbed her toes against a loose stone, stumbled and fell, she muttered to herself, got up and walked to the exit.

As she got to the opening, she noticed movement and lights by the ancient and large knobbly tree. It was as thick as a fortified tower as if standing guard on the edge of the enchanted forest. She stopped and knelt behind the devil's nettle, with its glistening lacey cream flowers that hid the exit of the tunnel. Here she spied a gathering of tree sprites, they appeared to be circling the tree without moving. She sat there mesmerised by this spectacle of colourful hues dancing around their mother tree. Morgan had told her that these creatures were guardians of ancient trees, this was the first time she had seen them for herself. They were petite, just above ankle high to Laura and wore dark green leaf-like garments, but nothing on their tiny feet. They stopped circling and sank into the bark of the tree. The last one hesitated and looked around at Laura, eyes as green as the first grass of spring. Laura took in her appearance, she was in no doubt the sprite was female, with pleasing lips and long brown hair, turning black at the tips; her skin was a hazel. Within a heartbeat, she disappeared.

Laura would often creep out of the tunnel, sometimes she was fortunate to look upon the tree sprites. Most times she looked out; they were nowhere to be seen.

‡

Late afternoon two riders came into sight.

Morgan called Raoul, "beware we never see strangers in these parts. Tell Martha and Laura to stay inside, we will send them away."

"Hello, we're looking for a bed for the night, can you help?" asked one of the riders.

"Sorry," said Raoul, "we have no room, a large family is living here."

The strangers, without speaking turned and rode away.

Morgan, turning to Raoul as they rode down the farm track said, "they're a raggle-taggle pair, I've seen people like that when I was travelling; they were usually villains of sorts."

When they were out of sight the two riders stopped where their gang of ten thieves sat waiting. Their names were Aldwin and Edmund Nash, highway bandits. They wore bandanas around their necks which they used to cover their faces when out attacking and robbing.

"There are only a few people in the farmhouse, we'll return at dusk with the gang, and move in," grinned Aldwin.

‡

In the farmhouse, later that evening, Martha was in the kitchen baking bread, pies, and preparing flapjacks to cook, whilst Laura sat watching. Raoul and Morgan were in the family room eating

35

their supper of porridge when the door burst open. Twelve men stormed into the farmhouse, led by the two strangers that had ridden by earlier that day. This gang of robbers quickly surrounded them.

Aldwin and Edmund stood in front of Morgan and Raoul. In an intimidating manner, they unsheathed their shiny knives and picked the grime from under their fingernails. The rest of the gang wandered around the farmhouse, looking for any inhabitants, searching the annexe, sleeping quarters and main rooms.

Hearing the commotion, Martha pushed Laura into the pantry, "quick, hide in the tunnel, there's trouble in the family room, keep out of sight. I will come back and tell you what's happening."

Laura made her way behind the barrels of flour to the secret tunnel, one of the robbers entered the kitchen as Laura disappeared into the tunnel.

Giving Martha a sharp look he demanded, "anyone else in here?"

"No—who are you, what are you doing in our home?"

"You oughta come and join your menfolk in the parlour," he said, in a tone that suggested it was an order, not a request.

As Martha entered the room, she saw a rabble of unkempt men, she counted twelve. Immediately she knew they were outlaws. Most wore bandanas, their trousers were covered in patches, they all carried knives. They had long dishevelled hair and beards; they were all wearing cloaks.

Morgan and Raoul looked at Martha quizzically where's Laura? in their faces, she mouthed 'in the tunnel'.

"What do you want?" asked Raoul. "we're poor farmers, there's nothing of value here."

The two leaders stood side by side. One removed his dirt stained bandana that was wrapped around his surly face. He sported a wispy beard that couldn't quite hide the scar under his jawline. "We are the Nash brothers, Aldwin and Edmund," announced Aldwin.

Edmund with a hint of ruthlessness behind his smile lifted his unshaven, pockmarked face. Wearing shabby clothes, he took on the persona of an animated scarecrow.

Raoul and Morgan glanced at each other, they knew these names, they were infamous bandits, they ambushed merchants on small isolated paths.

"What have you come here for?" Morgan asked.

With a smile, Aldwin replied, "we only want to rest up here for a night or two."

Looking at Martha, "that's impressive porridge, we would be grateful for a bowl of that each, we've been riding all day. Jak, tether the horses in that big shed."

Martha just muttered to herself, *smirking horrible beggars*, and stamped into the kitchen.

Aldwin shouted after Martha, "perhaps a slice of bread—maybe ale as well."

Back in the kitchen, Martha told Laura what had happened and to stay hidden. Whilst mixing the porridge, she found and passed her a blanket to sleep on.

That night none of the Lovet family had much sleep, they were dispatched to the cellar, whilst the robbers took the best sleeping quarters. Next morning, they were expected to feed the rowdy bunch of robbers their breakfast.

"Porridge and bread please, with cider," they demanded, thumping the table with wooden spoons.

They were a dirty bunch, gulping the porridge, not bothering with spoons, just tipping the wooden bowl to their mouths and slurping. Only two loaves of bread were laid out, so they fought over it, tearing pieces off with their dirty hands. Martha had made three loaves of bread but hid one for the family to eat later.

In the kitchen Morgan was helping Martha, he was fuming, "at this rate, our supplies won't last the winter."

After they finished breakfast, Aldwin called all the robbers into the great room. "I want you all to search the farm for any weapons the family may try to use against us."

Edun said, "it's a farm, there are plenty of tools that could be used as weapons against us."

"Search the place anyway, there may be things of interest to us, and check the outside buildings," replied Aldwin.

Laura was lying outside by the tunnel, alongside the devil's nettle, when Edun and Jak ambled around the corner. They were both eating an apple, our apples noted Laura, as she slid back into the tunnel.

"This is the famous Catacomb forest, doesn't look that eerie," said Edun, throwing his apple core at the trees.

"See, nothing has happened."

Jak nudged Edun, "go on then, I bet you won't go one hundred steps into it."

"I . . . er don't want to now, maybe tomorrow, how long are we going to hide out here," said Edun.

Jak replied, "don't know, maybe throughout the winter, that's what Aldwin says," throwing his apple core into the forest.

They carried on around to the chicken coop, and into the large shed. Laura saw her chance and crept out alongside the forest and ran to the river. Crossing the river, she raced up the river bank looking for her friend Snowy. He came scampering through the long grass, and ran towards her with his eyes wide, sensing Laura was worried.

Running up to him she says, "wicked men have come to our home, I dare not come to meet you while they are living at the farm. I will stop today, but after, I will have to stay away, I don't want them following me."

They meandered around the forests and fields but mostly lay in the grass enjoying each other's company. As dusk fell, Laura got up to leave for the farmhouse. She headed back to the river, for the first time apprehensive about returning to the farm. Back home, after eating freshly cooked flat cakes, Laura crept out to where the hole from the chamber led to the inglenook where the robbers sat drinking. Listening to their conversations made her anxious for her family's safety.

Aldwin addressed all his men, "this place is ideal, hidden from the main highway, it's isolated and well stocked with food; soldiers will never find us here."

Edmund added, "It's large enough for all of us, we'll be here until spring, maybe longer."

They celebrated, by drinking the barrel of cider they had found in the cellar. Laura was now fearful for her family; they were expecting them to move on after a few days.

Next day Laura was hiding behind the stone wall in the inglenook, one of her secret places, listening to the robbers. She was seething, watching them etching their names into their table and chairs. One of the robbers, an offensive man who looked like he had just lost a fight with a bear twisted around, looking for a place to rest his drink. He swept his callous hand across the shelf, sending all Martha's ornaments to the floor. Those that didn't break he stamped on, his black leather boots ground everything to shards. Laura's eyes widened with disgust. She had never felt this emotion of hatred before, it consumed her body.

Edmund called Edun and Jac, "first thing tomorrow morning I want that large tree chopped into small logs, we won't be sitting in the freezing weather throughout the winter."

Those words turned Laura's anger to sadness, she loved the tree and feared for the safety of the tree sprites. *I must try to warn them; maybe I can get them to leave the tree.* She made her way back to the kitchen and glided through the tunnel and ran straight outside. Rushing across the neglected land, she flung her arms around the tree, it was so large her arms didn't go halfway around the trunk. Laura had never touched the tree before; she pressed her face against the trunk. It was soft and warm due to the moss growing on the bark, which weaved itself around the coarse and bumpy tree bark.

She pressed her cheek hard against the trunk, quietly sobbing, "evil men will chop down your tree, can you hear me; I know you're there; can you understand me? you must leave. They're coming tomorrow to use this lovely tree as kindle. Please leave I cannot save your tree; you must leave now."

She fell to her knees, sobbing and imploring the tree sprites to leave, not knowing if they understood her, or even knew she was there.

Unexpectedly, she perceived a warm presence wrapped around her body, she stopped snivelling and looked around, but could see nothing.

A fusion of thoughts formed inside her head, a perception, *stop crying, relax.* She held the tears, sat and calmed her pounding heart.

A voice, a thought in her head, like the soft strings of a flute. *We do not have vocal cords as you, we communicate with thought. Do not speak reflect your words into your mind.*

Wicked men are coming tomorrow morning to chop down this tree.

Do not worry yourself, nothing will injure this tree—we are the trees armour, we will protect it.

As she arose, she saw a glow and three tree sprites standing on a branch just above her head.

One of the tree sprites unfolded her hands towards Laura.

We have been aware of you watching us, I looked into your eyes and saw you have a kindly nature, so we permitted you to observe us. We appreciate the forewarning and will shield our tree from any harm, now go back to your dwelling. Do not return, tomorrow the tree will be shielded.

‡

Next morning, she spied Edun and Jac leaving the house, both carrying a large axe each. She was tempted to watch what happened but heeded the warning not to venture there today. She wondered around the tunnel fretting about her newfound friends, she wanted to look out many times during the morning.

After midday, she heard Edmund bellow, "where's Edun and Jac? they should have come back with logs. You two," he testily hollered at Cliff and Stretch, "go and find out what's happened."

The two robbers stopped their knife throwing game and ambled outside and around the farmyard where they found Edun and Jac asleep on the grass.

41

"Best fetch Edmund, those two are in for a beating!"

When Edmund arrived, no amount of kicking, shaking, or heaving woke them up.

"You two," Edmund snapped, "get those axes, and cut it down now!"

Snatching the axes, and throwing them over their shoulder, they trudged towards the tree. Both men raised their axe above their head, as they brought the axes towards the tree, a dancing circle of red and green fluorescent light surrounded the tree. As the axes moved towards the tree, the green light emanated towards the blades, hitting them with a lightning bolt sending both axes twirling into the air. The red light flashed into the two men; they collapsed onto the floor into a deep sleep.

Edmund's face whitened, he looked on speechless. He started walking backwards with his hands raised, palms pointing at the tree.

He turned and stumbled back into the farmhouse shouting, "that tree—it's bewitched, fetch our men, drag them into the annexe."

Next morning, Laura ventured out of the passage, to the tree.

Placing her hands on the bark she filled her head with words, *I'm glad you are safe.*

Two of the tree sprites dropped onto Laura's shoulders, *we were able to stop the men before their axes cut into the tree. Had you not warned us, they may have inflicted much harm before we could have stopped them. It would have taken many years to heal had they inflicted just one bite with their axes. So, we thank you for warning us, we are indebted to you. Whenever you need any help, we will try to help you.*

The thugs, what happened to them.

They have been given a sleeping enchantment; they will sleep for two days.

We have many wicked men move into our dwelling; can you remove them?

Sadly, we cannot leave our tree, nor can we interfere in your world, intoned the tree sprites.

✢

Morgan, with Casper at his heels, walked into the great room where most of the bandits sat drinking and lounging in chairs. Martha had asked him to collect the food bowls. As he walked through, Casper rubbed against Aldwin Nash's leg, in his friendly manner. Aldwin half-drunk put his foot under Casper and sent him flying across the room; he landed by Edmund, on his side whimpering. That brought cries of laughter from all the vicious criminals. Edmund, who was sprawling across a seat, jumped to his feet in shock. He stood over Casper, and with one big blow, stamped on Casper, breaking his neck, killing him instantly.

A deathly shadow crept throughout the room, killing a dog for no reason shocked all the robbers. The only sounds were of noxious Perry, sniggering. The rest of the robbers stopped their activities and turned their eyes on Morgan. With his head looking at the floor he was walking slowly with heavy footsteps towards Casper. His hands were shaking with rage. As he got closer, he turned and grabbed Edmund around the neck with both of his hands. They locked around his neck instantly cutting off his air supply. Edmund's hands flapped around, like a bird trying to take off. For a few moments the bandits looked on in shock, then two gripped Morgan, and tried to pull him from their leader. Such was his anger; none could get him to release. Edmund had become limp, the thugs were getting worried now, more grabbed Morgan, but they couldn't get his hands to release.

Aldwin shouted, "move."

He raised an oak chair over his head, and brought it hard down onto Morgan's back, he collapsed, releasing his grip on Edmund's neck.

He then shouted to Edun, "you, drag Morgan to the cellar, there's no telling what Edmund will do when he recovers."

"Jac, you make a bolt and secure the storeroom, you three grinning maggots, round-up Martha and Raoul. We will keep them locked in the cellar, the woman can come out to cook," stated Aldwin. "They are not wandering around free anymore. You, throw that dog into the yard, out of my sight," he said to the remaining villainous specimen.

"Why can't we slit their throats and dump them in the forest?" asked Edun.

"The woman is a good cook, since coming here we have been fed well, for now, they can stop here," replied Aldwin.

Edmund lay on the floor gasping for air; he took a long time to recover, as he did his face turned red, his eyes bulged.

"Where's that man gone?" He roared, picking up the food bowls and throwing them at the wall, smashing everyone.

"Calm down," stressed Aldwin, "I have a plan. We will let them fester in the cellar for a few weeks, then we will bind and tie the men to a horse, and take them to a hold-up, making sure their faces are seen. Eventually, they will have to join our band."

Morgan, still unconscious, had been dragged to the cellar storeroom and thrown in. Raoul and Martha were hauled from the kitchen and cast in with him.

Jac crafted a bolt, and put it on the storeroom door, they were now imprisoned.

When Morgan came around, his back ached from the strike of the chair. He looked devastated as he explained why they were incarcerated in the cellar.

The next morning, Jac called Martha out of the cellar's storeroom, to make breakfast, which, for her own reasons she readily obliged. After preparing the robbers their breakfast, she crept into the tunnel to Laura.

When Laura saw her mother she said, "what's the matter: you look upset, has something happened?"

Martha, taking Laura's hand, sat with her on the makeshift bed and said, "I need to tell you something quick before I'm missed."

She took a deep breath, "the robber Edmund—has killed, Casper."

The pain inside grew and grew, she couldn't hold it back, a wail so loud emitted from Laura. It was so piercing, it raised the flock of tree sparrows outside the farm, from their roost.

Martha was ready and pulled Laura's head into her chest, placed her free hand onto the back of her head, said, "let it out—quietly."

Morgan looked at Raoul, "Martha has just told Laura about Casper, hope those despicable men didn't hear."

Martha, holding Laura, closed her eyes, *my fearless tomboy daughter has returned to a vulnerable child. This is her first encounter with vile men and the evil they do*. Martha sat swaying Laura as if she was a newborn baby.

Then a plaintive howl could be heard in the distance, it was Kylo, he sensed Laura's sadness. Laura knew at once who it was, it gave her a little comfort knowing her friend shared her pain.

Aldwin sprang up with a start, "what's that noise?"

"Wild animals are about," replied Jac.

"I cannot stop with you long, they have locked us in the cellar, Morgan tried to kill Edmund," Martha said.

Laura drew a deep breath, "what has happened to Casper's body?"

"They threw him outside; he's lying by the barn."

Martha, with one last hug, kissed Laura on the forehead, and returned to the kitchen, ready to be thrown back into the underground cell.

Laura lay on her stomach, with her hands over her face crying for several minutes. With a jolt, she sat up and composed herself. She knew there was no one else, she had to attend to Casper.

Sneaking out of the tunnel, she went into the tool store. She purposely selected Morgan's trowel, which hung on a peg. It was a worn tool; she could feel Morgan's essence over the wooden handle. Outside she picked up Casper and wrapped him in the blanket she used to sleep on; then she stole to the fields by the river.

It was a chilly damp morning, a grey sky and a mist rolled over the river which noisily swirled around the yearning edge rock. With the trowel, she started digging. It took all morning to dig the hole, using such a small implement. Her hands had blisters by the time the hole was deep enough.

There she laid Casper to rest, under the Willow tree. After filling the hole, she collected a load of round stones from the river bank and made a marker where Casper was buried. Next, she dug up a few blue cornflowers and replanted them around Casper's grave. Finally, she pushed the trowel into the head of the grave, leaving just the handle showing. For several minutes she knelt, her teardrops falling down her cheeks, dripping onto the stones. Returning to her hideaway she sat, all afternoon in quiet contemplation.

Later that night, when the robbers were asleep, Laura went to the cellar and stood by the locked door. Morgan sat hunched up in the corner.

Laura gently voiced, "I have buried Casper by our outdoor school, he will forever be with us at lessons, like always."

Morgan crossed the storeroom, through a crack in the door, reached out to Laura taking her hands in his.

He dropped his head, "thank you for taking care of Casper."

Now they were locked in the cellar, things were getting desperate for the family; they sat around discussing their situation.

Morgan said, "they will never leave, someone needs to reach Nerbank Garrison and get help from the soldiers, but it's a long trek, they would soon notice if someone was missing."

"And catch them on the road," retorted Martha.

Raoul suggested. "take one of their horses . . ."

Laura piped up, "there's always one man in the farmyard, and they have two watching on the embankment, looking out for strangers. They would soon see someone leaving."

"Yes, Laura's right," said Morgan, "that won't work, anyway we have got to get out of this prison first."

Laura chipped in, "I could be there in eight days, from the kitchen tunnel into the forest. They don't even know I'm here."

"That's a possibility," said Morgan.

Raoul disagreed, "no, it's far too dangerous in that forest, Laura is only a child."

Laura interjected, "I can look after myself have you forgotten I'm eleven almost a full-grown woman. I am not a child."

"No," this time she was cut short by Martha.

"We will hear no more of this silly idea, we must think of something else, and bide our time," said Raoul.

"I can do it."

"No," shouted Martha and Raoul.

"But . . ."

Martha gripped the door and looked her squarely in the eyes, "no, you will not go."

"Our only hope is that someone on the Piran road will come down our lane and notice there is something wrong here," continued Martha.

"That's unlikely," said Raoul, "it's rare for anyone to wander this far from the trail."

Laura sat dejected; Morgan came over to comfort her.

"I could do it; I've made friends with the forest guardians."

She told Morgan how she helped save the ancient tree with the tree sprites. Morgan looked at Laura in awe. He said, "If anyone can get through the forest, it's you, but they're right, it is dangerous. Your mother and father have spoken and forbid it. Go back to your hideout, I'm sure we will come up with an idea."

Laura left the cellar and made her way back to the kitchen, and her hideout.

Next morning, Martha was cooking in the kitchen, when Edmund sauntered in with a red and white bandana around his neck, hiding his bruises.

"Cook these for us, we're having chicken tonight," said Edmund, throwing three dead chickens onto the table.

"You stupid man," said Martha through gritted teeth. "You have taken away half our supply of eggs, haven't you any sense!"

Edmund wasn't used to people criticising him, especially a woman, he went red in the face, "just you get on with cooking, or else!"

Edmund noticed that Martha had concealed something under her apron. "What have you got there?" he asked, pointing at her apron.

Martha just muttered something inaudible, but Edmund had caught sight of a loaf hanging out of her apron, exposing the food she was hiding.

Edmund grabbed Martha's arm, and spun her to the floor saying, "where do you think you're going with all that food?"

"My family need food, please, you're not giving us enough to eat," she pleaded, getting to her feet, whilst picking up the bread, cakes and pies.

"We come first; my men need their energy to go out robbing."

"No, I cooked this for my family, they're starving."

Edmund hit Martha with the back of his hand, knocking her back into the food cupboard, knocking milk and small clay pots of her homemade jam, all over the floor. She collapses onto the mess now on the floor, semi-conscious. He proceeds to spitefully, stamp on the food Martha had cooked, making it inedible.

That morning Laura awoke at dawn and hid behind the devil's nettle to watch the tree sprites. Hearing a ruckus in the kitchen, ran along the tunnel as Edmund was leaving. Her mother, bruised from the fall, a swollen face from the blow was on her knees in a mixture of broken pots, jam and milk; trying to stand; tears spilling from her eyes. In that instant, Laura decided, she was leaving for help, regardless of her own safety.

Going over to her mother said, "stay where you are, I will get a cool wet cloth."

Fighting back the tears, she bathed her mother's swollen face. She held her mother in a tight embrace, daughter comforting her mother.

Laura's expression hardened, "everything will be back to normal when those violent men leave, and that one will pay for doing this to you."

Martha gave Laura a gentle prod on her back, "go back into the passage, I must take those vile men their food." She tried to smile at Laura. It only highlighted the bruise forming on her cheek.

Back in her hideout, she vents her frustration out on the cloth, by wringing it dry. Laura had decided enough is enough *I can and must do something, going through the forest couldn't be that dangerous.* Laura started to construct a plan; convincing herself it would be an easy hike through the mystic forest. *It's only a group of trees; it can't be that dangerous I must get to Nerbank Garrison.* One by one Laura gathered the equipment she needed to make the journey. Another blanket was acquired from the storeroom, a discarded leather drinking vessel found at the back of the kitchen larder. The more items she collected, the higher her confidence grew in undertaking the journey.

Now it was getting close to leaving, Laura's thoughts were about her family, they will be so worried, but if I don't go, they will die. She was torn, I know mother will be distraught, she closed her eyes for a moment and decided to leave a note.

On the parchment, Laura wrote.

Mommy daddy and uncle Morgan.

I have decided to get help.

Do not worry, I will be back in two weeks with soldiers.

The road will take too long I will use the catacomb forest.

I am not afraid.

Do not be afraid for me.

I love you all.

Your daughter Laura.

Mommy, please don't worry.

An opportunity to steal a short knife from the bandits came her way. she was watching them, through a crack in the inglenook, they were throwing knives into the wooden door.

"The nearest blade to the mark wins," quipped Aldwin.

"What do we win," asked flabby flack, "I want an extra slice of cake."

Everyone laughed, "thinking of your stomach again," said Aldwin as he roared with laughter.

The night got rowdier and rowdier, finally, tired and drunk Edmund signalled, "I win, time to retire."

When they left to bed down for the night, Laura crept in and selected the one with the sharpest edge, which happened to be the one that was also the most ornate. She pulled the knife out of the door and slipped it into her belt. All the items she had collected were stored in the secret tunnel, ready for the journey.

That night Laura made herself two loaves, they tasted sour, but were editable—just. Martha had tried in vain to teach Laura to cook, but it was one skill she couldn't and didn't want to master.

Chapter 5

Trinity.

On the other side of the enchanted forest, Trinity was bounding through the undergrowth heading for the open country. Issuing a joyful cry, she leapt out of the forest into the countryside. With the sun on her back, and renewed energy, she started sprinting around in open fields, enjoying the feel of soft grass under her hoofs. She stopped and drew in the smell of the morning dew, filling her nostrils with the juicy flavours of the open country. She raised herself on her hind legs, reaching for the sky. She released a soft squeal of glee; unaware three men were setting a trap.

She ran across the meadow, down to the river making for her favourite tree, an old twisted hazel whose branches hung over the river and intertwined with each other as if reaching down for a drink.

She dipped her head under a branch and jumped over the river. Her neck jarred back forcing her legs up, missing the bank; she fell backwards into the water. She scrambled out the river, pulling Bill out of the tree with the rope he had lassoed around her neck. Gram burst out of a ditch and threw another rope around her neck.

Trinity had plenty of fight, kicking her hind leg at Gram; her hoof shaved his forehead. She spun about, trying to break free of the rope. She lowered her head her amethyst eyes burning hot with anxiety. She focussed her horn on Bill. Before she could thrust forward, Silo, the third man wrapped another rope around both her hind legs. She toppled over, landing onto her side. Kicking her hind legs out she caught Silo on his Left arm.

He screamed out, "she's broken my arm." He rolled on the ground in agony.

Bill was pulled along the ground, as she pulled herself up by her front legs. She then raised her right leg above Bill and stamped hard. He rolled out of the way as the hoof sank into the moist bank of the river. She was inhaling deep and prolonged, dragging out her strength; fighting for survival. Gram jerked another rope around her rear legs, bringing Trinity to her knees. Panic seeped into her head. Although both rear legs were trussed, she kicked them out at Gram, grazing his shoulder. With her eyes distracted, Bill strung another rope about Trinity's front legs, pulling her over, onto her side. She rolled onto her back with a roar of rage, kicking and rolling from side to side, trying to strike one of her captors.

Gram Bill and Silo stood to one side, waiting for Trinity to tire. After several minutes she flopped on her side gasping for air. Gram rushed at her and tied another length of rope around her front legs. She got to her knees on her hind legs, and with one last push, lurched herself at Bill, with her horn aiming at his head. Gram pushed Bill clear. Trinity landed face down on the ground, gasping for air. Bill and Gram unhurriedly wrapped more ropes around her legs. She was trussed up like a hog over a fire pit, unable to move.

Trinity, a unicorn, mustard body and head, with amethyst eyes, on her forehead a sparkling red horn.

"Bring the animal cart around now," shouted Gram to Bill.

Silo, standing holding his broken arm cussed Trinity, "that beast has broken my arm the maggot! let me cut her throat."

"No," shouted Bill, "she's worth more alive."

The two men, with Silo watching, dragged and pulled Trinity towards the cart. Although Trinity continued to fight hard, rolling

53

and swinging her tied legs out, she tired. Trinity was dragged into the iron-barred pen.

She lay there panting, *why did I ignore Storms warnings about playing in open fields; I was so arrogant, telling him I'm much too clever and fast to be captured. What does the future hold for me now? I have no future, in a pen to be put on display, or will my enchanted horn be removed? I will die, I have no doubt.*

Trinity had been discovered by Bill, who came across her whilst looking for foxes to capture for their show. He was hiding behind a common broom bush watching the fox cubs when they scattered and ran back to their den. He turned to the forest as Trinity emerged leaping around the open field, unaware someone was watching. For a few minutes, he was mesmerised by the sight of a unicorn. breaking free from the spectacle, deciding he must capture the rare creature. He told Gram, who, along with Silo, came and hid in the shrubs planning how they could ambush the unicorn. Her downfall was, she always liked to jump the river in the same place. So that's where they set up the trap. Gram, Silo and Bill were the owners of a travelling show, they went around the country displaying what they called rare animals. Until now they displayed normal forest animals, now they had a rare unicorn.

Chapter 6

The journey.

Laura left just before sunrise, with the two loaves in her leather bag, the short knife in her belt. The small blanket was tied around her back with her rope, the leather drinking vessel, full of fresh water from the well.

As she passed the ancient tree, she put her hand on the trunk and said, "farewell my friends, I must journey through this forest to get help for my family. If I don't leave now I never will, then what will become of my mother and father—and uncle Morgan."

Standing by the tree, silently contemplating, going over her words, repeating them inside her head. Still worrying about her family, and how they will react, once they know she has gone. *I must go, they will die, or be killed if I don't try.*

With much trepidation, she set foot into the enchanted forest.

Although they didn't answer, the tree sprites caught Laura's thoughts, her anxieties. They relayed a message to their kindred that resided deep in the forest. *A young human female is travelling through your forest, she is a kindly soul, give her assistance.*

Laura followed by what appeared to be a track, albeit barely noticeable. She had only taken a few steps inside, her body shivered, not from the cold, but the aura emanating from everything in the forest. She felt all the living creatures and plants were aware of her presence. And were resentful she had invaded their space. The disquiet of the trees was real. Looking up she imagined they were muttering words of alienation. Stopping for a moment, she shut her eyes and placed her hands over her ears, she could hear the palpitation of her heart. Apprehension entered her mind. She swallowed, *why have I allowed myself to become scared of trees and plants. I cannot forget why I am here.* Opening her dark, brindle coloured eyes, she took a deep breath and pushed forward. The floor soon became thick with fallen leaves, twigs, and broken branches. *I should have brought a scythe with me, if this route gets any denser, I will never get through this forest. I need a quarterstaff.*

She got on her hands and knees sweeping away the loose foliage. She found and picked up one long solid branch. With the knife, she shaved off the side-shoots and trimmed the ends until it was as long as she was tall. Pushing forward, using the staff to steady herself, she saw how useful her new possession would be in helping to push through, and clear a path.

‡

Laura had put her note inside Martha's apron that hangs on a peg inside the larder, she knew her mother always put it on before cooking. She had folded the note in half and wrote in big letters, Laura, on the outside. She knew Martha didn't read or write, but she could recognise her name.

Martha found the note and took it to Raoul and Morgan to read. Morgan took it from Martha's hand and read it to himself. He shook his head and passed it to Morgan.

"What has she done? Tell me, don't lie I want to know what she has written. Tell me—now," screeched Martha. She knew she felt it in her bones, her daughter had left home to get help.

Morgan read the note aloud, Raoul placed his arm around Martha, caressing her back, as she started to cry. She took the note from Morgan and hugged it to her chest as if cuddling Laura herself.

"She was cooking last night, the smell still lingered when I entered the kitchen; she must have made herself food for the journey," mused Martha, wiping her eyes.

56

"Someone should tell her," said Morgan, thinking about the last time he ate something Laura had cooked.

Raoul tried to console Martha, "now we have something to look forward to if Laura . . ."

Morgan intervened, "when Laura reaches the garrison soldiers will arrive, arrest these villains, then we will go back to a quiet life." Trying to sound positive continued, "she is a resourceful girl, I'm sure she will be fine."

Martha started sobbing again, "she has an abnormal fear of being surrounded by tall structures. You told me how she reacted in the town,"

Morgan told Raoul and Martha how she had befriended the tree sprites and had helped save the tree. "I looked upon tree sprites once before; she befriended a company, at her young age. She has accomplished more than us three," said Morgan.

This brought little comfort to Martha, "I've never seen one of those creatures in my life, I don't care if I never do. That forest is something different, it's dangerous, we have all heard the dreadful sounds coming from that place."

Raoul, who had squeezed his eyes to stop tears falling, put his arm around Martha. She asked Morgan to read and re-read the note.

‡

All morning Laura pushed forward through the dense undergrowth, thankful she had picked up that branch and created the staff. The path, small as it was, had disappeared.

The environment became unrelentingly dense. The tall trees had created a canopy blocking out most of the light. Following the sunrise became challenging; her knees wobbled every time she looked up into the trees. Shutting her eyes momentarily, she didn't understand how anything so natural could trouble her mind so much. She gritted her teeth and pressed forward. More mysterious sounds surrounded and echoed throughout the forest, the creaking trees felt alive. A family of disturbed common dormice, on the forest floor, went scampering off into the undergrowth. Tree roots were spreading across the floor, the veins of the forest. Every tree looked identical after the day's toil.

Dusk was approaching, she stopped for the night and settled down between the roots of an enormous tree. Resting against the tree, she ate a slice of bread, then slept with knees against her chest and the blanket wrapped tightly around her body. She slept soundly after the days walk.

A sliver of sunlight shone onto Laura's face, chasing her nightmares away. After nibbling on a slice of bread, she rose and tracked the sunrise. She had only been walking for a short time when she heard a peculiar chattering sound coming from the underbrush to her left. *Its only birds foraging for insects, or small forest animals*. She frowned, *there's an abnormal creature lurked in the shadows. It's bigger than a rabbit.* Gripping her staff, she turned away from the thicket and quickened her step.

Before long, little grey stone-like scrawny creatures appeared, they had thin bony arms and legs, and long fingers. She couldn't guess how many, they danced in and out of the trees.

They came towards her skipping around and squealing, "you are going the wrong way, wrong way, wrong way, you're going the wrong way."

Laura didn't know what to make of these weird beings, gripping the knife, expecting them to attack.

"Go away! Shoo! Leave me alone!" she shrieked swinging her staff in the air.

She carried on walking, but quickened her pace, when two of these creatures ran across her feet, tripping her. As she fell, one loaf flipped out of the bag, an imp grabbed it and ran off. Laura got to her feet, now incensed, she started swinging her staff around and gave chase trying to retrieve the stolen bread. They taunted and mocked her, sometimes a wide grin spread across a face, exposing needle-like fangs. The surroundings became as gloomy as a winter's night sky. Their leader turned back on Laura and sniggered. She looked, the creature had the eyes of a darkling, ugly and deceitful. With one flit, he ran past Laura and was gone. She looked around; they were all gone.

Without realising it they had tricked and led her a long way from the route she was taking. Laura stood still, looked around, the air hushed and tranquil. The only sounds were insects buzzing, and a light breeze blowing the treetop leaves. All she could see were tall and impregnable bushes concealing the forest beyond. She had been led into a trap—a labyrinth.

First, she tried to climb up a bush; they were a species she had never come across before, they were strong, thick and dark green. She got a little way off the ground but encountered thorns, long and sharp, everywhere. Her rope was of no use, she couldn't attach it anywhere, it was as if the bushes were enchanted.

Next, she tried to figure out which way to go, wandering haphazardly around, advancing deeper into the labyrinth. After a while Laura panicked, dashing back and forth. A fiery temper coursed through her mind, a reaction she had never experienced before. She ran down passages that turned into dead ends. She turned a corner and saw a piece of her tunic that, a few minutes earlier, had snagged on one of the thorns.

 She soon became exhausted, fell to her knees and with her hands over her face started sobbing. Rubbing her red eyes, acknowledging her parents were right, she was too young to undertake such a journey. *Those dreadful creatures have tricked me. What else had they in store? Will they attack me; kill me?* It was now getting late; she huddled up into a corner, threw the blanket around herself, and covered the blanket with bracken she had collected.

"If anything wants to bite me tonight, you will have to find me first," she warned anyone that might be listening.

She lay shivering with fear, trying to stay awake, holding back her eyelids from dropping. Midnight passed, she slipped into a troubled sleep.

‡

Tad, followed by the rest of the imps, ran into the stone-walled abode built by Tad the Minotaur many seasons ago. He had created the maze to keep hunters out and trap unsuspecting victims. Inside the dimly lit room, Zee sat at a large spruce coloured table mixing various ingredients. The room was filled with the fragrance of Patchouli, one of Zee's passions.

Tad ran to Zee, tugging her sleeve, "mistress we have trapped another victim in the maze, a lost child, young human girl."

Zee spun and lifted Tad, her distorted face sparkled like a star shining on the moon. "a girl just what I need. My dear little numbskulls I will soon be free from this distorted skeleton I'm forced to walk inside. I could almost kiss you. Do you know where she is?

"Yes, we followed, she's hiding under some leaves, crying."

Zee started laughing, "by tomorrow, she will be a blubbering mess. At dawn, bring her back here. Tonight, I will prepare my new elixir, the soul destruction potion. Her essence will rejuvenate my body back to its former beauty; I miss my locks. You may feast on her body."

Tad grinned at Zee; his teeth itched to bite into the soft skin of Laura.

‡

The moon was still high in the night sky when Laura awoke to the sounds of a chilly night breeze rustling in the treetops. It had been a restless night; she felt as lonely as a desert ship. Tears burnt her eyes, fearing death was approaching in the form of several tiny monsters. Lying on her back, Laura looked up; the wall of shrubbery looked taller and closer. Throwing off the blanket, bracken dust settled on her auburn hair. She brushed the debris off; took a small piece of bread from her bag and sat nibbling on the crust.

Those bony devils stole half my food. "Hope you choke on it," she bawled out in frustration.

Standing with her back against one part of the hedge, she stood and took a few deep breaths. *Morgan told me there is always a solution to a problem. You must dig into your mind to find the answer. Think.* She became calmer.

Shutting her eyes, she created a circular maze within her head. She used her mind's eye to trace the path, a solution to the problem an idea formed. She placed her hands on the back of her head, and sucked her bottom lip, decided the answer was to follow one side of the maze. With her right hand pressed against the right edge, she started walking. To test her theory, at every bend she twisted a branch. Passing none of the twisted branches, at around midday she emerged from the labyrinth, half a day lost, tired and hungry, but delighted.

‡

The imps arrived at Laura's refuge a little after dawn.

Tad kicked a pinecone. "she gone he squealed, my soft tasty flesh, gone!" His heart seized, "mistress will be violent and bloodthirsty. We must return and face her rage."

Like a snail's trail, the imps made their way back to the centre of the labyrinth. Led by Tad, they sidled into Zee's lair. Zee lifted herself out of her chair and shuffled over to the nervous imps.

Tad whimpered, "she's gone her crying corner was empty."

Zee stared at Tad, the white pinprick in the centre of her black orbs turned red and drilled into Tad, "did you look for her?"

"No, we came straight back to tell you."

"You bunch of boneheads, this is a huge maze, there are only three entrances. She's wandering around, lost. Get out and bring her back."

It took a moment for Tad to catch his breath. He ran outside issuing instructions to the imps, "explore every avenue, we know the false trails, she doesn't. Meet back here when the sun shines on Zee's home."

For three hours they searched every passage and blind alley; all returned, despondent. Tad the last to return went straight to Zee.

"Did you bring the crybaby girl back?

"Mistress, she escaped, I saw her footprints outside the north gateway."

She gestured to Tad, "take your puppets and track the wretched minx. If you return without her . . ."

He acknowledged with a groan; her words chilled him.

Chapter 7

The Withered forest.

L aura stood looking around, trying to ascertain where she was and what direction to follow. She stared at the treetops, looking for an opening. A small vent in the canopy allowed the sun to strike through, allowing Laura to determine her bearings. She continued her journey in an easterly direction.

Mid-afternoon, Laura sat and took a rest. After the encounter with the imps, she decided to make herself another weapon, a club. Searching the woodland floor, she found a nice stout branch. It took Laura an hour to whittle it into shape. It had a tapered body, with a good hand grip. She tied the club around her waist, staff in hand, prepared to fight if those creatures dare to come near her again. *I have a staff, a knife and a club, come near me again and you will feel my temper.*

Moving forward, the rest of the afternoon passed uneventfully. Laura felt an irritation on the ball of her feet. Removed her boots; sharp twigs had poked holes in the soles. She placed some spongy leaves inside the boots, sat and ate a small piece of bread, finished her water and looked for somewhere to sleep for the night. With little food and no water, Laura considered walking through the night. She looked up, lowered her head and tried to envisage the route in her mind. As the sun sank and the shadow of dusk approached, she continued forward, but the atmosphere in the forest changed, it became dark and menacing. Undeterred, she pressed on, feeling each step. She tripped over a moss-covered stone, falling with outstretched arms; her hand sunk into a slimy hollow. Rolling onto her back, a patch of moonlight that had found a break in the trees shone down. The trees took on a new persona, trunks reaching skyward, the branches were arms reaching out to grab her. She started to tremble, fearful of the new form the woods had taken. She heard the trees talking amongst themselves. The trunks moved, clinging to each other, leaning over her body like a miniscule ant about to be crushed. A night breeze rattled the branches; the rustling leaves spoke in sarcastic whispers; *what is this silly girl doing?*

"No!" she shouted out aloud. *I must overcome this fear—trees cannot move, cannot speak. I will overcome this fear.*

A colony of bats, startled by Laura's outburst, went screeching up towards the moon. Grimacing, she turned to her side, her hand wrapped around a narrow, round spongy animal, it fell in half; she squealed. Her head fell in exasperation; it was only a decaying branch. She got to her feet; the bitter taste of nightshade chewed on her tongue. The last straw of light from the fading pale moon was consumed by the dead soul of the night sky. She was surrounded by the stillness of the forest; everything was obscured by a dreary grey haze. She had only taken a few steps; to her right, a twig snapped. In the darkness, she saw a white dash carrying a pair of red eyes. Her wavering hand held the knife to her front. Her other hand wrapped around the club. Like the eyes of a dark lord, the unseen entity inched closer. She lost all sense, *is it a sprite, troll an evil fae.* It was almost upon her. Now closer, she saw the black body with a white splash down its back, a polecat. She moved to the side as the animal shuffled past.

With no moon or stars for a guide, she lost all sense of direction. Feeling her way into a clump of ferns, she decided to stop. She flopped, shut her eyes and tried to sleep. It was dark and cold, not the cold of a winter's night but the bone-chilling cold of fear. She stifled a tear and pulled the blanket tighter. She tried to think about happier times, summer nights with her family, running with Snowy. A wave of wind stirred the leaves. She shivered. Her eyes closed, finally finding comfort in sleep.

She was started awake by a pencil of light touching her eyes; the darkness had yielded to the dawn. For a moment, she was disoriented, still at home curled up in her comfy bed. Her eyes opened, staring wildly at the moody trees until gradually, her mind focused.

She heard a noise, a scurrying along the forest floor; it sounded as if an army of mice were on the move. Shaking the leaves from the blanket, she rolled it up, then moved back onto the obscure trail. The first thing she saw, appeared to be balls of pointed sticks moving, she stared harder; it was a colony of spiny pigs Morgan called porcupines. They were feasting on a poor animal; it looked like a dead elk, with spines sticking out of its half-eaten body.

Laura tried to sidle around the porcupines, she considered them harmless, but as she moved, they turned, twenty pairs of eyes staring at Laura; she found this disconcerting. Without warning, one turned on its side and shot one of its quills. She skillfully sidestepped the shot. They all clattered their teeth, another with its quill erect shot a spine, again she sidestepped the shot. Another did the same, then another. She hastily backed into the undergrowth. *Morgan never told me they could do that!* Now she understood the quills in the elk's body, *that's how they hunt.* Laura decided to loiter out of sight from the archer porcupines, the name she had given to the creatures.

She settled down and ate the remaining bread. After an hour had passed, and hoping the archer porcupines had moved on, she ventured back to the trail. They were still there, a horrible odour emitted from them. More spines came shooting her way.

Knowing she couldn't keep dodging those missiles, she turned back into the thick undergrowth. Now she had no choice but to push through the thicket and re-join the path past those creatures. So, with the staff, she beats a new path, hoping to turn into the trail, beyond the archer porcupines.

65

Following the trail was hard, but trying to create her own path, near impossible; her progress was agonisingly slow. Stopping for a few seconds to get her breath back she decided it was time to head back to the trail.

Which way do I go? She had lost all sense of direction. Seeing a space open up to her left, Laura decided to head into the clearing, and get her bearings.

Approaching the small thicket, she felt the atmosphere change; the trees had stopped whispering, no animals were scurrying on the ground, it had grown darker. Laura looked up, trying to decide the correct direction to go.

A frosty chill ran through her body. Pausing, she folded her arms tightly about herself. Laura was becoming anxious. She slowly looked around; everything looks decayed, death oozes out everywhere. *What is this place? It's a forest within a forest, a withered forest.*

Deep in the earth, something shrieked. She shivers, her heart wrestled, trying to break out of her rib cage. As she moved forward to make her way out, she saw movements out of the corner of her eyes, shadows drifting in between the black walnut trees. Was she imagining things? No, she saw something lurking. Depression now entered her mind. A sense of impending doom struck. She started to cry uncontrollably. Deep down inside she couldn't understand why—why she couldn't shake off this fear. The back of her mind was confused, a muddled mess. Her conscious wanting to know what was happening; she continued sobbing. She could feel beads of sweat crawl down the curve of her backbone.

Laura was now fighting the desire to sleep, voices whispering into her ears, *sleep—you must sleep.* She fought against the urge, no must stay awake . . . *relax and sleep,* she cannot fight it, her eyelids droop, she can't help herself, *you must . . . sleep.* She stopped walking; her head dropped forward, it filled her with fear—those voices, now melodic, breathing hopelessness into her ears. *Sleep little baby sleep, shut your eyes, little baby, sleep.*

Mommy, daddy—help me, Uncle—please help me, she sobbed, no words left her mouth, she gripped her knife tightly in her right hand, ready to fight, but there's no one, nothing to fight. She staggers, falls, her knees hit the muddy floor. She feels herself sinking. *Must move.*

Her vision was fading, greying, becoming dreamy; scrambling along the floor in utter despair. Tears pouring from her eyes onto her cheeks. Laura is now crawling on her knees, she collapsed, her hands outspread, her face falls into a pool of slime. Prostrate on the soft forest floor, arms reaching out, she grabs a tree root. Her mind falters, she cannot understand why she is so lost. She pulls herself along the floor, her fingers, forklike bore into the soft soil, filling her nails with filthy sludge. Her face is covered in mud, she tries to move, but her spirit is crushed. The smells of the unearthly realm are drawn into her nose and lungs, filling her head with fog; her mind is intoxicated; she sinks into an abyss.

Three; four shadowy figures appear and gradually surround her. *Come little forest spirit, live in our secret place. You will be safe.* Ghostly hands reach out, caressing her body, her face. Her bones bite of frost. She tries to scream; a hollow sound spills out. All feelings are now lost, her mind empty, her spirit is leaving, casting her body aside; until finally, she is gone. Her body stops working, her mind has sunk into an abyss of nothingness.

‡

Kylo was lazily observing the landscape, sitting atop the lookout, between Baron and Sheena. Wafting away an irritating mosquito with his tail, his head inexplicably jerked, his blue eyes darkened.

"Sheena, I can feel a burning spark inside my heart, what's happening to me?"

Sheena pushed herself against Kylo's side, "it's your perceptive power, let me help."

She pushed her power into Kylo, "I can feel your friend."

Kylo moved to his feet, "its sister, she dead, dying, I want to reach out to Laura, mother help me."

"She's many leagues away, we need to get closer, run to our border, the river, I will help you."

Baron watched from atop as Sheena and Kylo, taking flying like strides, raced to the river.

Stopping on the water's edge Sheena pushed her body against Kylo's side, "connect your perceptive ability onto the back of my power and reach out to your friend. Reach inside her mind, talk to her."

He felt the strands of Sheena's power stretching his own ability. He reached Laura's mind and coursed inside her head. *Laura . . . Laura . . . Laura my friend, Laura where have you gone. Sister return to me, live, fight death live. Laura come back to me.*

‡

A flicker in the depths of Laura's mind.

Live.

The muscles of her jaws twitched.

fight death, live.

A colourful buzz of words barely perceptible circle inside.

Laura come back to me.

She felt her spirit, her lifeforce moving, detaching from her body being carried away. She broke away from the spectre and surged back home to her source of consciousness.

Her body gushed with life. She awakened from the nightmarish phantasm. *No—no must stop.* "release me!"

Her body is uncontrollable, convulsing. Finger reach inside for her lifeforce. She still had the knife in her hand, she flails the blade slicing nothing but the chilled air. Sinking again, *wake up—wake.* She stabs herself in the left upper arm, the knife slicing through soft skin. Searing pain ripped through Laura's body; a scream as high as the mountains leapt from her open mouth. Extracting the blade, she hollowed, deep and ghastly, like the mournful cry of the waking dead. Blood flooded out, seeping through her tunic. The shadowy figures fade and shrink back into the underworld trees.

Laura sluggishly pushed herself up from the ground, her legs wobbled, blood dripping down her arm. She hauls herself up onto her knees and kneels, trying to gather her thoughts; slowly coming back into herself. She had no recollection of the earlier events but knew something dreadful had happened. Clasping her arm where she stabbed herself, she struggles to her feet with the aid of the staff.

The demons are returning, slithering from their odious pit; edging closer, shadowy arms reaching out. They are also upon her; gnarled skinless fingers stroke her body. The feeling of self-doubt and worthlessness begin to overwhelm Laura. This time she was ready, biting her lip, widening her eyes. In the swirling mist of bleakness, for a moment she saw the head of the phantom. He had a face that looked like a crab, oval with barbed feelers protruding where ears should be. She screamed from the depth of her soul, into the spawn of death, "leave me be."

The fingers recoil. She drives her body forward, walking, crawling on her knees. With sheer determination, she reached the edge of the withered forest. With an extra rush of energy, she drove herself on, far away from the evil sorcery that had fouled the land.

Resting briefly to gather her thoughts, her breath, she pressed on. Endured the pain in her arm, determined to get far away from the Withered forest. After hours of hard slog, weary and dispirited, she collapsed into a bed of wild mushrooms that smelt of rotting meat. They soaked into her clothes; she was past caring; she wrapped the blanket around herself and went into a deep sleep.

Chapter 8

Return of the Imps.

It was late morning; she was roused by itching on her eyelid and nose. Sitting up and wiping her nose, she discovered a profusion of little red bugs attached to her face. Leaping to her feet, she saw her body was covered by a colony of tiny spiders. Running her hands down her body, shaking her blanket. Like a gust of wind, she moved away from the spider's nest she had slept in. Finding a small clearing, she rolled over on the forest floor like a tumbleweed in the desert.

Laura's head was now beating like the rhythm of a drum. She curled on the ground and started sobbing. The gash in her arm burnt like the ember of a fire. Pushing the tears back, she examined the wound and knew it needed treating. She crawled around foraging around the forest floor for herbal plants. Below a juniper plant, she found a small clump of chamomile flowers. After picking a bunch of the flowers, she collects some fleshy cones from the juniper plant. Further on, a small witch hazel tree provided her with a handful of leaves.

Sitting cross-legged she places some ingredients into her bag, the rest she rubs vigorously between her hands. With great care she applies the poultice to the wound, and wraps a sweet coltsfoot leaf around, tied with a piece of vine. Her tunic, being a little on the large size, rolled the sleeve down her arm, helping to keep the poultice in place.

Pushing her back against a tree, her legs stretched out; her mind started to struggle with the burden, the responsibility Her eyes closed, wishing she was back at home, regretting everything. Crying quietly to herself, she saw an image of her mother, lying on

71

the kitchen floor, beaten up, bruised and hurting. Raising her eyelids, her vow, made in haste now pressed heavily on her mind. She swallowed; *they will pay for beating Martha.* Using her staff to stand, she set forth following the sunrise.

‡

Laura was now moving deeper and deeper into the heart of the forest, she was becoming more fearful. *What other acts of dark sorcery will this forest throw at me?* Slashing at the compacted undergrowth with her staff, unaware of eyes in the shadows watching her every move. The knife is drawn and slashed at the creepers that hang down; they swing loosely, wrapping themselves around her body.

Smashing her way through a mass of vegetation, she enters a small pleasant glade. There were orange berries she had never seen before, she was tempted; they looked mouth-watering juicy. Pulling one from a branch she slips it into her mouth. As she did, she heard a snigger. With her tongue, she flipped out the berry and looked around. A group of those little imps came charging out of the bushes and circled Laura.

They start chanting, "no one gets out of our maze and lives to tell the tale. We are going to beat you, bind you and drag your body back to mistress."

Laura's stomach tightened; her skin prickled; she shook with fear. They were more of a nuisance when she first encountered these creatures, this time they looked dangerous and vicious. Laura guessed there were eleven crawling towards her, their pitchy eyes danced around dark eyelashes. Everyone had long dagger-like nails displayed. One particular imp appeared to be directing the others. He was grinning and baring his needle-sharp teeth.

Laura's mind fortified, she pulls her club out and pitched a raw demoralising scream, not a fearful or scared scream, but an attacking cry. "If you want my body, you will have a fight of epic proportions."

She ran at the leader, the club swinging to the left and right, lashing the imps that stood in her path. Tad stepped back from the impending battle as the sprightly youngster and the lively club approached. She raised the club to her shoulder, and with an arched swing, hit the side of his body, knocking him flying through the air. He landed with a crash, on his back, on top of two imps. This not only shocked Laura of her own strength and deftness but also the imps. They took a step or two back.

A twig snapped at her back, she swung around, holding the club in outstretched hands, whacked two that had tried to sneak up on her back. Both fell to the floor, knocked out, but not before one had bitten her leg the other had scratched her arm, drawing blood. They had moved further back, out of reach of the club, but still circled her.

The leader rose, dazed and unsteady hissed, "attack, everyone charge, she can't defeat us all."

With nothing to lose, Laura ran at the imps swinging the club, as if swatting flies. She hit two with one thwack, three more were smashed into the shrubs. The few still standing fled, scurrying to the undergrowth.

Laura grabbed the leader around its neck, lifted him to her face and said, "what's your name?"

His tongue lolls out of his mouth, "not telling." His breath smelt of rotting skin and bone.

"If you don't tell, I will crush your head like squashing a snail's shell. Your innards will be left on the forest floor for the birds of the air to feast on." Squeezing his neck, "what's your name?"

Through its quivering mouth hissed, "Tad."

"Well, Tad—see this club," pushing it under his chin, "I will call it Tad basher, come after me again and you will receive Tad basher whacked on your skull, it will break like cracking an egg. Understand?"

"Yes," Tad babbled through trembling jaws.

She released her grip and let him plummet to the forest floor, landing with a dull thud. He hobbled into the undergrowth to join the rest of the pack.

Now tired, after whacking the imps, she decided that this was a comfortable place to sleep.

After tramping through the outskirts of this glade, she was sure the imps had gone. Collecting bracken, she threw it around the base of a tree; followed by her blanket. She then pulled the sides of the blanket around her body, with one hand on the knife, the other gripping Tad basher.

‡

Zee paced around her table. She grabbed a vial of green viscous and threw it at Tad. He sidestepped the missile.

She raged, "I must have that girl's spirit, it's my chance of freedom from this distorted body. First, she escapes my labyrinth, next she batters my wee soldiers."

She stopped pacing and glared at the imps, "why couldn't eleven of you overpower one child?"

"But she has got Tad basher," Tad whined, in a feeble voice.

"You spineless imp! You've got razor teeth and sword sharp claws," replied Zee.

Irked, she started pacing around her lair, kicking any imp that was stupid enough not to take evasive action when she passed by. She sat at her table, staring at all the vials, chewing on her bony fingers; thinking.

Her voice came out in a threatening tone. "I have a plan for you; run like the rapids, following her route. Move ahead; dig a deep wide hole, then cover it with bracken, sticks and moss, then wait for her to fall in. Leave nothing inside the trap, no vines that will enable her to climb out. She will be around the central clearing now. Bring her back to me; I don't care what you do to her, as long as she is still breathing. Otherwise."

With that warning, they scampered away, with fear shooting through their tiny bodies. They scurried through the forest, sometimes using the trees, swinging from branch to branch like deviant monkeys, desperate to get ahead of Laura. They ran throughout the day and night, arriving at the clearing in front of Laura. Further on, they found an ideal spot to set the trap. They dug with their claws and feet, deeper and deeper, they toiled all day and throughout the night. By dawn they had created a deep hole, they covered it with twigs, bracken and moss. The rest of the morning they laughed and danced.

Chapter 9

Storm.

The throbbing in her arm woke Laura. She prepared and applied a fresh poultice on her wound. Pulling her tunic on, she got to her feet and continued the journey. There was a refreshing, crisp chill in the air. She breathed in the fragrance of fallen pines, giving Laura fresh impetus.

By noon she had made good progress and was ready to take a rest when she spied a bush filled with ground plums. Most had gone over, but she found eight fit to eat. She sat munching her prize, letting the juices trickle around her chin, onto her bloodied tunic. With a full stomach, she felt pleased and more confident with herself. She pressed on, humming her favourite lullaby, the golden moonbeam. Most of the journey had been dank and dark, up ahead it looked lighter, she quickened her pace to see what was there.

The forest astonishingly opened up. Laura had come to a large clearing with the sun sending golden rays of light penetrating through the leafy canopy; illuminating the glade. Looking around she saw a small pine marten foraging on the woodland floor; she could just make out a peregrine hovering above the treetops.

Her eyes caught a movement in the opposite end of the clearing, a unicorn stood feeding on juniper berries. The sight mesmerised Laura. It looked so magnificent, dusty grey, around his fetlocks hung a tress of brown like ankle socks, below four brilliant white hooves. Its horn was stunning, glistening from a sunbeam of light. A translucent golden colour, rising from its forehead like an icicle, it spiralled to a point.

His silver eyes, as bitter as the devil's touch studied Laura for a few seconds. He swished his tail and scraped his left hoof into the soil, sending a cloud of decaying leaves into the air. He gave a loud snort and charged at Laura, his hooves crushing the vegetation, brush and wildflowers. He lowered his head, its horn pointed directly at her. Not knowing which way to run, but aware she could never outrun this creature, she looked around for a tree to climb.

With her back against the tree, her palm pushed against the smooth bark she started to edge around the tree. The green blades of grass she stood on began to sparkle. She watched as green specks crawled up her body. She looked down as the horn of the unicorn passed under her feet. She stopped breathing; her whole body was floating up the tree. Looking left and right, around her body, six tree sprites materialised, holding her arms and legs. Her alarm at travelling into the highest branches of a tree was eased by one of the sprites singing in her mind. *Relax your arms, your legs, your fear. Shut your eyes, think of the sun setting on a summer solstice.*

High up they journeyed to the forest canopy, where they alighted onto a wooden nest, shaped from the branches of the tree. It felt so good to be breathing in fresh air, the sweet smell of the treetop leaves. These tree sprites differed from those she had seen by the farm. They were dressed in a red-brownish outfit, had the same colour hair, but had it tied back with a decorative band.

The shock of been lifted so high subsided, she dropped her eyelids and formed words in her head. *You saved me from being gored by that awful unicorn, thank you.*

A noise purred inside. *My name is Ivy, our neighbours asked us to watch over you if you ventured into this part of the forest. They relayed a message by the trees.*

By the trees? Inquired Laura.

The tree roots touch, talk and sent messages, your journey has passed from tree to tree.

These tree sprites communicate with a soothing singing voice, it's so relaxing Laura mused.

Ivy continued, *do not think badly of the unicorn. He is called Storm; a few days ago, his companion, Trinity disappeared. She loved to run free in the pasture; Storm believes men from the village caught her. He assumes they killed her for her horn, he's probably right. So now he hates humans, he wanders around the forest calling her name. It's sad to see such a fabulous creature who has lost the will to live.*

Laura's head droops. *That is so sad, I have seen the evil that some men can do.*

You may spend the night here; you will be refreshed by tomorrow morning.

They gave Laura a vessel of water, it tasted of lavender flowers. *It's wonderful*, she thought, sipping the drink.

They provided a willow hammock; she had a restful night's sleep.

Laura was woken by speckles of dewdrops and dappled light dancing across her face. The breeze in the air was so energising. She stretched out her arms and lifted her eyes up to the sun. Reapplying a fresh poultice, she surveyed the crown of the tree. How could anything so cold, foreboding and evil lay at the bottom of these trees?

She was given another vessel of water; it tasted of the essence of elderberry flowers; she shut her eyes *if only I could stay here.* Laura informed Ivy, *I must move; my family are in danger.*

Ivy mused, *Storm has moved away, your paths will not cross, he has gone towards the north side of the forest. We have filled your water vessel; you are only a few days away from the exit.*

‡

Warily making her way across the clearing, heading towards the juniper plant; the one Storm had been eating berries from; she had perceived a slight trail behind the bush. Pushing back the overhanging stems, the grass was flatter, loose twigs were brushed either side of the path. Looking up, the sun beamed back into her face. She smiled; *this trail is going to lead me out of the forest.* A few steps to her left, hiding behind the wrinkled trunk of a crocked hazel tree, Tad grinned, his dark eyes glistened like jet.

With stealth and guile, he hurried back to the prepared trap. "Quick hide," Tad shouted, "she's coming."

Within a trice, they were hiding behind the closely knit trees, barbed bushes, and the large fronds of the ferns that were scattered everywhere. They heard Laura approaching, swishing her staff as she followed the path.

"Sssh, no sounds or giggling," warned Tad.

Laura came into view, took a few steps forward, and stopped dead. Her body hedged with disquiet. She perceived something was wrong. Morgan's teachings triggered an alarm. The path she had just emerged from was full of brambles. Here the path widened into a small tidy clearing, filled with soft moss. Further on, the path narrows. Her breathing slowed. *No, something is wrong.*

She took a slow step back. Two imps dived at her from behind, driving their nails through her tunic, into her back. she winced, it felt like the stinging of a multitude of bees. She screamed in pain as the claws bore deeper into her skin. She wavered unsteadily. One slashed the back of her neck; she cried out; a tear of pain fell onto her cheek. A river of blood seep into her tunic and flow down her back. Another imp ripped his jagged claws into the back of her knees and ran the barb down to her ankles. The burst of pain crawled up her leg she choked, and stumbled forward, onto her knees, splaying her arms out. Her hands hit the moss and passed

79

through; she fell headlong into the trap, landing face down into a segment of gravel, cutting her forehead.

She lay there covered in sticky sweat from the day's trek, her grimy hands still gripping her staff; it had become her companion, her friend. Her blackened scratched and bloody face pressed against the hard earth. She took a deep breath to compose herself and realised the dank smell she breathed in was her own body. Above she heard the imps laughing and whooping. Those vile creatures had transformed from inconvenient pests to deadly monsters; *will this pit be my grave?* Laura lay still. *I can't allow them to kill me—mommy, my family, they are all waiting for me.*

They were taking turns looking over the pit, throwing pebbles at her prostrate body. Tongues sloshed around lips.

Tad pushed to the edge of the pit, "we've done it, we've caught her at last; no escaping now. Zee will drain and consume her life-force; we will feast on her flesh and bones." A vein of drool trickled out the corner of his mouth, "I want to eat her warm heart while it is still beating."

One imp asked, "how do we get her out of the pit?"

Another said, "and back to Zee?"

She lay still, listening to the sinister words of Tad. *Who is Zee, a bloodthirsty ghoul; a stony monster like the little imps; what's their plan?*

The imps were silent, no one knew what to do. They moved away from the pit and sat assembled in a circle, jabbering amongst themselves. Now no one was watching, Laura, ignoring the sting in her back and the gash in her leg, cautiously got to her feet. Looking around, trying to assess the snare she was in. she saw plant roots were protruding from the sides, which were covered in ants scurrying everywhere. Laura, looking around; the pit was long, but narrow, with outstretched arms, she could easily touch both sides with the palms of her hands. The imps had dug, by their reckoning dug a deep hole, but they hadn't considered Laura's full height, which was equivalent to four imps.

When she stood full height, the hole was not deep. *With my arms stretched out, and a small leap, I could reach the top.* She was about to jump up but hesitated? *They would hear me scrambling up, then they would bite, stamp and tear my fingers and hands. I would fall back in. That would be the end; they would set a watch. I need to get out quick.* Squatting in a corner like a glum gnome, she sunk her head into her arms. Her mind was racing. *I must escape; I'm getting close to my goal.*

Meanwhile, the imps were arguing amongst themselves on how to incapacitate her.

"Let's throw stones and rocks at her, knock her unconscious, bind her with vines, then we can drag her to Zee."

"Yes, mistress will be elated; she will be good to us."

Sitting in the corner, she ran her hands along the staff. A shiver of expectation flashed across her eyes, a revelation; the staff is longer than the sides of the hole. Rising to her feet, she crouched down low, holding the staff out in two hands. She leapt up as high as possible. As she reached the peak of her jump, she swung the staff around and held on tight. The staff smacked onto the edges of the pit, like a perch. She somersaulted around the staff like a circus acrobat. The momentum carried her right over the staff, into the air and above the hole; she flipped onto the ground.

The imps had started to rise when they heard the thud of the staff. They saw Laura flying out of the hole, still holding her staff in her right outstretched arm. Her tunic was loosely flapping about her body with strands of thread weaving in the air like a broken yarn wheel. Her mud-caked hair, now dishevelled, was lying tangled across her crabbed face; her eyes clouded blood-red from the forehead cut.

One imp shouted, "a witch! She's flying out on a broomstick."

As Laura landed on the clearing, she dropped her staff and pulled Tad basher from her belt.

Clasping it tightly in both hands, she raised it high above her head and brought it down hard into the ground with a tremendous crack.

Loose twigs, dry dust, and fallen leaves flew into the air. An explosion of sunshine fell through the canopy, throwing shafts of light against Laura's back. She emerged. from the dust storm with starry specks floating around her body.

The imps were caught unawares, their mouths open, staring in astonishment.

Laura was outraged they had tried a third time to capture her, light flared behind her eyes

"The witch eye is going to curse us," another squealed.

With Tad basher held high, eyes ablaze, jaws clenched baring her teeth. roared, "where's Tad?"

A scream from amongst the imps and Tad flew away. Laura raised Tad basher high as if reaching for the sky, advanced towards the remaining imps, first one ran, another followed, soon they were all fleeing.

Looking elated as she retrieved her staff, she couldn't prevent a look of triumph splash across her face.

‡

Back at Zee's lair, the imps came staggering back, it had been two days since the failed trap on Laura.

"Where's the girl?" screeched Zee, "has she defeated you again?"

"She's a witch," cried out Tad, "she flew out the trap on a broomstick. Her red eyes would have bewitched us."

"Yes," cried the others, "she flew out, into the air and attacked us, we ran for our lives."

Zee didn't know what to make of this explanation, her imps couldn't lie to her, but a flying girl, a witch, it made little sense. She pondered over this girl and her escapades for many days. It festered in her mind, another girl teasing me.

Grabbing the nearest imp by the throat, screeched, "she's taunting me, calling me stupid with her actions. We will dispel this—this witch girl."

Chapter 10

Starfall.

Laura had spent the night alongside a fallen tree trunk but had slept little, worrying about the imps returning. A scampering noise alarmed Laura, she peers over the tree and had to squint her eyes through the forest haze; she saw a pair of wild boars. They were both meandering around, searching the undergrowth for food. They both raise their noses in the air and turned as one as they picked up Laura's scent. Laura held her breath as she looked around for the easiest tree to climb. Two strides and a leap, she had caught the lowest limb of the tree, swung herself up and sprang up to the next branch. There she sat watching the boars, which gave a short snort and wandered away.

The boars hadn't bothered Laura; what did was the figure she glimpsed hiding amidst a buckthorn. He appeared to fade into the environment, but a ray of sunlight caught strands of his leafy hair.

Laura slithered down the tree and skilfully hid from this stranger; here she waited until midmorning. Hoping the watcher had moved on, Laura—crouching, stealthfully returned to her route.

As Laura followed a bend in the track, sitting on a branch of a tree was the young boy.

"Hello," he said, swinging his legs loosely, "I've been following you throughout the afternoon."

"I saw you in the buckthorn bush this morning!" retorted Laura.

"I spied you trying to hide behind that tree you had climbed."

"I saw you a few times, following me, hiding behind bushes, above in the trees."

The boy's voice wobbled, "you couldn't, you lie. I'm nimble, disguised, and glide in the trees."

"A few moments ago, you were hiding behind a fern, as I approached you slid into that ditch," replied Laura, pointing to the ditch. She added, "your clothes do blend into the forest, but your eyes shine like will-o'-the-wisps on a midnight lake."

His eyelids widened, exposing his jewel-like emerald eyes. "What's your name; what are you doing here; where are you going; where are you from; don't you know it's dangerous in here?" he gushed out.

She took in his appearance He wore a tan and apple green tunic, with short jade green boots. She could distinguish a few strands of his curly forest green hair peeking from under his pine coloured hood. He was fair skinned. She twirls her head away from him, ignoring the questions.

"Have you got lost; do you live in the village?"

She gave him a warning glare, turned away and continued to beat a path with her staff.

"Can't you find your way back home?"

"You're a talkative and nosy person, where I'm going is my business," she replied sharply.

In an exasperated tone, "well you're a dirty little girl who needs a good wash."

"Well so would you, if you had done only half of what I have done," she stated smugly.

This was her first encounter with someone her own age. He intrigued her, at the same time he infuriated her.

"Your face is grotesquely murky—is that blood on your tunic?" he asked.

She ignored him, embarrassed. Laura knew her face was covered in dried mud; she looked grubby with her dirty, torn clothes and she was surrounded by an offensive odour that clung to her body.

He tried again, "will you tell me what you are doing in this forest?"

"What I am doing is none of your business," she replied whilst swinging her staff clearing a path.

"Do you want me to show you the way out?" he asked.

"No, I don't need any help from a nosy boy who keeps chattering and asking questions all the time."

Laura gave him a sideward glance. *It would be nice to have someone for company, but who is he; and can I trust him?*

"In that case," he offered, "I will walk in front, and you can follow a few steps behind, I won't speak unless you ask me something."

Laura's instinct was to trust this boy, "you lead the way then," she said, leaning on a tree, and waving him forward.

Stepping past Laura, he pointed to the left, "a path through the forest!"

So off they set, walking with the lad in front, Laura walking just behind, and true to his word he kept quiet. He led Laura to a path where she didn't have to beat the overgrown vegetation.

Laura broke the silence first, "who are you; what are you doing in this forest; how old are you?" she asked.

"Oh, it's your turn to be nosy now, my name is Jayden, I'm twelve," he replied. "I live in this forest with my parents," cautiously he asked, "what are you doing in here?"

Wary of telling him anything, she replied casually, "I'm eleven, I must get out of this forest."

"Do you have any friends; what're their names; are you here alone?" Asked Jayden, hoping for a reply.

"I'm here alone, my best friend is Snowy, we . . ." She bit her lip; she didn't want to tell him about Snowy.

Jayden, downheartedly lamented, "I don't have any friends. I live with my parents; they say it's not safe for me to have friends. Will you be my friend?"

"I don't know", but seeing Jayden look disappointed added, "maybe when I accomplice my task."

He suggested they go back to his home, "it's called Starfall," he said. "You can meet my parents, it's just a short distance from the path. My mother will give you food and drink, you must be hungry."

Laura cautiously agreed, but kept one hand on Tad basher, ready for any surprises.

They had only followed the path for a short time, when Jayden next jumped over a briar bush and pointed, "This way, we're here!"

They were alongside the dwelling before Laura realised. It was surrounded by five dwarf birch trees, the branches of which conjoined to make the structure. If Jayden hadn't pointed out the access, she or anyone else wouldn't have known there was a home here.

They both entered, it was a huge warren, passageways snaking to the left and right, like a spider's web. Tree branches shaped the sides and floor. No doors or windows; it was lit by shards of light pouring in from above, where the treetops opened. The sunrays were reflected by orbs of agate creating a blaze of light and colour.

What is this place, she wondered; *what have I come to, another trap?*

"Gav, Sylviana come, look what I found wandering in the forest; a smelly ragamuffin girl in need of a wash."

His parents appeared from a passage on the left, Sylviana, Jayden's mother was dressed in a long white dress with a silver belt around her middle. Her long flaxen hair flowed like waves of the sea; her skin shone with a golden lustre. A circlet sat on her crown. Her ears were leaf-shaped.

Sylviana took Jayden's arm, and pulled him to a corner, "why have you brought a stranger here, you know the dangers if she tells anyone about us."

"I have observed children from the village; she's not like them. She's well educated, and here for a reason. I watched her all morning; she's observant, she knew I was following. There's a determination driving her forward, but she needs help; look at the state she is in. I trust her."

Sylviana walked over to Laura, aware of her staring said, "yes, I'm an elf, don't be worried, you're safe here."

Laura had never seen an elf before, she had heard Morgan tell stories of elves, but found it strange to come across one living in a forest.

"You're extremely muddy and threadbare; is that blood on your face and tunic?" said Sylviana, "come with me, there's a spring at the back of this passage, where you can wash. You can loan Jayden's clothes, we'll wash yours, they'll be clean and ready by tomorrow morning."

A wash sounded good, but stopping—she wasn't so sure.

"I would love to take a bath; I haven't had one for a few days."

Sylviana, taking Laura's hand, led her through a short passage of miniature saplings. Each one was adorned with beads of glass, stone and wood, that delicately tinkled as they walked along; the floor, like a tree carpet, felt silky underfoot.

When they reached the end, it opened out to a small grotto, with a spring surrounded by amethyst rock. It looked a magical place with violet light dancing off the roof. Water fell into the pool like the colours dripping from a painting box, creating a blend of shining whirls over the clear pool.

Laura looked astonished, "how can a horrid place have something so beautiful in it?"

"I formed the spring, and Gavin created the dell. Now young lady you badly need a wash before we send you home."

For the first time since entering the forest she looked at her clothes, they were covered in dirt, the true colours unidentifiable. Rips and tears everywhere, blood covered the sleeve where she stabbed herself.

"I'm sorry, my clothes—they're disgusting!" she said apologetically. "Mother made this tunic for my birthday; I've ruined it."

 She put her staff against a tree, removed her drinking vessel, knife and Tad basher, her rope she carefully draped over a stool.

Sylviana picked up the rope and running her hands over it, asked, "who gave you this; it's so light, like?"

"My uncle Morgan fashioned it, and gave it to me for my birthday," interrupted Laura as she removed her tunic.

"How did you get that cut on your arm; and those bites on your back, and legs, why have you got so many?"

"Imps," replied Laura, "they tried to capture me—three times."

"That's strange, those interfering folks don't venture this side of the forest," said Sylviana believing Laura had only travelled from the village.

"And the arm wound?"

"I did it to myself, I can't remember what happened, I know I needed to awaken myself from a nightmare."

Laura's knees buckled; she held the stool for support. The imp's attack and exhaustion had taken its toll. Sylviana placed her arm around Laura's shoulders, "you're in a terrible state, you need rest. I have berry leaves and root potion to help soothe those injuries. After you have bathed, I will rub some onto your wounds. Whilst you wash, I'll collect my ointments and some clothes for you to wear."

Laura, feeling more relaxed, stepped into the spring water, "oh it's warm."

Sylviana nodded and disappeared down the passageway.

She removes the poultice and lay in the spring water for longer than she intended; it was so relaxing she didn't want to get out. She cleaned her hair, which had mud caked in; it was back to a reddish-brown colour.

Sylviana returned and looked at the discarded poultice, "you know your herbs and healing plants, who taught you?

"My uncle Morgan, he's my teacher."

"He is an intelligent man. Let me take care of those imp wounds. First, I will glide my fingertips over your injuries."

Laura winced when her knife wound was touched; gradually all the discomfort eased. She felt an inner glow and saw a colourful phenomenon; her entire body was shimmering.

"What's happening; what are you doing?"

"I have basic elfin healing power," she replied silkily. "I will need to rub the potions on afterwards."

Sylviana rubbed her potion mix into the bites and scratches, it was so refreshing.

"Now for the knife wound, I have a special ointment for cuts." Her eyes dulled, "it's infected."

Sylviana cleaned, treated, and dressed the gash, applying a new poultice. "Put these clothes on, they're Jayden's, but they will do for tonight. We will eat now."

"Thanks, my bread ran out days ago, the imps stole one of my loaves."

"The water, how . . .?"

"It's elf warming stones, I created them," interrupted Sylviana.

After Laura dressed, they moved along another of the passages, meeting Gavin. He reminded Laura of Morgan. He was tall, a little taller than Morgan, dresses in a biscuit coloured intricately woven shirt and chestnut trousers.

He brushed aside a skirt of hanging vines, leading Laura into a round room. It was like walking into the innards of a tree, mousey brown walls, with a beautifully decorated table as a centrepiece where Jayden was sitting. Laura sat next to him. Sylviana disappeared into another passage, and soon returned with a brown topped mushroom pie, bowls of herbal soup, and lots of cakes; freshly baked bread and scented water. Laura took a deep breath, the aroma swirled around the room, she salivated, everything smelt so appetising. She bit into her piece of the pie, the first meal since starting the journey. It tasted delicious, melting on her tongue. She was eating as leisurely as possible, savouring every mouthful.

Jayden kept trying to learn why Laura was alone in the forest, "have you run away from the village; your family; did you get lost?"

Gavin, realised that Laura hadn't eaten a proper meal for a while said, "wait, let Laura eat, she hasn't had any good food since entering this forest."

Laura, with a mouthful of food, just nodded her head in agreement, they ate in relative silence.

After swallowing the last morsel, Laura sat back in her chair, her stomach full and satisfied. Now comfortable with Jayden and his family, she told them she was from a farmhouse on the opposite side of the forest.

"What!" exclaimed Sylviana her head shooting up, "you have journeyed throughout this forest—alone; I find that hard to believe."

"Yes, it's true," said Laura.

She proceeded to tell her tale, why she was here, and the exploits since entering the forest.

When Laura reached the part of the journey where she entered the withered forest, her voice trembles.

Breathing heavily, "I see something . . . I hear . . ." her voice faltered.

"On my knees," her eyes staring into nothing, hands turn white gripping the table.

"I . . . saw . . . felt," tears now streaming down her face, her body starts shaking.

Jumping to his feet, the chair crashing backwards to the ground, Gavin cried out, "SYLVIANA."

Sylviana was instantly up, took Laura into her arms and held her tight. Laura's body went into spasms. Sylviana stepped back and slapped Laura in the face, she was now limply hanging in Sylviana's arms. She held her tighter, letting her body radiate into Laura. There was an aura of iridescent between the two, the demon inside was driven back.

Gavin had his hands resting on Jayden's shoulders, who was visibly shaken by Laura's incident. He said, "you did the right thing by bringing Laura back here."

Laura slowly recovered, opened her eyes, ". . . what happened?"

Sylviana took both of Laura's hands into hers and said, "something from the forest has blackened your soul. You must never talk about that place, or what you experienced—to anyone. It lingers within you, bringing you into a deep depression, it's something you cannot control. I perceived that you were lost last time. Someone who loves you immensely must have known your mind was clouded and reached out to you; how I don't know."

Whilst Sylviana was holding her hands, Laura shut her eyes, feeling a warmth radiate deep inside her body; she became tranquil. *Elves have a sensitive and kindly touch. I'm glad I trusted Jayden.* When she raised her eyelids, she saw Sylviana's arms looked suntanned, her fingertips, like flower stems, were verdant and moist.

Deep down inside Sylviana had a tear forming, not since leaving her parents had she shed a tear. Now holding Laura, she identified empathy towards her. *So much burden for one so young.*

Sylviana turned her head, looked to Gavin and whispered, "I must help this young girl."

After a few moments, Gavin spoke, "come, we'll leave it for today, you can continue your story tomorrow when you have rested."

Laura, now regaining her composure, asked Gavin and Sylviana how they came to live in a dark and dangerous forest. "Don't elves live in an Elven Tribe, in the open air?"

"My people live in an enclave where the sunlight shines on our dwellings," said Sylviana, "but our experience is something special. Come let us move to our central chamber and relax, I will tell you our story."

They moved down a passage, to a smaller, intimate room.

Sylviana said to Laura, "Sit here, we will have a drink whilst I tell our story."

She left the room and soon returned with four beakers full of water. Laura took a sip, refreshingly cool, with a hint of honey.

Sylviana began, "fourteen years ago, I was playing in a dell, with two friends when four human boys came upon us; we ran away. Our leader forbids elves to engage with humans. Whilst my two friends went back to our dwelling, I lingered behind watching these boys, as they destroyed our flower dolls. When they had wrecked everything, they scurried off back to the village. One boy, who had just watched the others destroying our handiwork, stayed behind examining our creations and tried to repair one.

Fascinated, I approached this lad and asked him why they wanted to destroy our work? He told me it was because they did not understand it, but he found the work creative and intricate. His honesty struck me, so I sat with him, talking about the country, animals and insects. I explained how plants, flowers and herbs are useful. Before we realised it, the evening was upon us, and it was time to go home. He asked if we could meet again, I said yes, I was enthralled by this human, his name was Gavin."

Sylviana paused and looked across the room at Gavin, with a pleasing smile.

"We met the next day, then the following day, we continued to meet all season. He told me he couldn't imagine his life without me in it, I told him I felt the same. He suggested meeting my family, reluctantly I agreed, not sure what they would say. Back home I told my family I had someone I wanted them to meet, Gavin, my human friend. They were horrified, my father raised his hand as if to strike me, but my mother stood between, and stopped him. He sneered at me, saying elves do not mix with humans. Next morning, he appeared to have calmed down and told me to bring him back. I said I would bring him back tomorrow morning, I returned to my chamber extremely happy. Later that evening my friend Flora came into my room, she looked distressed. I asked her what was troubling her. Flora told me that Gavin would be killed if I brought him home. I was distraught and argued with Flora, defending my family. She convinced me to follow her to our assembly room where all the elders were in a meeting. Hiding in the chamber above listening, I soon realised that Flora was correct when my father stated that I would never see any humans again."

Sylviana paused, and took a long drink, sweeping her hair back, she continued.

"I had to stifle my tears as Flora led me back to my dwelling. Making me sit, she asked me two questions. Did I want to spend the rest of my life with Gavin and does he feel the same? I answered yes to both questions. A third question was asked, will I leave the safety of the elfin enclave, and never see my parents again. This was hard for me to answer, but my feeling for Gavin was so strong, I answered yes. She told me to rise before dawn, take all my belongings, and meet her in the glen. When Flora arrived, I was told to fetch Gavin, with all his essential items. Gavin wanted to know our destination, but I was more concerned with the elf trackers finding our route. She told us she had been up all night, laying false trails, and they would never find our path.

Flora is one of the most gifted elves I know. We eventually ended up in this forest."

‡

Whilst Flora and Sylviana were absconding, Agish, the elf king's advisor was pacing around waiting for the elf trackers return. He had sent three trackers out, immediately news of their disappearance had been reported. They returned around midday, reporting that Flora had laid several false trails that kept splitting into two paths. Three they followed circled and re-joined another one led to a stream, whilst others just came to a dead-end. This news angered Agish, he swore to the elf king that he would track and return the two elf females by whatever means possible.

‡

Sylviana continued, "Flora is most gifted. She had spent her life learning and gaining knowledge. Leaving fake trails came easily to Flora. She spent a few weeks here, helping us shape and hide this dwelling. After five weeks, Flora revealed it was time for her to leave. Gavin and I pleaded with her to stay, I told her they will know it was you who helped us, they will not welcome you back into the clan unless you reveal our whereabouts. She insisted on leaving but said she had a mind to stay close by where she could watch and warn us if any trackers came close to discovering our new home. we knew Starfall would be hidden from humans but elves could easily find us, so Flora left to set up her own place, hidden in a forest."

Laura looked up, fascinated by the life of elves and these stories, but had something on her mind. "Why did Flora give up her life in the enclave to help you escape?"

"I asked Flora the same question, she said it was similar to our story, this is what she told us. I was walking out one day when I can upon a lad studying the flora and fauna in a dell. Unaware I

96

was there I watched this lad for many days, he was at home with the forest. One day I approached him, he was a friendly, good-natured tall and handsome. I taught him about the environment, wildlife and elfin skills. He was an exceptionally good pupil, absorbing everything.

We continued to meet throughout the year, learning from each other, our friendship developed into something much deeper. I asked if he'd come and meet my kinsfolk, I felt sure they would welcome him. I told everyone in the elfinglen I was bringing someone special home. The following day, I took my mother and father to the dell where we meet. When he arrived, ten elves that had followed us, grabbed and bound him. Father held me around the neck, what's going on I cried. You will not promise yourself to a human, you will never see him again. My father hollered, take him away and throw him into the gorge.

They destroyed me on that faithless day, I have only existed since then. They tried to match me many times, I refused to meet with any of the suitors. When I saw you in the same situation as me, I guessed your family would react the same way mine did. So, I observed your parents after you had left, and it confirmed my worst fears, that's when I came to your room."

Laura's eyes narrowed making her eyebrows crinkle. She sat with her hands twinned tapping her thumbs, "they killed the man Flora was in love with—for no reason other than he was human?"

Sylviana closed her eyes and nodded her head.

Breaking the silence, "mother, will you please sing for us before we sleep," asked Jayden.

"Fetch my lyre," she replied.

Sylviana sat cross-legged on the floor, her fingers dancing across the strings of the lyre. She started singing the cry of the wolf song. Her voice sent a chill through Laura, the notes danced from her like a flute, so soothing. Laura sat mesmerised, watching Sylviana's lithe fingers fade from green to a flowery amber.

After she finished, Sylviana said to Laura, "I know you are keen to reach the garrison, but it's best for you to rest here tonight, and tomorrow. The next morning, we will travel with you, to the side of the forest."

Laura started to protest, but Sylviana said, "you need to recover from your wounds, especially the knife injury, I can treat you tomorrow, please—for your own health. It will take you another two days to reach the forest edge alone, we will get you there in one day; you won't lose any time."

Sylviana put her arm around Laura, it was such a warm embrace, Laura believed she spoke sincerely.

"Yes, I am exhausted, it was more dangerous than I imagined, they were right I shouldn't have taken this journey."

"No," retorted Sylviana, "your family are in great danger, you took the only option open. You are here now, they will soon be freed from their captors, thanks to your bravery. They will be so pleased when you return home."

Sylviana took Laura down a small corridor under an arch and into a doorless room. As she entered, Laura took a deep breath; the sparse room had the fragrance of lavender. A large cot pushed against the side wall, with a fleece cover. A wooden chair alongside, and a small round barrel with a washbasin and a carafe of fresh spring water.

Sylviana gave Laura a tender hug, "you can rest here tonight."

"May I ask you something, personal?"

"Perhaps, what's your question?"

"How does your skin tone change? It's like the seasons move across your body."

"Rest back and I'll tell you our history. Many centuries ago, princess Aurora, a human and her lover, a mage, lay together beside a sycamore tree, on the harvest eve. The silver moon threw down a star ray of life onto the couple. The princess bore the seed of man and the fruits of the tree. Their offspring was called Argent, part human, part tree with sap and blood running through her veins. Her body was mostly human with the ears of a leaf and the skin of the tree; the first elf. Argent became one with nature, coupling with humans, none could resist her beauty, charm and magical entrapment. The fruits she bore were of lesser elves; she became their queen. Many more elves were conceived on that special night, ensuring our succession line continued. But it's not necessary anymore. With the essence of nature in our skin, we learnt to control and alter the colour, as the changing season's change the colour of plants. We have developed into two races, the silver maple, of which I am one. The others are Skeltonian, dark and mysterious, they keep to themselves, hidden deep in the ground. They do not respect nature, the changing seasons; they hate humans. They also avoid contact with us."

Sylviana stopped talking, Laura's eyelids were drooping. She kissed her on the cheek and left.

Laura lay on the bed, unable to sleep, her mind was on Sylviana's reasoning, someone had reached out to her, who could it be; Snowy, but how did he call my name? Shutting her eyes, she snuggled into the fleece and slept soundly.

‡

Sylviana said to Gavin, "I fear for Laura if the demon materialises, she will be lost."

"I know you want to keep her here, but she will not stay, completing her journey is paramount to saving her family," Gavin reasoned. "Maybe we can travel to her home, and you can care for Laura with her family. I know it will be dangerous for us, but I agree we should help. Someone that is prepared to undertake such a perilous journey for their family deserves any help we can give. Possibly go to Flora and ask for her help."

"That's been on my mind, but first let's get Laura home."

The next morning, Laura awoke just as Sylviana called out, "did you have a good night sleep?"

"Best night since I entered this forest," replied Laura, as she arose.

Sylviana gave Laura her own clothes back, not only were they clean, but repaired, the rips had been stitched, the bloodstain removed. They were as new, a red and gold coloured tunic, it felt so soft, she put her face right into the fabric, it smelt of almonds, so fresh. The khaki leggings were stitched with colourful patchwork, and the shiny conker coloured boots had a mild smell of leather.

She spent the day with Jayden, he took Laura over their home; it was how she imagined an elf would live, filled with sweet-smelling herbs and spices. They had a flower, herb and vegetable plots, concealed from prying eyes. He told her the reason for the shape of their home, was to provide an escape if they were discovered.

They talked of elf history, Jayden said, "mother didn't tell you everything about Argent. When her time was due, she walked into the elf realm forest and became one with the elements. Her feet and legs became roots connecting with the earth. Her body grew bark; arms and fingers became branches and leaves. She became a mighty sycamore tree known as the Fountain of Argent. The tree reaches to the heavens, the branches spread out wide. It is said she still watches over us."

Throughout the day, Sylviana treated Laura's wounds, the knife gash had become infected, but by the end of the day, it had cleared. Laura, optimistically upbeat, delighted she had trusted Jayden, and grateful to everyone. Tomorrow, fit, healthy, and clean, she could complete her mission, things were looking better.

During the evening they sat together, and she completed her story of the unicorn attack, the tree sprites and the imp traps. They were astonished at her bravery and cleverness in finding a way out of the imp pit.

"You are so knowledgeable; how did you learn so much?" Asked Sylviana.

"My uncle Morgan has been my teacher from an early age," replied Laura.

Chapter 11

The Moss Garden.

Laura was given the same room to sleep in, but this time she arose at dawn, ready to travel to the garrison. They gave Laura a hearty meal, filled her leather bag with freshly baked bread; her leather drinking vessel was filled with fresh, flavoured water. With her clean, freshly washed clothes on, it was like the first day of her journey. Now she had company, to the end of the forest.

Before they set out, Jayden asked if he could accompany Laura to Nerbank Garrison.

"I can help Laura, I know the way to the garrison, it's just past the village," he said. "I have been that way many times."

Sylviana took Jayden to one side, "I'm glad you want to accompany Laura, for I have an enormous task for you. Don't let Laura mention her journey, especially that withered forest, you must stop her. If she has another spasm, hold her tight, as tight as you can. You have got elfin aura within you; it will help to drive back her demon. You saw what I did, a slap, the shock will bring her back, can you do that?"

"I will do my best."

"That's all I ask."

They both re-joined Laura and Gavin.

"It would do Jayden good to be in the company of someone his own age, and to be in the sunlight," said Sylviana.

With a big grin, Laura joked, "don't worry, I will look after Jayden, and bring him home safely."

Gavin put his arms around Jayden, smiling said, "It's settled, Laura will look after you!"

Jayden stood there, muttering and shuffling his feet in embarrassment.

Sylviana agreed, "you must wear your hooded cloak; you must not enter the village. If you see anyone, you must pull the hood over your head, your hair will make people ask you awkward questions." Looking at Laura she continued, "Gavin will get you a cloak to wear, it will cover your knife, rope and Tad basher."

Gavin, selecting a matching slate coloured cloak for Laura added, "if you meet anyone, tell them you are brother and sister, visiting your aunt in Drewcott."

They all left Starfall, Gavin and Sylviana leading the way, Jayden and Laura a few steps behind.

After walking side by side for a few moments, Jayden twirled around, "you need to walk behind me now, the secret path is narrow, it takes us to the edge of the forest. You won't need your staff, but it bends and twists, so stay close."

The route they took was easy walking, but difficult to follow, sometimes it turned right and went back on itself, veered sharply left and right. Although a longer distance, it was much quicker, and an easier walk. They came to the boundary of the forest at nightfall, they saw the moon shining through the branches of the trees, crafting eerie shapes and shadows as dusk fell.

Laura said, "I wish the route I took from the beginning, had been this easy."

"We have a place to bed down, a short walk in that direction," Gavin pointed past a clump of white berried bushes.

Within a few moments, they reached a small secluded clearing covered in moss, surrounded by small bushes of lavender. It was a haven of apple green, in a dark foreboding forest.

Gavin said, "we call this our moss garden, I cleared and planted this place so we had a comfortable bed. We often come here, and venture out to walk in the open fields, and to absorb the sun on our backs."

"It's exquisite," responded Laura, looking at the pure white rocks, inter-planted with coneflowers. She spread her blanket over the moss. "It's like a soft bed, you have made a perfect place to rest."

Sylviana opened her body bag and laid out four portions of food on a blanket in the fashion of a picnic. After eating bread, a slice of pie, and cakes, they settled down for the night, this haven was the perfect retreat.

As they lay on their blankets, Jayden said to Laura, "the day after tomorrow, we will be at Nerbank Garrison, the end of your journey; your family will soon be free of those bandits."

The words of Jayden made Laura feel good, she felt a warm glow, shut her eyes and whispered, "thanks."

When they woke, Laura said, "let's get out of this forest, and eat out in the fresh air."

Gavin replied, "it's only a short walk to the forest boundary, come, we'll walk a little way into the countryside with you."

Squeezing between a group of snowberry shrubs. they left the forest behind and entered the open space. Laura, taking in the sunlight flew her arms around Sylviana. No words were spoken, Sylviana felt the sense of relief in Laura.

Gavin turned to Jayden, "at the garrison, wait on the outskirts for Laura to return to you, but watch when the soldiers leave, they may take Laura. If they take Laura, return here—and don't try any spells."

Instantly becoming attentive, Laura's head swivelled towards Jayden, "you can do magic?"

Sylviana sighed, "elves have a degree of magic, Jayden has inherited the gift from my father, but he is still learning how to harness his power—so no magic. Do not draw attention to yourself," she said, whilst moving her finger back and forth.

Sylviana gave both Laura and Jayden extra cookies, "Put these with your bread," adding, "I expect you back in three days, we'll be waiting here."

Laura took her staff and pushed it forcefully into the earth by the edge of the forest. "I won't need a staff out here; it will be waiting here if I have to return this way."

Chapter 12

The Garrison.

As Jayden and Laura walked away, they both turned around and waved to Sylviana and Gavin, "see you soon."

"I wish we could go with them, they're only children," said Sylviana.

Gavin, still waving replied, "If anyone sees you, your kinfolk will be swarming all around here. Remember those cloaked men that passed by last year, we were lucky they didn't notice us. Why can't they leave us in peace? Besides, they're more like young adults, Jayden is sensible, and Laura is, well remarkable, they'll be fine."

"Yes," muttered Sylviana, in an inaudible tone, her mind had wandered elsewhere.

It was late autumn; the golden sun rays were glistening on the early morning dew that had settled on the blades of grass. There were delicate patterns of silvery threads made from spider's webs. The horizon was covered in a cool mist. Laura drank in the cool air with relief. She felt grateful Jayden had offered to accompany her on the rest of the journey. They walked across the open fields.

Laura, looking at the landscape said, "this is so scenic, how sad that you must live in that terrible forest."

"I'm used to it."

"I'm glad your parents let you accompany me to the garrison."

"I come out quite often, they're looking for two adults, not someone my age. This is the first time I have stayed away overnight."

"Let's stop and rest for a few moments, I want to savour the sun and crisp air."

Jayden agreed, "we should eat the cookies, they're so good."

Laura, catching her crumbs, not wanting to waste anything said, "I have never tasted anything so good in my entire life, your mother is the best cook in the world."

"We should reach the village by dusk if we follow this track," remarked Jayden.

After resting they set off, both agreeing it was nice to be walking out in the sunlight. Most of the morning they kept asking each other questions, neither had known anyone their own age. Laura said she was sorry he had to stay in hiding, afraid the Elvin company, that tried to separate Sylviana and Gavin, found out where they were hiding.

"You can come and visit me at the farm when it's safe, and the bandits have been removed, maybe stay a few days."

Jayden turned and looked at Laura, "I would like that, it gets lonely in the forest." He stopped walking, "your friend Snowy, why didn't he accompany you on this journey?"

Laura didn't know what to say, she bitterly regretted telling Jayden she had a friend called Snowy.

"Could you . . . forget Snowy?"

Jayden was taken aback by this response, now he didn't know how to respond, he merely gave a quick nod of the head.

They spent the morning in competition, naming the wildflowers and animals they came upon. When do they flower; what is the colour of the flowers; were they edible?

Laura pointed at a plant.

"That's easy, teasel," answered Jayden, pointing at another.

"Meadow Buttercup," replied Laura.

The game continued, they were both equally matched in their knowledge of flora and fauna.

After rambling across the country, Jayden pointed, "over there in the distance is the village called Drewcott, we'll be there before nightfall. You can see Nerbank Garrison just past the village."

Nearing the village, Laura said to Jayden, "what's going on over there, lots of cages on wheels, and two tents."

Jayden replied, "it's a travelling fayre, they travel around displaying animals for a halfpenny. They're only common animals you see in the wild, like foxes, hedgehogs and stoats, I'm sure you have seen all those running free."

"Why is there a tent in a different field, separated from the others?" asked Laura.

"Intriguing. let's go around the back and find out what inside. We can crawl underneath the sheets," answered Jayden.

They both strode into the field, and ambled around to the rear of the tent, once there Jayden removed one hook holding the sheet. Jayden crawled underneath, followed by Laura. Once inside they were both filled with disappointment, it was empty, except, in one corner stood a small crate covered with a cloak.

Gingerly approaching the crate, Laura took a deep breath, "lemon—lemon and honey."

"I know that smell," exclaimed Jayden.

Jayden hastily made his way towards the crate and spotted the fabric was tied in four corners. Laura got her knife out and quickly cut through one of the corner strands. With the corner now loose, they nervously pushed their heads inside the sheet. Inside the crate was a rusty old cage, with iron bars, and a big padlock on the door.

What they saw inside made them both gasp with disbelief, for curled up asleep was a white unicorn.

Jayden's eyes lit up, "it's Trinity—Storms mate, she's still alive!"

Trinity stirred, raised her head and opened her eyes. She recognized Jayden, and tried to walk over to him, but was pulled up by a rope around her neck, the other end tied to a bar.

Trinity, frustrated but pleased to see Jayden, made a whinny noise.

Laura whispered, "be quiet, else you have your captors here before we can help you. Do you need a drink? Have this," cupping her hand and pouring a little water into it.

"Can you get me out of here?" asked Trinity, slurping her water, and pulling at the rope.

Laura gripped the cage bars to stop herself from falling to the floor, "you can talk," she gasped.

"We only talk to people we can trust, you're with Jayden so I feel I can confide in you."

"Stay quiet," hissed Jayden, "we need to get you out."

"Your right," said Laura. "Listen—there someone outside. Trinity, get back to the corner, we'll hide under the cage."

They had barely got under the cage when two men walked into the tent, it was Gram and Bill.

Gram said, "ever since that unicorn broke Silo's arm he has wanted to kill it and sell its cone, but it will be a nice money maker once we travel to the big towns. We've wasted enough time here, I suggest we pack up and leave for the town of Piran, without Silo."

"I agree," complained Bill, "he does nothing but moan all the time, and drink every night, we can split our earnings two ways instead of three."

"We'll leave tonight, as soon as he goes to the tavern, he'll be there all night," added Bill.

"Good, he won't even notice we have left until midday when he gets up," said Gram. "We can pack and leave within the next hour, and be on our way, maybe travel throughout the night."

"Okay, we'll meet here in an hour, take the tent down, hook that cage to the horses, and scarper."

With that Gram and Bill slipped out of the tent, arms around each other, smirking and laughing.

Laura and Jayden emerged from their hiding place.

"There's no time, we have to act now, before they return," urged Laura. "How do we get Trinity out? Iron bars won't bend, and that lock looks indestructible."

Jayden replied with a smirk, "leave it to me."

He tinkered with the lock, it quivered, a sparkle, the lock burst open.

"Magic! you opened it with magic didn't you."

"Yes, now untie Trinity, and get her out, I have an idea," grinned Jayden.

Laura jumped into the cage and untied the rope from the iron bar, Trinity was getting excited.

"Calm down, we don't want anyone to come in now, we're almost done," said Laura, stroking her neck.

Jayden untied the tent at the back where they had entered until it was large enough for Trinity to pass through. Laura led Trinity outside, then cut the rope from Trinity's neck.

She whispered into her ear, "run Trinity, run home to Storm."

They stood and watched her disappear over the horizon, racing towards her home.

Jayden said to Laura, "collect a cluster of barley from outside, and put it into the cage."

Laura, nodding her head guessing what Jayden was going to do. The barley was tied into a bale, using the rope that had bound Trinity. The other end of the rope was tied to the bar as they found it. To finish, the blanket was thrown over the bale, and Jayden shut the lock.

"It looks like Trinity is under the blanket, asleep," giggled Laura.

☦

Trinity ran like the river rapids gushing over the land; it felt exhilarating to stretch her legs after being locked in a cage. As she approached the forest, Sylviana stirred, then ran to the forest boundary.

"What's the matter?" asked Gavin, "is there something wrong?"

"Someone is galloping towards the forest," replied Sylviana, as they reached the forest boundary.

"Look its Trinity, whoa stop, where have you been? We thought you were dead or taken by humans, it's so good to see you again," said Gavin.

"Three men captured me, and I was locked in a horrid cage, your son Jayden and his girlfriend released me."

"They're too young to be attached like that," Gavin angrily answered.

"Your coat looks raggedy, next time we meet I will give you a good brush; for now, go to Storm, he's been a misery since you went missing," said Sylviana.

Gavin added, "tell him the girl he tried to gore was the one who released you."

Trinity looked dismayed.

"He'll tell you, now go," Sylviana bade.

Trinity made her way through the forest, it was getting dark, Sylviana and Gavin made their way back to the moss garden.

Sylviana said, "so much for not straying from the path, but I'm glad they did, best add another day on their journey."

Now Trinity was free, Laura and Jayden hastily journeyed to the woods near the garrison. Just inside, they found a dell to sleep in.

Laura, tingling with excitement, sat up most of the night keenly waiting for the sun to peep over the horizon. When the first sunray flashed through the trees, Laura sprang to her feet and rushed over to Jayden, to wake him.

"Give the soldiers time to wake before you go charging down," advised Jayden. "Let's sit at the edge of this wood, we can watch from here."

Laura, pacing around, "do you think I can go now?"

"Go, men are moving around."

Before he had finished speaking, Laura was running, arms swinging around, towards the garrison.

Laura confidently approached the garrison, after a long and hazardous journey, help was in sight. she hurried towards the entrance. Two men were lounging against the door, both were dressed in shabby dark blue uniforms, with scuffed boots that were old and worn. Both men wore a petite moustache.

Laura confidently approached these two men.

"Who's in charge? I must speak to the captain of the soldiers, it's extremely urgent," said Laura.

"Can we help?" asked Pete looking at Laura.

Laura, getting frustrated insisted, "bandits have got my family, we need help."

Laura was now standing with a pinched lip, her arms hanging stiff, and fists shaking.

Seeing Laura's obvious distress Pete said, "follow us, we'll take you to our captain, his name is Ives."

Ely butting in stressing, "Ives won't like it, being disturbed, whilst he's eating."

Laura followed the two men to a dilapidated side door, Pete tapped the door and entered, Laura followed, with Ely.

They entered a small clammy room. Ives, the captain of the guards, a burly man was sitting behind a small desk, eating biscuits. He was dressed in the same blue uniform, with a large badge, affirming his position as captain.

Laura looked around the room, one window high up with bars, another door stood behind Ives.

Pete whispered in his ear, "this girl wants to speak to you."

"What is it, child?" Ives said, his voice as coarse as a winter's storm.

Laura, looking around at the three faces, took a deep breath, and told the story of the Nash gang storming their farmhouse. As she told her story Ives brushed biscuit crumbs off the table on to the grubby floor.

She finished with glassy eyes, "they're holding my family prisoner in the cellar."

Ives, now leaning back on his creaking chair asked, "where is your home; how did you get here?"

"My home is called the Lovet farm, it's on the other side of the catacomb forest, I got here by walking through the forest," replied Laura.

"You expect us to believe you walked through that Gruesome place, on your own," laughed Ives.

Pete had already started laughing, this set Ely off, who said, "she walked through that dark enchanted forest—alone."

Ives, with tears running down his cheeks laughed, "grown men won't venture into that place, people have disappeared. Now I know you are lying, is this a childish prank?"

Laura's eyes narrowed, wrung her hands together, her screwed-up face turned blood red. Shaking, she reached inside her cloak, and pulled out the knife, raised it way above her head and slammed it into Ives desk. The blade sank into the wood with such force, causing a deep chasm and sending splinters of wood across the desk, Ives slid backwards, falling from his chair.

In the loudest voice, she could muster, screeched, "this blade belonged to Aldwin Nash, one of the bandits!"

A deadly hush fell on the room, all eyes were on Ives, who got to his feet, sat, and composed himself. He reached over to the knife, and with all his strength, pulled it from the desk.

He pointed the knife at Laura, waving it up and down saying, "you dare to come in here, damaging my property."

As he spoke, he noticed the inscription that had been scratched onto the handle, two letters A.N.

He slammed the knife flat onto the desk, making Laura flinch.

Leaning back in his chair, "most of the soldiers have gone to the main fort in Piran, to get a new leader. We are only guards to lock up any villains the soldier's capture."

Laura was crestfallen, "why have they gone; when will they be back?" she asked.

"Six weeks ago, the captain of the soldiers was bored, so he announced that he would kill every beast in the catacomb forest to make it safe for everyone. With his mighty black sword, he marched in with two soldiers, they have never been seen since. The soldiers have gone to the town of Piran to report his disappearance, and get a new captain, only six soldiers are remaining. I don't expect the rest to return until next year."

Laura's eyes welled up, she looked at the floor and blinked to stop herself crying, her whole body sagged.

"Who knows of this farm?" asked Ives.

It was silent for a few seconds, Pete admitted he knew of the farm.

"Many years ago, I met a traveller from that place, it's far off the beaten track."

Ives motioned to Pete and Ely to come nearer, he whispered, "the soldiers are always bragging and boasting, yet they have never caught any proper robbers. If she is telling the truth, and it's the Nash gang then they will be trapped, and we could capture them— easily. The soldiers have been trying for years to capture those robbers."

With a big grin boomed, "the soldiers will be so dejected."

Pete readily agreed, adding, "It's boring sitting here doing nothing."

Turning to Laura, "young lady, I have heard of the Nash brothers, so we will investigate your claim, but if you are lying you will be in serious trouble."

Laura's eyes were aglow, placing her hands on the desk said, "thank you, my family are in great danger."

Turning to Pete, "tomorrow morning, at dawn we leave for this farm, with eighteen men, twelve guards and the six soldiers. I'm in charge, so I will command the soldiers to accompany us. Get the horses ready, two prison carts, and provisions for six days, go and prepare."

"Sir, I have never ridden a horse, but I will be content to travel inside the prison cart."

"Oh no, you're not coming, I don't want you absconding, you are stopping here under lock and key."

"Lock her up in a pen," he instructed Ely.

Ely looked shocked, "she is only a child."

Looking at Laura, crunching his lips said, "she can stay in this room, but secure the door until we return."

Turning to Ely, "she is your responsibility, get her a blanket to sleep on, and feed her. Do not let her leave this room until we return."

Ely nodding his head, "yes, she won't be going anywhere with me watching."

Turning to Laura, Ives said bluntly, "if you're lying, you will be put into a cell, regardless of your age."

He departed the room by the inner door, followed by Ely and Pete. Laura noted the knife was still lying on the table, as soon as the door shut, she grabbed the knife and returned it to her belt. She inspected the room, looking for a weak spot to try to escape. There was nothing, the only window was high up, as every window in the garrison, it had several iron bars running from top to bottom. Laura settled and sat on the desk thinking.

Jayden, wondering what had happened to Laura decided to spend the night in the dell.

Next morning, noises outside woke Laura, she jumped up to the window and peered out to the scene of Ives directing his men, ready to move out. At the same time, Jayden had watched the guards and soldiers mount their horses and take the route around the forest, there was no sign of Laura.

Although she had plenty of supplies in her backpack, Laura accepted the food offered by the guard Ely.

She tried different methods to escape, using the knife to prise the door open, dig the window frame out. She even tried to remove a panel from the wall, nothing worked. When Ely came in with the food, she tried to run past him, but he slammed the door shut.

Jayden watched throughout the day, expecting Laura to leave the garrison and join him for the journey back to Starfall. By nightfall, ignoring his mother's warning, he crept to the garrison.

Nerbank Garrison was a small, stone-built rectangular single-storey building, with a large door on each of the four walls. In the centre, six iron cages like cells, large enough to hold three prisoners in each cell. At one end the horses were stabled, the opposite end was Ives office, with a storeroom at each side. Along the length was the guard's and soldier's quarters.

All the guards and the six soldiers travelled with Ives, only Ely was left at the garrison to guard Laura. Jayden stealthily made for the door Laura had entered the garrison, first, he tried the handle, it was locked, so he made for the window. He jumped up, grabbing the iron bars and looked inside. As he jumped Laura heard a scraping on the wall outside, so she jumped up to the window, grabbing the bars. They both faced each other, barely a hands length apart, the iron bars keeping them separated.

Laura spurted out, "he didn't believe me at first, but now he's going to check out my story, but he has locked me in here!"

"Don't go anywhere," he quipped sarcastically, "I will get you out, and look after you!"

The jab was not lost on Laura, "all right we're even, now can you get the door open?"

"Easy," he crowed as he dropped to the floor, Laura ran to the door, she could hear Jayden fiddling with the lock.

Jayden made a triumphant entrance, grabbing Laura's hand said, "quick it's time to leave."

Once outside, Jayden weaved his magic on the lock, it gave a shudder, a click and was locked.

They ran noiselessly through the early evening mist as if a dangerous beast was in pursuit, not daring to look back. They were still holding hands as they ran. The guard wouldn't discover Laura had escaped until he had his breakfast. He would spend many hours scratching his head, wondering how a child got out of a locked room.

They ran until they were exhausted, both flopping to the ground panting, neither had the energy to speak.

Laura, still gasping said, "I would like to be your friend."

Jayden just lay there, happy he finally had someone to call a friend.

They got their blankets out and found a safe spot to bed down. Lying on their backs looking up at the stars, both fell asleep and slept soundly throughout the night.

Chapter 13

The Roth Family

They awoke to the blush of dawn colouring the landscape. Laura rolled up their blankets, and using them as seats, sat and ate a portion of bread, and one of Sylviana's cookies. Laura stood and stretched her arms into the air, turning her head from side to side, trying to decide which way to Catacomb forest.

Turning to Jayden she asked, "which way do we go?"

"I think we ran the wrong way; the Catacomb forest is that way," he nervously said pointing to a small grassy mound. "Drewcott is in-between, there's nothing for it, we will have to skirt the village. If we're late Gav and Syl will leave the forest and come looking for us. I don't want them coming out, it's dangerous, the elves are still tracking them."

Avoiding the main path through the village, they found a small trail to follow that took them around a small woodland onto a hillock. From this point, they spied the stream, and the main highway on their right, looking the other way was the village.

"That's the road the guards have taken to my farm," said Laura.

The village had become alive, teeming with activity. People pushing carts, a few working the land, and a bunch of children playing. They followed the shale path avoiding the village. As the centre of the Drewcott faded from sight, the path folded closer to the outskirts of the village.

Jayden said, "up ahead, there's the field where we released Trinity, from there we can make it back before nightfall. I will fill our water from the stream, wait here, I won't be too long."

Laura watched Jayden disappear down the dusty bank, sat on a fallen branch and nibbled another cake.

"What do you think you're doing on our land?" shouted a voice, that startled Laura.

Jumping up she saw three boys, one tall and slim, the other two were smaller, they were twins. Laura noted they were carrying sticks. They were older than Laura, the tallest who had shouted looked the eldest, maybe fourteen. The twins looked twelve.

In the shadow of the bushes stood three girls. One had a cloth full of raspberries; she looked Laura's age. Two younger girls stood on each side, she guessed nine and seven. They were slim pasty-faced and wore ragged clothes; the youngest girl's dress looked as if a wild animal had torn the hem. Only the eldest boy and girl wore clothes that fitted. The others were dressed in oversize garments. They were all barefooted, had scuffed dirty faces and looked scared, maltreated.

"We don't want strangers around here, what you doin'?" challenged the eldest, as he stepped in front of Laura.

"W—, I'm visiting my aunt, who are you?" she replied, hoping Jayden kept out of sight.

"We are the Roth's clan, my name is Walter, these are me, brothers and sisters," he said swinging his arms around and pointing at the others behind him.

As he finished pointing, he unexpectedly brought both hands onto Laura's shoulders and shoved her. She fell backwards, swinging her right arm around onto the damp grass, stopping herself from hitting the ground. The girls looked shocked, the other two boys stood, hands on their hips, smirking.

She sprang to her feet, a hairs breath away from this bully and looked him in the eye, "don't try that again!"

"No girl tells me what to do," he clenched a fist, swung his arm, and tried to hit Laura on the nose.

This time she was ready and easily dodged the punch, his fist hitting nothing but the cool air.

"I don't want to hurt you, just leave me in peace, I'll be on my way," Laura said, as she loosened her cloak.

Walter wasn't having any of this, to be shown up in front of his siblings. He laughed, "you hurt me; I'll show you," he turned to his two brothers, "grab her, I'm gonna show her who's boss around here, you'll be leaving with two black eyes."

The twins rushed at her, one each side as Walter came forward. Laura pulled out Tad basher, with one swing hit both brothers, sending them onto their backs. For Walter it was a thump onto the side of his face, sending him to his knees; crying.

Her encounter with the imps had honed her skill with Tad basher, three boys were easy prey.

"My name is Laura the witch, from the Catacomb forest. I'm looking for boys to cook in my cauldron; I want you to come with me."

The three boys, in panic, dropped their sticks and ran blindly away, leaving their sisters huddled together in each other's arms.

Laura approached the girls and said, "don't worry, I'm not going to harm or take you away, what's your names; does your brother bully you?"

The eldest plucked up the courage to speak, through trembling lips said, "I . . . I'm Clare, my sisters are Giselle and Anna, he always bullies us."

"Clare, those bruises on your arm—your cheek, it's all red, did he hit you?" asked Laura.

"No, the monster hits us, when he's been drinking," snivelled Anna.

"The monster?" asked Laura.

"Our pa is the monster," answered Giselle. "He makes us go around the village begging, they don't give us money, just food. They make us eat it in front of them, they know the monster takes it off us. If we don't earn anything, we go along the hedgerows picking berries."

"When we get home with no money, he beats me," whimpered Clare, lowering her head.

"he always picks on Clare and Walter," disclosed Giselle.

"What about your mother, what does she . . ."

"She left just after I was born," said Anna, wiping her nose.

Clare folding her arms, "Walter once told us he saw the monster punch her in the face, later that night she abandoned us."

"Do you have many friends in the village?"

"We don't have any friends, the village children call us names," replied Giselle looking downcast.

Laura put Tad basher back into her belt, put her arms around the three girls and pulled them closer together. Laura's stomach was churning from the rancid smell.

Whispering into their ears, "next time your brother picks on you, say to him, Laura the witch is our friend, if you don't stop, we will send for her."

They looked at Laura with eyes wide, Clare asked, "are you really a witch?"

Anna sank onto her knees and wrapped her arms around Laura's legs, pleadingly asked, "will you be our friend?"

"Some little folk I know believe I am. Now walk home with self-respect, don't show you were afraid."

Laura hugged each girl and said, "take care, and don't forget to stand up to bullies—and yes, I will be your friend."

She then whispered into Clare's ear, "tell him . . ."

Clare swallowed, "you are the first person to have ever looked at us."

"I don't understand, what do you mean?"

"You see us, three sisters, three girls. Everyone else sees us as something lower than dirt on their shoes."

Laura pulled Clare into a tight embrace and kissed her cheek, "I would be proud to call you a friend."

As the three girls walked away, Laura's fist flew into the nearest tree, grazing and bloodening her knuckles. "Why? their own father—so brutal, why?"

Jayden came out of hiding and put his arms around her, "some men are despicable, you've seen it at your farm."

"Those three boys, I was ready to help if you needed me."

"Yes, I saw you, behind those dogwoods, I hate bullies," replied Laura, "It's that brutes' fault, the boys just copy him. Come on we had better get going."

"You head towards that coppice and wait, I will cover our path and set a false one, something Flora showed me. It'll be enough to stop those boys trying to follow us," said Jayden.

‡

When the three sisters got home, the boys were telling their father, Bryok, who had beaten them. Walter was desperately trying to save face. He had his hand over his cheek, trying to hide the red mark where Tad basher had struck.

"Big boys attacked us from behind, about six or seven."

Bryok, turning to Clare asked, "did you witness those lads that attacked your brothers?"

No longer afraid of Walter, she answered, "no, that's not true, Walter attacked a girl in the woods, she beat him."

"Yes, we saw, they tried to grab her, Walter said he would black her eyes, she bashed them," confirmed Giselle and Anna.

Walter, shot a furious look at his sisters mouthed, "I'm going to beat you."

"Is this true, was you thrashed by a girl?"

Walter just hung his head in shame, staring at his feet, slightly raising his head, "she's a witch from the catacomb forest."

Bryok pushed Walter to the floor and strode angrily out the hut. Where's he going now, they wondered?

Walter, jumped up, grabbed Clare by her neck and lifted her off the floor.

Before he could speak, she cautioned him, "lay one finger on me, and my friend Laura the witch said she would come for you. She will turn you into a toad and put you in a jar and take you to her secret nest and use you in one of her spells. She will put you on the floor and put her foot on your slimy back and press hard until your eyes pop out. They would be thrown in her cauldron when she is concocting a witch's brew."

Walters mouth becoming flaccid, his face blanched, his shaky hands released Clare. He ran out of the hut, into the countryside, looking for somewhere to hide.

For the first time in an age Clare was mollified; she grinned.

Chapter 14

The chase.

Laura noticed that the fayre was on the side of the path they were walking along.

"Let's hurry past, we must get to the forest before nightfall," Laura said, striding forward.

Jayden agreed, "Gavin and Syl will be worried if we don't return on time—look, there's the tent that Trinity was locked in."

Laura, sniggering, "do you suppose they would imagine a unicorn could turn into barley?"

Just as she spoke, Silo scrambled out of a ditch he had fallen into, on his way home from the village. He was recovering from a hangover from having spent the night drinking cider in the village tavern. He grabbed Jayden around the neck with his good arm, in his Left hand, which was in a sling, he held a long-curved dagger to Jayden's back.

"You make any funny moves and he gets it in his back," he threatened. "You're the ones that let our unicorn free, well me mates will want a word with you two."

"Your mates were running out on you, we overheard them planning to abandon you here," stated Laura.

"I know, they came back and blamed me, said I was hiding it somewhere," grumbled Silo, gritting his teeth and kicking fragments of shingles. "They beat me up, now it's your turn to suffer their rage, you won't be laughing then!"

Laura looked despondently at Jayden, shut her eyes trying to conjure up an idea, nothing came.

Silo said, "you, walk in front towards that tent, the one with the empty cage."

Silo was walking at the rear, with the knife in Jayden's back, Laura was leading. As they walked past the animal containers Laura discreetly loosened her cloak. She guessed Silo would lock them in the cage, then call Gram and Bill out; Jayden wouldn't have time to use his 'open lock' magic.

"Get in," he ordered Laura.

The cage was unlocked. She pushed the door open and jumped up, stood on the edge with an outstretched hand to help Jayden. As she pulled him up and his back separated from the knife, her other hand pulled out the knife from her belt. Laura jumped out and stabbed it into Silos hand. He screamed and dropped his knife.

Laura, still holding her knife and Jayden's hand in the other said, "run!"

They dashed out the tent, almost stumbling on the discarded food strewn everywhere. As they disappeared behind the tent, Gram and Bill arrived to find out who was screaming. They found Silo leaning against the cage holding his hand, blood dripping onto the floor. He was writhing in pain.

"Two kids did it, one of 'em stabbed me, the ones that let the unicorn out, I caught 'em, then the girl did this to me. They ran out a moment ago, catch 'em, they can't get far; they're only kids, go on get after 'em," he sputtered.

Gram and Bill looked at each other, looked at the wound on Silos left hand, turned and rushed outside. They dithered on which way to go, deciding to split up. Bill ran around the back, Gram headed towards the village.

Laura and Jayden were running up the hillock hoping to disappear over the top. They stopped at the crest and looked back, no sign of anyone.

Jayden said, "make for that collection of birch trees, where we can rest up and hide."

They ran down the hillock and stumbled into the thicket; they both held onto the white bark of a tree, head drooping gulping in deep breaths.

"That was close, I dread to think of the beating we would have got if the other two got their hands on us," said Jayden. "Let's get further back behind these trees, we're still exposed. We can have a drink of water and move on. It's midday now, we can still get to the forest by dusk if we keep moving."

"Yes, we need to find a safe path, I'm sure they will come looking for us," said Laura.

The sun was lying low, casting long shadows. A chill was in the air as they left the cover of the white birch trees.

Laura was thinking of her mother, "Martha calls those ghost trees," she fretted sorrowfully.

"Cheer up, the guards will be at your farm tomorrow, your mother, and all your family will be free," said Jayden.

Laura didn't answer, she felt warm inside, he knows the right things to say.

"Let's hurry along, give me your hand, we'll run together. I'm not happy with those villains looking for us, we're too exposed on this grassy plain," said Jayden.

They ran at an easy pace, supporting each other across fields, into a vale, and across a small stream. Up ahead they spied a briar, here they decided to stop for a rest. They ran in still holding hands,

Jayden abruptly stopped, he was lying on the floor, dazed, and unaware of what had happened. It was Bryok, he had followed them, raced in front, waited in the bush and whacked Jayden.

With one hand, he grabbed Laura around the neck and lifted her off the ground. Her legs swung loose, she instinctively lashed out, trying to kick him.

He growled, "you're the girl that humiliated my son. I'm going to throttle you, and your friend, then I will drag your body back, to show him you're not a witch."

She calmed, "do you want your entrails spilt all over the ground?"

Laura had her knife pressed into his stomach. He could feel the point of the knife, he looked down and saw it pressed into his portly stomach, he released his grip on Laura's neck. Her feet tentatively touched the dry sandy ground. Keeping the point pressed against his stomach, she looked him over; Bryok was an uncouth, stout, compact man, not much taller than Laura, he stank of skunk, his broad unshaven chin was covered in sores.

"You're a nasty parcel of filth, no wonder your son is such a bully, you should be ashamed of yourself, beating your own sons and daughters."

Jayden dazed and bloodied, got to his feet. The hood on his cloak had fallen back, exposing his green hair.

Laura said, "tie his hands and feet, and tether him to the brambles."

Jayden unravelled a short rope, which all elves carry, tied Bryok's hands behind his back, and wrapped it around his legs and feet. He then tied it to the stem of a bramble bush, whilst Laura kept the knife pressed into his belly.

"I'll get both of you when I'm free, I'm coming after you," Bryok kept shouting, whilst squirming around, making it hard for Jayden to tie him.

Laura, shaking with rage, held the knife, erratically moving it under his chin, "you're a vile disgusting man."

Bryok swallowed hard, the colour drained from his face. Jayden put his hand on Laura's arm. She returned the knife into her belt and pushed Bryok to the ground. He landed sprawled out on his back.

Laura stood over him and said, "you can wait here for my friend Ives, captain of the guards. Trying to murder two children, he will lock you inside the garrison."

Laura, looking at Jayden's face, "your nose, it's bleeding, let me treat it."

"Later, let's keep moving, I'll feel safer when we're in the forest, I want to sleep in the moss garden tonight."

After a few minutes, Jayden stopped walking, "you're adept with that knife, did Morgan coach you?"

"No, I learnt by necessity."

"We've travelled some distance, I can still hear Bryok shouting, someone will find him soon."

"There, over the horizon, the catacomb forest and our way back in, I can just make it out," Laura said. "We can still reach it before it gets too dark."

‡

Bryok was now getting hoarse with the constant shouting when he heard horses sauntering around the briar.

"Help, in here," he cried out.

It went quiet, then footsteps trampling across the grass, it was Gram and Bill.

"It's that tramp from the village," said Gram.

Bill was untying Bryok, "why are you tied up inside these brambles?"

Bryok, trying to be evasive replied, "there were two of 'em."

Bill bluntly asked, "was it a boy and girl?"

Bryok, nodding his head, "that girl is dangerous, she had a knife on my stomach."

"That's the ones we're after, she stabbed our mate in the hand, do you know where they are going?" asked Bill.

"The catacomb forest and the moss garden, whatever that is, that's the direction they travelled," said Bryok pointing towards the route they had taken.

They mounted their horses and galloped towards Laura's and Jayden's trail, climbing up a tor where they stopped to scan the horizon. The sun was now setting, causing a haze on the horizon, making it difficult to see anyone moving in the distance. A flock of roosting crows flew out of a tree, drawing Grams eye. Placing his hand to his forehead he saw them running past the tree.

"Over there, they're heading for the Catacomb forest, quick we can get there before they disappear," said Gram.

Both horses reared up as they were instructed to gallop after Laura and Jayden.

Jayden and Laura stopped running to take a rest, they sat on the grass, Jayden turned around to watch the sunset and saw two horsemen bearing down on them. He turned and looked at the forest, then back at the horses, realising that they would catch them before they reached the safety of the forest.

"Laura they're coming, we need to reach the forest, quick get up and run."

Laura looked around, shut her eyes and said, "we can't give up, we must try."

With a deep breath, both staring at the ground, they ran, both knowing within minutes they would be caught.

An ear-splitting shout from Sylviana, "eeeaaaaaseee."

The horses pulled up, almost throwing Bill and Gram. Laura and Jayden kept running, swoosh an arrow flew over their heads, splicing Bills left ear. Sylviana and Gavin were standing on the edge of the forest, Sylviana had another arrow in her bow.

Gavin bellowed, "that was a warning, one more step forward, and the next arrow enters your heart."

Bill was holding his ear, blood dripping through his chubby fingers running onto his cloak. They sat there shocked and motionless, as their quarry reached the catacomb forest, and disappeared into the wood. The pain in Bill's ear gradually intensified, he shut his eyes tight, trying to stop himself crying out. They both dismounted; Gram took his mud-stained yellow bandana off, and tied it around Bills head, covering the cut ear.

"Only one type of woman can fire an arrow that accurate, an elf girl. I could see how elegant she was," said Gram.

"Well, while you were admiring her, I was the one with the arrowhead in my ear, come on let's get back," replied Bill.

Laura grabbed her staff as they ran pass Sylviana, who shouted, "you're a day late!"

They took a few paces into the wood and dropped onto the floor.

"Get your breath, then we will make our way back to our moss garden, those two men have turned around and are leaving," said Gavin.

They trampled back to the sanctuary of the secret garden. The slog from the village had taken its toll, Gavin was supporting Jayden and Sylviana supported Laura. In the safety of the moss garden, under the half-moon, they both detailed everything that had happened during their journey. Gavin and Sylviana were overjoyed they had released Trinity.

Chapter 15

Riding a unicorn.

Next morning refreshed after a good night's sleep, they travelled back to Starfall, arriving at dusk.

"Tonight, we sleep here, tomorrow we travel with Laura, back to her home," announced Sylviana.

Laura, a little confused said, "you are travelling with me?"

"Yes, I know a safer and quicker route, you won't encounter any disruptions."

Jayden grabbed Laura's hands, "we will stop friends a little longer, I am coming, you can't leave me alone—please?"

"Yes, we are all travelling with Laura, now rest, we start at dawn," said Sylviana.

A sweet melodic sound awakened Laura, she shut her eyes listening, it only lasted a few moments.

"Come on sleepyhead," called out Sylviana, "I have someone who wants to meet you."

Sylviana led Laura from Starfall, followed by Jayden and Gavin. Outside stood Trinity and Storm.

Storm looked at Laura and said, "I almost pieced you with my horn, yet you still released Trinity, I am so much in your debt."

Sylviana explained why Laura was in the forest, and said, "we want to get Laura safely back to her home. It's on the other side of this forest, can you help?"

Trinity looked at Storm and said, "it's time to repay our debt to Laura."

133

Storm lowered his head in front of Laura.

Jayden said, "he wants you to touch his horn."

Laura placed both hands around the horn, and half shut her eyes, the forest faded, and Laura saw her family. They were locked inside the cellar storeroom, she let go with a shudder.

Her voice quivered, "the guards haven't done anything, my family are still locked in the cellar," she welled up.

"Perhaps they can't find your farm," suggested Gavin.

"No, I gave Ives precise instructions," replied Laura.

Storm walked to one side, head held high, he gave a thunderous roar. Laura put her hands over her ears, wondering what was happening. She didn't have to wait long, first, there was a bellow, a herald reply. Two unicorns arrived, Laura and Jayden looked on in amazement.

Jayden's eyes glistened, "what an incredible sight, I didn't know two more unicorns were living in the forest."

Storm addressed the two unicorns, Hart, who was a mottled cream, and carried a grey horn, and Gilda also a mottled cream but bore a silvery horn.

Jayden said, "he's saying his friends need a ride, and he wants their help."

There were lots of discussions, finally, it went quiet, Storm left and came over to Laura and Jayden.

"We have our own trail around the edge of the forest, we will give you all a lift. Laura, you ride with me, you will be back at your farm by dusk tonight!" affirmed Storm.

Sylviana said, "everyone hang on tight and keep your head down, unicorns run at double the speed of a horse, it's called a unicorn flying charge."

Gavin helped Laura onto the back of storm, "tuck your head into his neck and hold tight onto his mane."

They started at a gallop; within a few moments, they were flying around the forest. Laura looked down and noticed that their hooves barely touched the ground as if they were silently gliding. They were carried past the central clearing, swerving to the left in an arc. Laura, lying with her head resting on Storm's neck, kept one eye open, watching the environment as they rode by.

The path was narrow but well-trodden. The forest didn't look so foreboding, riding high on the back of a unicorn. Around midday, they flew past an old wooden derelict cabin, through a tunnel of trees. True to his word, by taking the unicorn trail, they reached the edge of the forest at sunset.

Gavin said, "we'll bed down here tonight, and decide the best way forward tomorrow."

‡

It had been twenty days since Laura had left the farmhouse. Martha had become despondent, walking around in a daze, not eating. She was dragged out of the cellar and thrust into the kitchen to cook porridge. She sat down with a faraway look in her eyes.

All the villains were resting in the family room, waiting for their breakfast, creating an unpleasant clamour, with their noisy shouting and rantings. Arriving at the farm, they tried to give the impression they were kindly robbers. Their true nature had started unfolding since killing Casper.

Edmund said to his brother Aldwin, "next week we take those two men to a holdup, with no bandanas. We will threaten to kill Martha if they don't do our bidding. Morgan, the one that attempted to throttle me, will pay dearly; where's that woman with our food it should be here now?"

Aldwin wandered into the kitchen, to find Martha in the pantry, with her head in her arms resting on a barrel of flour, sobbing.

"Get out of here, and cook our breakfast," he demanded.

Martha looked up and shook her head.

Aldwin grabbed Martha around the neck, dragged her back to the kitchen, and let her fall to the floor. With a vicious look said, "you either cook or become a widow!"

That broke Martha.

"No don't harm him, I beg you, please; your food will be ready in a few moments."

Cast back into the cellar storeroom, Martha threw her arms around Raoul, "Laura our baby, she is . . ."

Morgan stood, "no, utterly not! she is still alive."

"I've been counting the days since she left. I know exactly how long she has been gone."

"We must have faith," said Raoul.

"Those two brothers—they're up to something, they were both sniggering when I laid out the food."

‡

That morning Sylviana was first to wake, she was aware of trampling and mutterings nearby. Waking the others, Sylviana pointed to the south of the farm, "there's movement around the farmyard; it's the guards and soldiers, it looks like they are about to mount an attack. From the safety of the forest, they watched the assault on the farmhouse unfold.

Laura pointed out Ives, "he's directing the guards, twelve are charging through the main door, with Ives leading the way in.

Three soldiers on each side of the farm, making sure none escape around the back."

They could hear the guards bellowing, "give up, surrender, you are surrounded!"

Within a few moments, the robbers came out of the farmhouse and thrown into the prison carts. Most surrendered without resistance, Edun and Jac came out lashing their knives at anyone that came in striking distance. They stood side by side, manoeuvring towards the shed where their horses were stabled. One soldier unwisely tried to tackle the two men, Edun slashed his face. Turning to join Jac, four guards grabbed him from behind and wrestled him to the floor. Edun was surrounded by three soldiers and three guards, he dropped his knife and surrendered; they were hurled into the carts with the rest of the gang.

‡

"Quiet," shouts Morgan, "there's a ruckus outside, it sounds like fighting."

They all stood silent, Raoul held Martha tight in his arms. Heavy footsteps came echoing down the cobbled steps.

Captain Ives entered the cellar with two guards, "you must be the Lovet family; we're here at your daughter's request."

Raoul caught Martha as she fainted.

"Pete, break that lock," ordered Ives.

Laura, where is she; is she well? Asked Morgan.

"She's safe, back at the garrison in my office."

Martha slowly came around, "she did it, she got through that forest, and saved us."

"Come on outside," beckoned Ives, "all the thieves are locked up."

‡

Sylviana turned to Laura, lifted her up in her arms saying, "your mission is over, I'm sure your parents will be out soon."

Sylviana had just finished talking when Jayden called Laura, "Ives is bringing two men and a woman out, your family?"

"Hold steady," Gavin said to Laura, as she started to rush out.

"Wait until the guards leave, they will wonder how you got back so quick."

Outside the farmhouse, they held the bandits in the two prison carts each with two horses and three soldiers on each cart. They were preparing to make their way back to the garrison, with their infamous prisoners. The guards were on horseback, Ives leading the way. Martha and Raoul both thanked the captain of the guard, Ives for freeing them and capturing the gang that had held them captive.

"I'm sorry we weren't able to apprehend the leaders, the Nash brothers," said Ives.

He asked Raoul, "do you want to return to the garrison with us, to collect your daughter, Laura?"

"Yes," replied Raoul, "we've been so worried, I expect she is wondering what's happening."

Gavin said to Laura, "you had better show yourself, otherwise your father will have a wasted journey, we will withdraw back into the forest, and wait."

Storm said to Hart and Gilda, "go back home, your help is no longer required this day."

Laura asked everyone, "will you stay until the guards leave, I'm sure my family would like to meet you."

"I want to meet everyone, perhaps I can meet your friend Snowy," hinted Jayden.

"I would like to talk to your uncle Morgan," said Sylviana. "Now go, before your father leaves."

Laura walked out of the forest, and paused, one hand holding her staff, the other hand over her mouth looking at her home, her family. Under her cloak, Tad basher and the knife in her belt, alongside the water vessel.

A stunned Ives was the first to perceive Laura as she stepped out.

Raoul, aware of Ives glazed stare turned around and uttered, "Laura?"

Everybody in the farmyard turned and stared in disbelief.

Martha threw her arms out and screamed, "Laura!"

Laura, throwing her staff aside was now running to her mother. Martha dropped to her knees to welcome Laura into her arms.

She threw herself at Martha crying, "mommy—I've missed you so much."

Martha spread her arms around Laura, pulling her close, nearly squeezed the life from her. She swallowed, trying to speak, her throat clogged, tears streaming over her cheeks. Taking in a gulp of air said, "I have been so worried about you—you are a stubborn child."

Laura felt Martha's body, she had lost weight, looked gaunt and pale. *Lack of food, those vile slimy men were starving my family. She'll soon be back to normal.* By this time, Raoul had his arms around both Martha and Laura. Everyone was talking at once.

Ives approached Laura and said, "I salute you; most grown men won't venture into that forest, you have done it twice. How you got home so fast is remarkable, how did you do it?"

Laura, fidgeting quipped, "I rode on the back of a unicorn."

This made everyone laugh, except Morgan, he looked quizzically at Laura, knowing Laura always tells the truth.

Morgan said, "she needs to rest now, don't you need to make a move, you've got a long journey with those robbers?"

Laura asked Ives, "why did it take you so long to capture and remove those bandits from our farmhouse?"

Ives, taken back by this direct question answered Laura. "After what you achieved, you deserve a proper answer."

"First, we couldn't just charge in without knowing how many; are they armed; do they have an escape route?"

"At the edge of the lane to the farm, we dismounted and hid in the lower glen. I despatched two of my best guards to observe the farm from a safe distance. We knew at once two lookouts were watching throughout the day and night. After two days, we had a good idea that twelve men were living inside the farmhouse."

"At dawn, the lookouts changed, but not at the same time, we guessed they had breakfast together. With no one watching for a short time, we stormed the farm front and back, whilst they were busy eating. The plan almost worked, we caught the robbers with little resistance, maybe because the Nash brothers weren't there to direct the men. Somehow, the brothers escaped, and left their men to their fate, most likely, they are far away by now."

Laura then asked Ives, "do you know a man in the village called Bryok Roth?"

"Yes, a lout, a bully, and a coward, he scrounges around, what he earns is spent in the tavern, his young ones take care of him. He sends them out begging, most of the villagers are kindly disposed towards the children, they would do menial tasks for a slice of bread. I've been told he sometimes beats his children, but I have no proof, else I would arrest him."

140

"He was going to strangle me, kill Jayden and take our bodies back to show his children."

Martha gripped Raoul's arm as Laura spoke.

"I will throw him in gaol when I return, the villagers will cheer."

"What will happen to Clare and the rest of his children?" Laura asked.

"The boys will be taken to work as labourers on farms, the girls will be sent to the nearest town, Ecrind to work as servants," replied Ives. "The eldest, Walter can do as he chooses, he is old enough to take care of himself."

"So, they will be split up?"

Ives just nodded his head.

"That's not right, they've done nothing wrong."

Laura cast her eyes down, dropped her head and firmly said, "don't put him behind bars—not yet."

Ives was taken aback, nonetheless replied, "If that's your wish."

Morgan put his arm around Laura, "It's a difficult decision, whatever you choose, the children suffer."

Ives interrupted, "I will record this unpleasant incident, if you change your mind, come back to the garrison before next spring."

Turning to his men he said, "make ready, it's time to go."

Before mounting his horse, Ives stood in front of Laura and gave a salute, saying "I will never forget you—not with that indentation in my desk!"

The guards trotted out of the farmyard, around the corner to the track that leads to the main highway.

Chapter 16

Friends and Foes.

M artha, taking Laura's hand said, "come in, I will make you something to eat, then you can tell us everything."

Laura stood back, "before we go in, I want you to meet my friends I made on the way through that forest."

Walking into the forest, she took Jayden's hand and drew him out, Gavin and Sylviana followed. Morgan inhaled deeply and dropped to his knees; his eyes glazed over.

Laura ran straight over to him, holding his hand asked, "what's wrong?"

Immediately Sylviana was there, she gently drew Laura away, dropped to her knees and put her arms around Morgan. In his eyes, she saw the vision of the young man with Flora. She cushioned Morgan's hand and said, "would you like to meet Flora again?"

"I would give my last breath," he answered, lowering his eyelids.

"You won't need to do that," she replied, "I will take you to her."

His eyes widened. "Is Flora far away; Is she well; isn't she still with her kin?" asked Morgan.

"She is well, living alone in her own dwelling; you will see her in two days," replied Sylviana.

Laura, standing nearby, realised that Morgan was the boy Flora believed was dead. She threw her arms around Morgan's neck. "Are you going to bring Flora back? I would love to meet her."

"Flora is coming back, I want her to meet you," said Sylviana. Turning to Morgan, "we will leave tomorrow morning when we have rested."

Laura asked Morgan, "what happened to you after you were taken to be tossed into the gorge?"

Morgan said, "they had no intention of killing me, elves are not murderers, they bound my hands, then took me far away, to a place I was not familiar. They left me with a warning to never try to find Flora. It took a long time to return to familiar lands. I went straight to the glen where Flora lived, but they had moved, I could never find their new home."

Sylviana said to Gavin, "it's time to repay Flora, I will take Morgan to her, we will depart tomorrow."

"Did you know who Morgan was?" asked Gavin.

"I suspected beyond hope when I saw Laura's rope, it was elfin weaved, but believing he was dead I kept it to myself."

"It will be dangerous for you, to travel in the open."

"I know, but we owe Flora everything."

"You are right, take care, the journey will be dangerous; I will wait here with Jayden. How are you going to travel?" inquired Gavin.

As Sylviana spoke, Laura shouted, "Storm, Trinity are you coming out," and beckoned them to come.

Hesitantly, both the unicorns stepped from the forest and made their way to Sylviana, looking around suspiciously at everyone. Sylviana wrapped her arms around Trinity's neck and whispered in her ear. After fidgeting around, she settled and agreed with Sylviana.

"Oh my, what a wondrous sight," said Martha.

"How did she—do this?" Raoul inquired.

Morgan just shook his head, "she did say she rode a unicorn to get home!"

"Is that where the tree spirits live?" Jayden said to Laura, pointing at the large tree.

Laura walked to the tree, placed her palm on it, "yes, this is where my friends live." She placed her cheek against the cascading bark, *thank you for* . . .

A rough callous hand gripped around her neck and lifted her off the ground. She felt a blade press into her back. She screamed. The hand around her neck tightened. Her legs flay, she gasped for air.

‡

The Nash brothers were in the kitchen when they heard a commotion in the main hall and the guards storming in the rear entrance. Edmund snatched a cleaver from the worktop. Aldwin withdrew a bread knife from the wooden holder.

"Quick hide in the larder," suggested Edmund, "there are too many to fight."

As they rushed in Aldwin tripped over a ladle and fell against the barrels of flour, exposing the tunnel entrance.

"Quick inside this passage, leave the creeps to fight the soldiers," Aldwin said, dipping into the tunnel. Once inside they pulled the barrels back, hiding the entrance.

"How did they find us," said Edmund.

"Forget about them, let's find out where this tunnel leads, maybe it's our escape route."

As they made their way along the tunnel Edmund said, "someone has been living in here, look, a makeshift bed, blankets and candles."

At the exit from the tunnel, they peered from behind the devil's nettle and saw six soldiers. They were searching the outbuildings animal pens, one had to crawl into the pigsty.

"They're looking for us," warned Edmund, "we had better lie low in this tunnel until they leave."

That's where they remained, whilst the guards secured their men in the prison carts. They heard the reunion of Laura.

"So that's how they discovered us, we never knew a child was living here," observed Edmund.

"That brat needs teaching a lesson," snapped Aldwin.

"She's hugging that tree, now's our chance, let's grab her. We can make that elf girl command those two unicorns to carry us away. We'll take that horrid child with us, and dump her in some remote land!" replied Edmund, with a sickening grin. "We won't kill her, we'll let the wild animals do the job for us. We'll kill the two unicorns; their horns are worth a tidy sum."

‡

It was late summer, Kylo was getting fretful, he hadn't seen Laura for a long time. Every day he ventured to the river's edge looking across to the other bank, wondering why his friend hadn't visited him. Laura's scent was on the opposite side of the river, mixed with more humans. Kylo turned and walked away. A piercing scream rolled on the faint breeze; he turned around, looking across the river. With one leap he landed on the yearning edge rock, one more bound he was on the other side.

On the bank he stood there taking in the fragrances on this new land, a strong scent of man and elf swirled nearby. Amongst the odours, a strong sense of fear from Laura, without hesitation he sped to the source, his adopted sister was in danger.

‡

145

Aldwin Nash held Laura's body high, "so, you're the little urchin that brought the guards upon us?"

Morgan made a move towards the brothers, Aldwin gripped Laura tighter, she was feeling lightheaded, going limp.

Brandishing the knife, growled, "anyone makes a move, and the girl dies."

He eased his grip and pressed the knife in Laura's back. A sharp intake of breath from Laura, as the knife cut through the cloak, into her tunic, and nicked the back of her skin. After enduring the long, and dangerous journey, the idea of dying by the hands of the vile men she was trying to save her family from, filled Laura with the resolve to survive.

Martha, dropping to her knees, and cried out, "please, please don't harm her, she is just a child."

Laura, remembering her vow to her mother, slowly and stealthily slid her hand under the cloak. Her hand reached for the knife, her fingers nimbly wrapped around the handle, she took a firm grip. Morgan, aware of Laura's intention, caught her eyes and shook his head. Her eyes turned away, lucid and determined. She pursed her lips.

Edmund shouted, "elf girl, I want you to . . ."

Laura in one movement swung around, pulled the knife out and sliced it into Edmunds hand that was holding the knife in her back.

"For Casper, and the misery you caused my family," cried out Laura.

Edmund screamed out in pain, dropping Laura. He looked at his hand in disbelief. She had used his brother's knife to slice the back of his hand. He glared at Laura. She was facing him with both hands on the handle of the knife, the blade pointed at his gut. Edmund's face coarsened. He held his knife high and took a step forward. Laura was backing away as Kylo emerged from behind the farmhouse. In an instant, he was upon Edmund. His jaw snapped Edmund's wrist. The knife fell to the floor. With one swipe of his paw, he sent Edmund flying through the air. He landed in a crumpled heap by the big tree. Aldwin was frozen to the spot as Kylo advanced towards him, his shaking hand let the cleaver slip from his fingers to the ground.

The turn of events changed the atmosphere from distress to terror. Everyone was unsure what to do. Raoul held Martha, with his free hand motioned to Laura to sidle to his side.

Sylviana pushed Jayden behind herself and whispered, "move into the forest, and hide—now!"

She was the only one armed. She slowly reached for her bow and quietly slipped an arrow onto her bowstring, wondering how many arrows it would take to bring the creature down. Or how many shots she could fire before the wolf was upon her.

To the utter amazement of everyone, Snowy came and stood beside Laura; she rested her head into his neck. Snowy thrust his head forward, almost touching Aldwin's face.

"My friend is hungry, he wants to snap your head off, chew the skin from your face and gnaw on your skull."

Snowy curling his lips back to reveal his teeth, still dripping Edmund's blood. His tongue wiped away the saliva dribbling around his lips. Aldwin has stopped breathing, his face as ashen as the sea of death.

"Go now!" bellowed Laura, pointing at the enchanted forest, "do not return here again, or he will crunch your bones in his jaws."

Cold shivers invaded Aldwin's body. He tentatively edged towards his brother and pulled him to his feet. They disappearing into the gloomy forest.

147

No one spoke; they stood staring at Laura, an eleven-year-old girl hugging a gigantic white wolf. Laura said to Snowy, "you saved me, oh, how I have missed you, thank you."

Ignoring Snowy, Martha ran to Laura and squeezed her tightly. "What's happened to you, my love, you left us with a heart as pure and innocent as the first snowfall. You have returned older, wiser and a little harder. Carrying and using a knife. Walking with a club hanging from your belt. Your eyes are steely hard. You're not my baby that left us all those days ago."

"I'm still your daughter, but I have seen the reality of life. It's not all beauty and sunshine. Those robbers opened my eyes to evil. During my journey, my heart felt the wickedness some men do. Yes, I have changed, I know life isn't always kind; I'm not going to be a victim."

Sylviana in a hushed voice said to Morgan, "is this your doing; did you teach Laura how to tame a wolf; a huge white wolf?"

"No," stammered Morgan, "I know nothing of this, she has exceeded anything I have taught her."

Sylviana turned to Martha, "you have an amazing daughter, elves can no longer walk with wolves, yet Laura has a great white to protect her!"

Jayden who had returned to Sylviana said, "that wolf—it's her best friend!"

"Laura," said Morgan, "you have surpassed yourself; I could not imagine you could achieve so much; you must have some amazing stories to tell. But why did you let those bandits go? we could have kept them in the cellar as they did us until the guards return."

"I wanted them out of my sight. In the forest, they may meet some of my friends, if they do, they won't reach the other end."

Everybody was now talking, Kylo was making his way back to the river.

Laura ran to join him, "you risked everything to save me, I will make sure they keep quiet."

Sylviana came running down to Laura, "can I walk with you? I want to talk to your friend."

To Laura's amazement, Sylviana seemed to be having a conversation with Snowy. "You can understand what Snowy is saying, and talk in his own tongue?" asked Laura.

"Yes, elves have always been able to communicate with wolves, would you like to learn? As we talk, I will translate, try to understand they use facial expressions as well as sounds, his wolf name is Kylo."

Kylo pessimistically said, "when Baron finds out I have shown myself to more humans, he and Sheena will move."

"I have an idea," confessed Sylviana, "can you keep it a secret from him for a few days, I must leave to reunite two people."

They sat by the river bank, which was trickling towards the valley. Sylviana did most of the talking, Laura occasionally interrupted with a wolf expression, which pleased Kylo. It was late afternoon; an icy breeze circled the group.

"Time to return to the farmhouse, it's getting chilly, and they'll be wondering what's happened to us," said Sylviana.

"Bye Kylo," said Laura in wolf tongue, as he ran up the opposite bank towards his cave.

‡

Back at the farmhouse, everyone had been busy, Martha cooking, Raoul Morgan and Gavin tidying up. The highway robbers had wrecked every room with their knife throwing competitions.

Overturned furniture, broken crockery and decaying parcels of food littered the floor.

Jayden was in the farmyard, feeding the farm animals; they had been neglected. "You're back just in time for something to eat," remarked Jayden, with a cheeky grin.

After they had eaten Raoul suggested they sit in the family room to reflect on the turn of events.

Morgan, turning to Laura said, "tell us about your adventures in the forest?"

Sylviana sprang out of her chair shouted, "No! Laura, you go to bed now! you need to rest."

When Laura had gone, Sylviana told everybody a demon possessed her.

"When Flora returns, we will cure Laura."

With that they retired, Sylviana telling Morgan to be ready to travel at first light.

Chapter 17

Zee meets the Nash brothers.

It was now late afternoon; the brothers had been struggling through the forest. The vines and bramble they battled with had attacked their clothes, Edmund's trousers were ragged, Aldwin's tunic now resembled a swathe of ribbons. Edmund struggled to walk, bruises covered his back and legs, the bite from Kylo had damaged his hand. Aldwin had taken to holding his brother as they ventured deeper into the forest.

"Curse that animal," said Edmund.

"Yes," replied Aldwin, "but did you see his coat, that pelt is worth a small fortune."

"What are you suggesting, that beast would have killed us if that girl hadn't called it off," said Edmund.

"That wolf child will be its downfall, it came to protect her, so we set a trap. We snatch the wolf girl, throw her into the pit, and cover the top, she's bound to start hollering. When the wolf comes to save the girl, it will fall into the trap. We'll throw spears into its body, she can stand by and watch the wolf die, that'll be our revenge on Laura."

"You make it sound so simple, I'm the one that was sent flying across the farmyard like a piece of leftover offal. Look at my hand, it's useless now, I'm severely bruised all over."

"When we get out of this forest, we will recruit more thugs, lay the trap and kill it. Don't forget it was that obnoxious Laura that sent us into this morbid forest," said Aldwin.

As he spoke something in the undergrowth overheard him. It was Tad the imp. He scratched his bony forehead, grinned and scampered back to Zee. Running into the lair he started flapping his arms like a bird trying to take flight, gabbling nonsense.

Zee shook him, "slow down, what have you seen?"

"There are two lost travellers, men. They said Laura had sent them into the forest, Laura the witch girl, they called her a wolf child."

Zee was perplexed, "why has she sent me a gift, after we tried to capture her."

Turning to Tad, "return and lead them to the labyrinth, I want those two men in here to question. Then I shall take their spirit."

With the rest of the imps, Tad found the Nash brothers a few paces from where he last saw them, he whispered, "It's now time to lure those men into the labyrinth, you know what to do."

They all ran around cajoling Aldwin and Edmund, "you're going the wrong way, the wrong way; follow us, we'll show you the way."

"What are these creatures; are they trying to help us?" wondered Aldwin.

"Let's follow them," said Edmund, "they look harmless enough."

They meekly followed the imps into the labyrinth, once deep inside, the imps disappeared as hastily as they appeared.

"What now?" queried Edmund.

"I don't know, it was your idea to follow those little creatures," replied Aldwin.

The brothers continued to argue, pushing each other, just falling short of fighting. They tried to find the exit, unlike Laura, they couldn't work out what to do; wandering deeper into the labyrinth.

152

Exhausted, they lay to rest, nightfall came, but strange and eerie noises kept the brothers awake most of the night.

‡

It was early morning the following day, when Tad, with his band of stalky imps behind him, left Zee's lair. They found the Nash brothers close to where they had left them, both looking disgruntled, tired and fearful.

Tad waved his stemlike arm, "come, we will show you the way."

Now tired, hungry and utterly lost, obediently they followed the imps, Tad was feeling particularly pleased with himself leading the Nash brothers to the centre of the labyrinth, and into the lair. Zee was out of sight. Her Silhouette stirred, hidden behind a shadowy curtain of lace.

In a low soft alluring voice, she said, "you must be hungry. I have prepared a broth for you, it's on the table, help yourselves."

They eagerly sat at the prepared table and devoured the broth. After they leaned back relaxed and contented, feeling safe in Zee's company.

"So, what brings you into my forest?"

"A wolf girl called Laura drove us in here," replied Aldwin, surprised by that question.

First, she's a witch, now she's a wolf girl. "What can you tell me about this, Laura?" Zee asked. "Where does she live?"

"She lives in a large farmhouse, with three adults."

"Where?" Zee hissed impatiently. Her voice splintering back to its coarse rasp.

"It's right on the edge of this forest, a day's walk from here. She has a powerful white wolf as a protector; It flung me across the

153

farmyard grounds. That's how she commanded us to enter this place, we couldn't argue with that beast."

"A wolf isn't that dangerous, why couldn't two men overpower it?"

"Its mouth is large enough to bite a man's head off with ease," replied Edmund, rubbing his hand.

"Tsk," *I need to think about this animal.* "So, the witch sent you— are you my gift from Laura?" grinned Zee.

Aldwin looked at Edmund and muttered, "what is she talking about?" He turned to the shadows, "what are you doing living in this maze: who are you?"

"I am Zee, queen of the forest, your mistress in waiting."

Zee moved out of the shadows like a jewelled crone she wore a crown of emeralds she had taken from the minotaur's hidden treasure. Her arms stretched out as if sleepwalking, the bony fingers with blueberry coloured rings on, pointing at the two Nash brothers. Her black piercing orb-like eyes were staring at the brothers, she was now muttering in an unearthly tongue. The sight of Zee terrified both the brothers. They rose to leave, but she had contaminated the broth with a sleeping potion mixed with her transformation elixir.

Zee started chanting her incantation.

"Ye of life,

Spirit of might,

Given to Zee,

Return and be,

Yielded by dawn,

An Impish form."

The Nash brothers collapsed onto the floor, convulsing, unable to speak. Aldwin tried to crawl away. Zee kicked his hands, he rolled onto his side; her clawlike toes tore into his stomach. He momentary screamed, fell onto his face and sunk into unconsciousness, alongside his brother.

Next morning, they awoke on the floor as imps, with no consciousness of their former life, just knowing they must serve Zee.

"Go, join my band outside," commanded Zee.

They both shuffled out, one with a damaged hand.

"Laura, I thank you for my gift, I must come and visit you sometime," roared Zee for everyone to hear.

‡

Returning to the fayre, Bill and Gram told Silo about Bryok, the elf girl and the children's escape.

Bill said, "do you remember when we were in Ecrind and we went into that rowdy tavern called the Hawk? A tall stranger in a long black cloak came in and said he would pay for information about elves."

"Horrid place, I didn't feel safe in there, it was full of ruffians," pointed out Gram.

Bill said, "tomorrow morning we ride to Ecrind, find that man, and tell him we saw an elf girl."

"They must be living in the Catacomb forest, so it should be worth a few silver coins for that information," grinned Silo.

"It won't be that easy, he will want to come and look around before he pays us, but let's go, we have nothing to lose," replied Gram.

The next morning, Gram and Bill took the well-worn track to Ecrind, arriving mid-afternoon. The town was bustling with people milling around, tradesmen, and stalls everywhere. They housed their horses and went to the Hawk Inn, which was down a dingy alleyway. The tavern, a well-known place for villains to hang out. From a distance, it had the colouring of a fresh green appearance. On closer inspection revealed it was decayed wood, covered in mould and mildew.

The owner, an unshaven, slovenly man slouched over the countertop, remembers the stranger. "Gave me the shivers," he said. "I only saw his eyes, but I knew he was a sinister person to avoid. He comes in always asking about elves, he never stops for a drink. Try one of the other three taverns in the town."

After giving them the names and directions of the three taverns, Bill suggested they split up, go to one each and meet at the third. Bill had no luck, neither did Gram, so they both arrived at the third tavern, The Green Ivy, at the same time. As they walked in, the tall stranger walked out, bumping into Bill and knocking him onto his back, the stranger just carried on walking.

Bill, sprawling across the floor, shouted after the man, "hey wait, are you looking for elves?"

In one movement the stranger turned around, reached out, lifted Bill from the floor, with a grip that could kill a person with little effort; he asked, "what do you know about elves?"

"See this ear," said Bill touching his cut ear, "an elf girl did it, fired an arrow at me, told us it was a warning."

"Where; When?" he asked bluntly.

"How many silver coins do we get?" asked Gram.

The stranger, turning to Gram said, "ten, if you show me, and prove that it happened."

"It happened yesterday, by a village called Drewcott. It's late now, and it's a day's ride, we'll take you tomorrow morning, meet us at dawn, by the blacksmiths," said Bill.

The stranger just nodded his head and walked away, leaving Bill and Gram wondering if they had done the right thing.

Gram said, "the innkeeper was right, that man is sinister and strong; his green ringed eyes were disconcerting. Can we trust him?"

Bill said, "there's two of us, he's only one man, keep your blades ready, if there's any trouble we'll knife and rob him."

That night they slept with their hands on their knives, in a dark smelly alleyway near the blacksmiths. Rats came sniffing around while they slept but left when they couldn't find any food. As the sun rose, streaming light across the rusty rooftops down the bleak wooden walls they stirred, stood up, stretched, and walked to the blacksmith's stables. Two strangers were waiting, both wore black capes up to their eyes. Bill and Gram looked at each other with sinking hearts.

They journeyed back in silence, Bill and Gram led the way, with the tall dark strangers following behind.

Bill whispered to Gram, "can you tell those two men apart, they're identical?"

"No, it's abnormal, I don't like it," replied Gram.

"Take us to the place where the archer fired at you."

Early afternoon, they reached the tor where they spotted Laura and Jayden.

Pointing, Gram said, "over there between those trees and the Catacomb forest, that's where she hit me with her arrow."

They rode on to where their horses stopped.

"The elf girl called to our horses and commanded them to stop, we were almost thrown off, then she fired her arrow," said Gram.

The two strangers, dismounted and looked inside the bushes.

"That's where she stood, on the edge of the Catacomb forest," Bill pointed to the spot Gavin and Sylviana were standing.

"Here, I've found the arrow, they're telling the truth."

"Is it an elf arrow?"

"Yes, an elf crafted this."

"You said another man was chasing these two children, where can we find him?" asked one of the strangers.

"He lives in Drewcott village, we'll take you there," said Bill.

They rode towards the village; the sun had started setting. When they reached their fayre camp, Bill and Gram stopped.

Bill said, "that's Drewcott village, the man you want is called Bryok Roth, this is our camp, do we get the ten silver coins now?"

As the strangers rode off, one tossed a small bag to Bill, containing the silver coins. They left without saying a word.

It was getting dark as the strangers walked into the village, the first person they asked, pointed out Bryok's hut, it was on the edge of the village. As they strode across the grimy path to the hut, the villagers that were still around could only wonder what mischief Bryok had done.

They walked to the entrance. There was only a piece of rotting timber propped up to stop anyone from entering. Without pausing, they pushed the timber to the floor and entered the hut. The first thing they saw was Bryok lying on the floor covered in vomit, in a drunken stupor; the room was drenched in the smell of stale fermented ale. The crash of the timber had woken the children;

158

they peered out from their rooms. The three boys slept together in one room, the three girls in the other.

With one hand, the stranger lifted Bryok by the neck and stuck his head into the pail of water they used for washing. He came out sputtering, not giving him time to recover, he was dunked into the pail again.

The stranger said, "why were you chasing those children two days ago; what did they look like; do you know where they were going?"

"The witch girl beat up my boys, I was going to . . ."

Clare came running out of the girl's bedroom. "No father," she shouted, "Laura is a friend."

Bryok, with the back of his hand, cracked Clare in the face, sending her splaying onto the floor, knocking her unconscious. Anna and Giselle crawled over to Clare, Giselle holding her hand glared at Bryok, with pure hatred dripping from her eyes. Anna's tears were washing over Clare's face.

Oake and Dudley looked to Walter; he turned away, his eyes clouded, "she'll be better off dead."

"What's in it for me?" said Bryok, sobering up and smelling money.

"Two silver coins, now answer our questions."

"They said they were going into the Catacomb forest to a moss garden, they both wore cloaks. The boy had greenish hair, his eyes were a greenish colour, like yours. He tied me up with this strange twine," he replied picking up the thread he had discarded on the floor.

Snatching the twine from Bryok, they tossed two silver coins onto the floor as they walked out.

Outside the hut they examined the twine, "green-eyed elf boy, elfin twine, it must be them. It's time to use the tracker."

The tracker, half-fae, half Skeltonian, shadowed the hunters, keeping hidden from human eyes. He was always a day's distance behind his fellow dark lords. The strangers, Skeltonians, only had to wait a day for him to arrive.

Chapter 18

Flora.

At the farmhouse, Sylviana and Morgan were preparing their journey to Flora's dwelling.

"We won't need any food, just two blankets," Sylviana told Morgan.

Morgan looked quizzical at Sylviana, "blankets?"

"Yes, to sit on," she said, as she opened the farmhouse door to reveal Trinity and Storm standing outside.

"They have agreed to take us to Flora, we will be there by tonight!" She continued, "throw your cover onto Trinity's back, shut your eyes and hold on tight. We are heading for the Ecrind Fargate crossroad."

Once mounted the unicorns cantered down the single track that joins the Ecrind road. Once there, they changed into a full gallop, charging up to a unicorn flying charge; Morgan shut his eyes.

‡

After Sylviana and Morgan rode away, Laura sat with her mother, Martha, and asked, "I've been thinking about Morgan, flora and my name; was I named after Flora?"

Martha nodded, "Yes—Morgan was becoming a vagabond, searching for something he could never find. When you were born, we told Morgan we were naming you after Flora and asked him if he could become your tutor. We hoped that would give his life a purpose. He refused and departed for another search. He was gone for three years. When he returned, we introduced you to him. He knelt down; you immediately put your arms around his neck. He agreed to stop for a short time. He taught you about animals, wildlife, reading and writing. You were a quick learner, he never left us again, but spent every morning educating you."

Laura said "I wouldn't have had the courage or ability to have made the journey if Flora hadn't taught Morgan, who taught me. I hope I get the chance to meet her."

✚

By late afternoon Storm shouted to Trinity, "a group ahead, divert."

Storm shot into a ditch followed by Trinity. As they moved past, Morgan opened one eye and recognised Ives with the Nash gang.

"What's that?" questioned Ives.

Before Ives had finished, the unicorns had leapt back onto the road and disappeared.

The light was fading as they reached the crossroads of the Drewcott Ecrind road. The unicorns slowed to a canter.

Sylviana said, "cross the river Ner, at the avenue of white eucalyptus trees, go straight to the large oak, and stop."

After dismounting, Sylviana stroked Storm, "wait here for a few moments, then follow us to the dingle. We'll get you oats and hay, and take you to a safe place to sleep, I want to surprise Flora first."

Following a path of stepping stones, Morgan followed Sylviana across a mossy bank to a group of mountain ash saplings. Sylviana approached two moss-covered saplings and stopped.

Turning to Morgan said, "count to ten and follow me."

She turned and sidled between the saplings and disappeared. Inside she saw Flora's back, she was preparing two raspberry drinks.

"Hello, you're taking a risk leaving the forest, what made you venture out?" Flora said while turning to face Sylviana.

"I've brought someone to see you," she replied.

"I sensed no one with you!"

"I masked his presence from you," she replied moving to her left as Morgan entered.

Two vessels smashed to the floor, spilling raspberry juice over her bare feet.

‡

Laura, Jayden and Kylo were lying in the grassy patch, just beside the river, relaxing and surveying the landscape when Kylo sat up with his ears perked.

"What is it, what's wrong?" asked Laura, as she sat bolt upright.

"It's your mother, she gave a shrill cry," replied Kylo.

Laura jumped up and sprinted towards the river. Kylo alongside gripped Laura's collar and flipped her onto his back. She held his neck as Kylo jumped to the yearning edge rock. He was on the other bank in a blaze of urgency, surging towards the farmhouse. Laura had never ridden Kylo before; it was so exhilarating, had it not been so urgent.

Sheena and Baron were sitting atop the crag, they both watched as Kylo crossed the river and made his way to the farmhouse.

"What is it?" asked Baron, as they both stood.

Sheena, with her eyes shut and gazing intensely, said, "there's trouble at the girl's home, her mothers in distress."

"Kylo can take care of himself, but let's go to the river, you can sense what's going on better down there," replied Baron.

163

"I agree," said Sheena as she bounded to the path that led to the river's edge.

At the farmhouse, Laura sprang off Kylo, and said, "you go around the back if there's trouble you can surprise them."

Laura ran across the yard, skidding around the corner to a sight that shocked her to the bone. Her mother was on the floor, bound from head to foot with twine, her mouth lashed tight, sheer terror was in her wide eyes. A pack of disorderly imps were dragging her into the Catacomb forest.

Laura didn't know what to do, she didn't have Tad basher or the knife, she panicked and yelled, "stop!"

A movement drew her eyes to another figure standing in the shadows of the farmhouse, it was Zee. She stepped out, into the light, wearing a raggedy black cloak, carrying a staff to help her bent body walk. Part human, part imp, she cast a grotesque figure.

Through her callous mouth, she said, "so you're the tiresome witch called Laura!"

Something in Laura's eyes shocked Zee, then she saw it.

Zee crowed, "you're possessed by my imps lost souls. I cast them out into the wilderness, you have their shells. I see it now; they're taking your soul. As the imp form will take me if I don't rejuvenate with the essence of beings that wander the forest."

These remarks shook Laura, she tried to push it to the back of her mind.

Kylo came around the back to attack Zee, but she was expecting him, as Kylo pounced Zee threw specks of powder at Kylo reciting,

"Sleep beast sleep,

Sleep until you weep,

Sleep like the unborn,

Sleep until dawn."

Kylo staggered and fell, tried to get up, fell again, staggered to his feet, fell a final time, he lay there motionless.

"No," screamed Laura, running towards Kylo.

Zee jumped upon Kylo's body, drew out a large black sword she had saved from one of her victims. She held it over his throat.

"Stop! witch girl, no tricks or magic, do as I say or this beast's blood will flow . . ." she faltered, staring beyond Laura.

✝

"Quick," said Sheena, "we must get to that building, Kylo has fallen, he needs our help!"

Kylo was fast getting across the river and reaching the farmyard, but Sheena and Baron got there much faster. They circled the farm, Baron ran to one side of the farmyard, Sheena skirted around the other. So it was, that Baron came behind Laura, and swerved to a stop seeing the sword over Kylo. Baron curled his jaw and bore his thick bone-crunching teeth.

Zee was trembling—terror crossed her face. Two fiery eyes shot at her imps; she would make those two suffer for not disclosing to her two beasts were living by the farm. She wasn't aware of Sheena standing behind her.

Sheena took the sword from Zee with one bite, grabbed her neck in her jaws and swung her around and around, finally letting her go. She flew high into the air, through the trees and crashed, somewhere in the forest.

The second Baron and Sheena showed the imps ran, scattering into the forest, leaving Martha still bound, prostrate on the floor.

Laura ran over to Martha untying her saying, "stay here, do not be afraid, they mean you no harm, that's their son."

She ran over to Kylo, where Sheena and Baron were kneeling with their heads on Kylo, believing he was dying.

Laura approached Sheena and said, "that creature cast a sleeping spell on Kylo, he will be back with us tomorrow." Her eyes wavered, she dug her nails into the palm of her hands, "he will awake."

Raoul had been showing Gavin around the farm when they heard the commotion. They came running from the top field into the farmyard. They hesitated, not sure what to expect from the wolves. They saw Martha, staggering with her arms around Laura for support.

Laura moved aside so Raoul and Gavin could support Martha into the farmhouse. As they disappeared through the door, a sensation of dread tugged at Laura's mind.

She slid into a heap on the floor.

‡

The two dark strangers, Skeltonians, a cheerless race of mountain dwellers, dark cousins to elves, were waiting in the alehouse for their tracker to arrive.

"Let's leave, this is the most revolting tavern we have ever been in, these humans are disgusting," whined Gim, one of the tall strangers. He continued, "I can sense the tracker, he's nearby."

Outside in the village square, against the moon, they saw their tracker prowling along the skyline.

"Come, we'll walk to the Catacomb forest tonight, there will be time to rest tomorrow," said Cyn, the other Skeltonian.

They intersected the tracker and made for the forest, stopping only to adjust their direction. Once at the entry point, the tracker led the way along the path, pointing to bent twigs and squashed leaves.

"There," said the tracker, pointing to the moss garden. They all rambled around trampling everything.

"One elf, one elfling, one human man, one human child," said the tracker.

"We can rest here and continue at sunrise," said Gim.

They awoke before dawn broke and followed the tracker all day. He stops and points to the trees, "elf dwelling."

Eyeing the forest floor, he continues, "they ride four horses, no, hoof prints far apart—unicorns!"

Pointing to his left, "unicorn trail, we go that way."

For three days they followed the unicorn trail, the tracker occasionally pointing out the wide strides the unicorns took. On the fourth day they reached the edge of the forest, skirting around its edge they sighted the farm.

The tracker, pointing at the Lovet farm, "they entered that building."

Like a reptile, he slithered across the farmyard and made his way to the farmhouse and the dirt track.

Returning to Cyn and Gim he said, "yesterday, one elf and one human took that dirt track."

"What do we do?" asked Cyn, "follow the trail, or interrogate the occupants of the farm?"

"They are friends to the elves, they will tell us nothing, or lies, we will wait here and watch before we follow the trail. Maybe this is their home," replied Gim.

Chapter 19

A new Elfin.

Laura was lying on her bed, deathly white, struggling for breath, Martha and Raoul were expecting the worst. No one said the words they were thinking, it's only a matter of time, one hour, maybe two hours before our brave daughter dies.

Jayden stood at the crossroads, at the dirt track to the farm and the highway, waiting for his mother to return. It was late afternoon, and far in the distance, he spotted Trinity and Storm. They were harnessed to a cart, inside sat his mother, with Flora and Morgan.

He ran like a hare, his heart pounding, almost breaking out of his ribcage. He reaches the cart, gasping for breath he said, "Its Laura, she's dying."

Storm stamped his hoof, "untie us and get on our backs."

Flora and Sylviana gripped the unicorn's necks as they sped off, immediately bursting into the unicorn flying gallop. Morgan and Jayden hid the cart, with Flora's belongings and walked to the farm.

As Flora and Sylviana reached the farm, both felt the despondency surrounding it. They jumped off the unicorns and ran through the farmyard, towards the house, unaware they were being watched.

They ran into Laura's room, a scene of desolation, Martha lying across Laura's body weeping, Raoul's hand was stroking Martha's back.

Flora shouted, "everyone out the way," as she raced to the bed, not giving Martha a chance to respond, but threw her aside.

Taking Laura's hand into her own, shouted at Sylviana, "she's almost lost, I need your help, hold her other hand. Now give me your other hand."

Sylviana reached over Laura's body, Flora grabbed the hand and tenderly placed hers and Sylviana hand onto Laura's chest.

The family sat in a corner of the room, watching the two elves trying to bring Laura back. Martha tried to speak, but there was a tightness in her throat. They witnessed an incredible sight, they had created an aura between Flora and Sylviana, which passed through Laura's body, an elfin figure eight healing circle. This is performed by one elf, never by two, but such was the dire situation of Laura, Flora decided this was the only chance she had.

The aura intensified, for a few seconds, the room was warmly illuminated. Sylviana could no longer handle the burden and collapsed onto the floor, breaking the connection. Laura jolted and gave a gasp of air, then started having convulsions. Flora, still holding Laura's hand, placed her other onto Laura's body, she now went into a trancelike state.

Sylviana, struggling to her knees asked, "have we succeeded?"

"No," replied Flora, "she had four rhysheba demons within, we have removed one, she is infected deeply inside, to her core, her actual essence. Gavin take Sylviana, she is spent and needs to rest, I will stay and do what I can."

"What can we do to help?" asked Morgan, as he walked in with Jayden.

"A chair for me to sit on, I need to stop with Laura tonight."

Everyone stayed the night, hoping Laura would regain consciousness, recover. The minutes passed into an hour, two hours three four; by morning there was no improvement. Flora sat

170

constantly holding Laura, fighting the demons within. The hours grew to a day, then two, three days; they saw no change in Laura.

The family took it in turns to sit with Laura. Flora was constant, she never moved, never slept, never took her hand off Laura's body. Her sole purpose was to rid Laura of her demons. It was affecting Flora. Everyone saw the changes, but no one spoke of it. Sylviana, although worn out, offered to help.

Flora said, "We did an extraordinary and arduous technique you must leave and rest."

☦

Watching Flora and Sylviana running into the farmhouse, Gim said to Cyn, "tomorrow at dawn, you travel to the elves at Elfield. Go to Agish and tell him we know where they are living. I will wait here and watch if they move, I will leave a trail."

It took Cyn five days to reach the elves of Elfield, passing through the white wolves' territory, over the pure mountains, into the plains of Tundra.

Arriving at Elfield, Cyn, wheeling his head around was unimpressed with the brilliant artistry of the elfinglade. He was used to the gloominess of the Skeltonian caves where he dwelt.

He bellows out, "I have business with Agish, where is his chamber?"

Roheck, striding forward answered, "I will take you, follow me." Turning to Dain, "tell my father Zilar to come to Agish's chamber."

They enter a large chamber, Agish is seated near a tall pillar. As Cyn approaches Agish, Zilar enters and joined his son seated by a pillar at the rear of the chamber.

171

Cyn addresses Agish, "the two you seek, they are both at a farm the other side of the Aswin River."

Agish mouth arched into a sardonic grin.

Drumming his fingers in excitement asked, "how many people are on this farm?"

"With the two elf women, we counted three men, one woman, and one boy, an elfling," replied Cyn.

"So Sylviana is a mother," Agish mumbled through gritted teeth.

Roheck glanced at his father, Zilar.

"Get Harwyn here, now," bawled out Agish, thumping a fist into his open hand. "Got you now!"

Loyal and respected Harwyn, leader of the archers entered and dropped his head, "Elder, you summon me?"

"Prepare twenty fighters for a five-day journey. We have two renegades to return home, we move out tomorrow morning."

When Harwyn had left, Roheck and Zilar came forward to discuss the latest developments with Agish.

Zilar spoke, "we will go with you on this journey."

"No, I will bring them back."

"Alive?" asked the Roheck.

"If possible," replied Agish.

Zilar, speaking forcefully, "with twenty armed soldiers—we will accompany you tomorrow."

"No, I will . . ."

"You dare to defy council dignities? We will have you removed from office."

"You may travel with us, as observers."

Midnight on the eighth-night, Flora was still holding Laura's hand when her eyes flickered, they opened the tiniest of slits.

Looking up she muttered, "Flora?"

At that moment a strong and passionate howl was heard all around the farm, it woke everyone at the farmhouse. Kylo knew Laura had returned. When he awoke from Zee's sleeping enchantment, Sheena insisted he returns to their side of the river. He sat at the river bank never moving, taking short naps, relying on Baron and Sheena to feed him.

Jayden was up and out of bed, running from his room fearing the worst. He was the first to reach Laura's room, almost yanking the door off its hinges as he snatched it open. The picture of Laura sitting up in Flora's arms, brought tears of joy.

He raced out shouting, "get up, Flora's done it, Laura is back."

Within minutes, the family were in Laura's room, everyone asked the same question, "is she cured?"

"Yes," declared Flora, "that dreadful place no longer has a hold, the demons are defeated." Flora continued, "the rhysheba demons from the withered forest have been cast out, the evilness is gone."

Flora stood and released her hold on Laura, for the first time since entering the room. Laura, sitting on the side of her bed, swung her feet onto the floor, and tried to stand. Her legs gave way, Flora caught her waist before she hit the floor. She scooped her up and lay Laura back on the bed.

"Don't rush it, give yourself time to recover."

Both Flora and Laura looked alarmingly drained. Laura's eyes were baggy, her skin was creamy white, but her eyes, like the stars blinking in the dark sky above, lit up as she looked at her mother.

Martha threw her arms around Flora, "I don't know how to thank you, you have returned my child, but it has taken so much out of you. I am forever in your debt."

"Morgan told me about Laura, and everything she accomplished, she is an exceptional and brave young woman."

"We know," replied both Raoul and Martha, "when will she be able to move from this room and live again?"

To their amazement, she replied, "tomorrow morning, we will both be up for breakfast. Laura needs to exercise her muscles as soon as possible, but for now everyone please leave; I have important information and advice I wish to tell Laura."

When they were alone Flora told Laura, "you are cured, but under no circumstances should you enter either the Catacomb forest or the Withered Forest. Three times they tried and failed, those evil spirits they tasted your soul, they will be waiting for another chance to take your body."

The rest of the night they sat up talking, Flora telling her how she will be affected by the events of the last few days.

As dawn broke, Flora said, "move over, I will rest on the bed beside you for a short time."

They had scarcely closed their eyes when they woke to the aroma of fresh bread.

"Wake up," whispered Flora we both need a good meal.

When they joined the family for breakfast, in the light of day, they could see the impact the last eight days had affected Flora. Emotionally and physically she was drained, her hair looked like it was made of silvery silk woven with moonlight dust, not a single strand of golden hair remained, her smooth satin like-skin was now discoloured. The veins on the back of her hands were raised, but her huge smile was radiant, now Laura was cured. After they had eaten a breakfast of freshly baked bread, boiled eggs and cakes, made by both Martha and Sylviana, they all moved to the great room.

Sylviana, questioning Flora, "what's happened to you? your appearance I can see has changed, but . . . I cannot sense—something has changed."

"I need everyone to understand there will be significant changes in Laura, due to the method I used to drive out the Rhysheba spirits within her body."

There was a respectful hush as Flora spoke, she now had everybody's attention.

She continued, "I could not remove the spirits from outside, for five days and nights I tried, my aura would not work, and I was tiring. From day six I gave my healing energy into Laura, by doing so I have drained my body."

She paused to give everyone a chance to absorb what she had disclosed.

Sylviana, half realising what Flora was saying, said, "you have let go of your . . ."

"With my power running through Laura's veins, her essence her heart, she was, with my help, able to defeat the Rhysheba spirits. All of my elf healing powers have gone, Laura has absorbed and retained everything. Laura has now got to learn to harness and control her new powers, I will be around to help."

Sylviana looked beyond Laura's eyes and saw. She took her hands and felt the radiance that elves possess.

Flora continued, "she has become an elf healer, not by birth but by transference—she is still Laura, but has the essence of elf sap running in her blood."

Morgan asked, "cannot you withdraw your power back out of Laura?"

"No, I didn't know if the process would work, it could have taken both our lives, but I had nothing to lose, Laura was going to die. No elf has ever performed such a dangerous process, reversing it would be impossible. Nor can Laura attempt to return my powers. She is still a human child with elf abilities."

In a hushed voice trying to stifle tears, Martha said, "you've given everything, everything you could to save my child."

Morgan was now holding Flora's hand said, "come, you need to rest, there's a room prepared for you, come sleep and recover."

Raoul, putting his arm around Laura, "did you understand what Flora has done?"

"Yes, she told me everything last night, when you had left," running her hand down Flora's arm as she walked out with Morgan.

Jayden tapped Laura on the shoulder, "there's someone outside waiting to see you."

They walked outside, waiting there was Kylo.

Chapter 20

Family feud.

The next day after the first meal, Flora and Sylviana sat in the family room discussing their future.

Sylviana stood and called Laura, "It's time to talk to the wolves, show us the way."

"We have to swim the Aswin River, my craft can only carry one," Laura replied gloomily.

"We'll swim you use your craft," said Flora.

"No, you use the craft, you're still worn out," Laura snapped pursing her mouth.

Throwing her hands up, Martha groaned, "don't argue, she can be very stubborn."

They all crossed the river, Flora in Laura's craft, Laura and Sylviana swimming side by side. Kylo warily appeared. Laura ran from Sylviana, Kylo bowed down, they both rubbed their head against each other.

Flora looked on in awe, "If I hadn't seen it with my own eyes, I wouldn't have believed it possible for a human to bond with a longclaw."

Kylo bounded away, Laura said, "he's going to fetch Baron and Sheena."

"You can communicate now?" asked Flora.

"Yes, Sylviana gave me the basics, I took it from there."

Flora whispered to Sylviana, "Morgan told me she was intelligent and a fast learner but this is beyond belief."

The three great wolves stepped down the bank, and with the poise of a divine Felidae sat a few paces from Flora and Sylviana. Kylo moved to Laura's side; she grooms behind his ears. He purred in approval.

Sylviana spoke in wolf's tongue, "I want to set up an elfin enclave nearby, with my family, Flora and Morgan. We vow to protect and hide you from any huntsmen. We understand your worries, hunters may become aware of you living here, we want to assure you that no one will reveal your whereabouts."

Baron snorted with disdain, "remember the last time in the plains of Tundra!"

"We were not part of that decision, we will not desert you but live amongst you, in the woodlands. Our enclave will be a hidden realm within the copse; humans will not be able to perceive its existence. We will create a passageway for you to pass through at will whenever you feel the need for safety," reassured Flora.

"What have we to lose? We leave now and travel into the wilderness. They abandon us, we go into the wilderness," argued Kylo.

Sheena stood and spoke, "I agree with Kylo, we stay." Turning to Baron, "come we will watch them closely."

Flora and Sylviana stood, held their hands as if in prayer, bowed their heads, said, "elves to wolves, we vow to protect you if hunters arrive here."

As the wolves wandered away Flora said, "we must find a place to create our new home."

Laura jumps up and pointed, "over there, inside the woodland, there's an idyllic spot near the stream."

Back at the farmhouse, they thanked Laura for showing them the site.

The next day Gavin and Morgan set about the manual work required to create the elves enclave. Sylviana and Flora weaved their magical enchantments to keep it hidden from unwelcome eyes.

On the way back to the farmhouse, Flora taking Morgan's hand sighed, "five, maybe six days and we will be ready to move into our home, together."

The following morning, as if hit by a lightning strike, Sylviana sat up, "they're here, we are uncovered. I can sense their presence fast approaching, we have scarcely time to run."

"What is it, what's wrong?" Morgan worriedly asked as he rounded the table to be at Flora's side.

Flora stood, and holding both Morgan's hands bemoaned, "my kin are on the way, I am not running, they are too close. I will fight, my life is nothing without you, they are not taking me back."

"I stand with you, if this is the end, I'm glad we found each other for these days we had together," replied Morgan.

Everyone talked at once, how far are they; how many will come; where can we go; what will they do?

Laura, gripping the table said, "why?"

Sylviana called for everyone to be quiet, "they will be here within the hour, I sense twenty-five elves on horseback. They will try to take me, along with Flora back to our own kinfolk, by force."

Resting her hand on Laura's shoulder, she said, "you asked the simplest and exploring question which I cannot answer. Our leaders are blinded by self- righteousness and they will not accept change, it makes me sad, after thirteen years they still hunt us."

Approaching Flora, Martha declared, "we will stand by your side, you came to us in our darkest hour, nothing—nothing will stop me. They will have to cut me down first before they take you."

"That applies to everybody in this room," added Raoul slamming his jug onto the table.

Both Laura and Jayden jumped to their feet and said, "and us," in unison.

"Oh no, you will stay in the farmhouse," said Martha.

"And you," said Sylviana, putting her arm around Jayden, "you children have been in enough danger lately."

Everyone agreed the children should stay secured in Laura's room.

"Children," murmured Laura pacing around the room, "children, you call me a child."

Morgan approached Laura, knelt in front of her, put his hands on her shoulder, "no, you're the bravest person I know, not a child. Someone has to stay behind and look after the livestock if they take us away. Don't worry, I'm sure we will be fine."

She knew he was lying. *Morgan is looking over my shoulder, he's lying, stay safe, if we're killed you will live, why didn't he say it.*

"Come," said Sylviana, and escorted Laura and Jayden to Laura's room, "you stay here, someone will fetch you when the elves have gone."

Sylviana pulled the door shut and put an enchantment on it. When they were alone, Jayden tried to open the door, his magic wouldn't work on his mother's spell.

Whilst he was trying a different spell to unlock the door, Laura was busy at her storage cupboard, where she kept her personal knick-knacks. She flushed out Tad basher and the robber's knife, both were placed into her leather belt. She moved her bed to one

180

side; Jayden was now becoming curious and stopped to watch Laura. With the bed moved she started to prise up one of the boards.

"What are you doing?" asked Jayden, as he came over and helped Laura remove the board.

"This hole is over the cellar I . . ."

"We will join our families and face the threat together," interrupted Jayden.

Twenty-five elves arrived at the farm; they rode on white stallions without saddles. There were ten archers and ten sword wielding elves, all dressed from head to toe in olive green. They were led by five riders, four carried bows, two wore cloaks of moss green which covered their faces, only their eyes were visible. The leader was Agish, with a bow around his shoulder, he carried a sword, and two knives in his belt. Alongside Agish was Cyn the Skeltonian.

The five leading elves dismounted, Agish stepped forward with Cyn; Gim emerged from the forest and joined alongside Agish. The two cloaked elves stood a few paces to the rear.

The fifth rider, Harwyn turned to the archers and shouted, "make ready."

The troops dismounted and made ready with their bows and swords, everyone pointing at the group standing.

In the farmyard side by side, stood Martha and Raoul, each with a bread knife. Morgan had a short sword and Sylviana held her bow, with a quiver on her back full of arrows. Gavin held the black sword Zee had discarded. Flora emerged from the farmhouse, striding as the princess she was, dressed in a tight-fitting garment of gold, with a gold belt around her waist. In her long white hair was a jewelled crown of gold leaf and silver. She carried a leather scabbard hanging from her hip, the golden grip of the sword was peeking out. Walking majestically across the courtyard, she stopped a few strides away from Agish.

In a clear tone of authority, she spoke, looking at Agish, addressing the soldiers at his rear, "how dare you enter this property with your threat of war, I command you to leave—now."

The archers lowered their bows, they had not been chosen to attack their princess.

Morgan stared aghast.

"Didn't you know?" Sylviana muttered, "she was giving up her crown for you."

Agish, standing in front of Flora said, "princess Flora, you hold no power since you deserted your people."

Turning to Sylviana said, "come with us we are taking you home, living with these heinous humans is dishonourable."

Turning back to Flora, he exclaimed, "you are a disgrace, leading Sylviana away from her family, you too are returning."

Martha moved in front of Flora and said in a menacing tone, "to take Flora you will have to kill me first."

"Do you want to die?" sneered Agish.

As he spoke Laura and Jayden came running from the farmhouse, Laura making for Flora, stood beside Martha.

Facing up to the elves cautioned Agish, "keep away from my family and friends."

"So, you use a child to protect yourself, come with us and no one is harmed, stay and you and these humans will be slain."

Flora steps forward, musing, *how did she get out of her room*, gripped Laura's arm and pulled her back.

She said, "everyone makes the mistake of calling this young woman a child. She is the bravest, and the most ingenious person I have ever known. You, for your stature—she towers above you."

Laura's whole body was now quivering with anger. With a shrug, she released herself and pushed forward; with a stiff back, looked up and addressed Agish. "Look at the field you're standing in, it's full of life, living things, insects, animals, plants and you want to cover it in blood. I was taught that elfin folk were a nature loving people, but you—you are no different to the evil humans I have met. You dare to come here with threats of violence and the murder of your own kin. You—and all you," pointing at the archers, "are a disgrace to the Fountain of Argent."

Laura looked at Agish, his face hidden under a veneer of bitterness. His mouth curled, emitting a murmur. She knew he had cast her words aside like a farmer sowing seeds. Flora, seeing Agish getting agitated, took a firmer grip on Laura and pulled her away. Laura saw there was disquiet amongst the archers, the last few words had severed their hearts, they all knew Argent would look upon them as wrongdoers. A few wavered. Laura swung her arm around, breaking the hold that Flora had on her, and moved towards the line of the sword wielding elf's, eying each one up.

She freighted a curt curtsy, "I bow to you all. You are bravest of the brave, you come to do battle against the mighty farmers and their fearless daughter."

She walked down the column of elves, pausing by one that had lowered his sword a shade. The cheeks on his wheat green face twitched when Laura moved within three paces.

She looked into his oak wood eyes, "when you return home, will they will sing into the night toasting your bravery? Do you want to be the one to remove the head of the child who conquered the catacomb forest? You could return and parade my head around your streets proving to your peers what a mighty warrior you are. But first, you must defeat me in battle."

Morgan and Raoul both made to grab and drag Laura back. Flora moved the palms of her hands, stopped them from moving. "Wait, if anyone is going to stop bloodshed it will be your daughter. Like knitting an intricate pattern, she is weaving her words with great care; remind me again how old Laura is. Sylviana has her sights on the elves in front of Laura. If any make a move towards her, she will pierce their heart with an elfin fused arrowhead."

Agish saw Flora's weakness. "Unless you want that child dead, surrender. Harwyn command your man to do as the child requested, take her head off, if Flora and Sylviana don't lay down their weapons."

Laura saw the sword creeping down, "I understand your hesitation you have heard I am dangerous with a hand knife and wooden club. I will even the odds." Turning her back said, "now swing your mighty sword." Laura stared at Flora. The truth dawned, she twirled back facing the elf. "After you take my life, what next? Will you cut down your own princess; stab her in the heart; will you parade her head next to mine?"

The sword blade was thrust deep into the soil.

Agish's face turned a toasted brown, "Harwyn, take command of your troop, I will not tolerate insubordination." He turned on Flora, "unless you want these two children dead . . ."

"The only ones dying here today will be you; my friends are coming," interrupted Laura with a sternness in her voice.

She was aware of three white figures approaching from behind the archers.

"Oh! There are more children," laughed Agish.

"No," answered Flora, "she's referring to the three gigantic wolves coming behind your rear and flank. These are not normal wolves; they are descendants from the great and ancient breed of longclaw white; they were once the friends of elves."

Sylviana came forward, with Jayden at her side, in a clear and cutting voice said, "these three fearless wolves are friends to this extraordinary young lady."

Kylo, Baron and Sheena had crossed the river, seeing their friends in trouble, came to help.

Baron, weighing up the situation said, "spread out, Sheena, you run to the left at a zigzag, I shall do the same to the right. Kylo, go and protect your sister."

As they moved forward, Kylo momentarily glanced at Baron.

Agish and the armed company of elves turned and watched the three wolves as they were surrounded.

Laura stood in front of the twenty elves, folded her arms and said, "sheaf your swords, lower your bows, they will not attack unless you show aggression."

One of the cloaked elves walked forward and asked, "who is that child?" pointing at Jayden.

"It's your grandson, Zilar—father," said Sylviana.

Zilar threw his cloak back, turning to Harwyn, "tell your archers to stand down, this ends now, there will be no blood spilt today."

Harwyn roared, "soldiers of the Ailanthus, do as Zilar—and the child command, lower your arms. We do not murder farmers, women," he bowed to Laura, "and brave young girls."

Agish swirled his head, losing his command, losing control. His whole body was now pounding with anger. He stepped forward, withdrawing his sword, and thrust it deep into Zilar's back.

Turning to the Skeltonians snapped, "brothers, bring them to their knees."

Before he could withdraw his sword from Zilar's back, Agish was struck in the neck and heart by two arrows. One fired by Sylviana and the other, by the hooded elf—he fell, his rich red blood flooded the ground.

The Skeltonians, with their swords raised, charged at the group. The wolves were standing alongside their friends; Sheena jaws wrapped around Gim. He flayed his sword, striking nothing but the soft morning breeze. His body flagged; the sword fell from his hand as Sheena squeezed the life from him.

Cyn lunged at Sylviana. Baron intercepted. Cyn fell back, slicing Baron's front left leg. Baron, with a yelp, sank his teeth into Cyn's torso, killing him instantly.

Sylviana ran to her father, holding his hand and resting his head in the palm of her other hand.

The other cloaked elf ran over to Sylviana and asked, "how is our father?"

Sylviana looked up at her brother Roheck and shook her head.

Baron was limping towards the great river, to return home.

Laura ran after him shouting, "stop."

"What does that girl want, can't she see I'm hurt," complained Baron to Sheena as he licked his wound.

"Wait, she wants to help," said Kylo walking in front of Baron.

Making Baron sit, Laura placed her hands on his wound, immediately Baron felt relief from the pain.

Laura smiled, "thank you for coming to help, the elves no longer wish us any harm."

Baron said, "I do not trust Elves, they are bad."

Laura understood the words Baron spoke. She replied, "these are good, they were being led by one who was misguided, he has been slain."

Laura now placed her other hand onto his paw, and continued, "Kylo told me you were a mighty warrior, but I see you are also kind. I'm glad we are now friends."

Baron, with a look of tenderness in his eyes, called Kylo and Sheena to his side, as they walked back towards the river, Sheena rubbed against Baron.

Harwyn approached Roheck, "we never wanted any of this, it took that girl, a human child," looking across at Laura, "to stop our arrows from flying, what she said cut deep into our fundamental values, she spoke true from the heart."

Everybody was watching Laura talking to the wolves, the elves were in admiration that a human had achieved what they could no longer do. As she walked back, the elves parted, laying their swords and bows at their feet, leaving a passage for Laura to walk.

Harwyn knelt in front of Laura, "that's their way of showing respect. Young lady, what's your name?"

"Laura Lovet."

"Laura Lovet, I bow my head to you, you are wise beyond your years. You talk of our people toasting the bravery of the elves on this mission. When I return, our halls will be filled with the tales of Laura Lovet, the girl that faced a troop of elves armed with a club and a knife and defeated them with her words of wisdom." Harwyn withdrew his sword, "It is written that a force in defeat surrenders their weapon." He placed the sword in Laura's hands, "I surrender my sword to you. Keep it safe and please do not think too unkindly of my soldiers."

Laura, overwrought, took the sword, lay it on the grass and put her arms around Harwyn's neck and gave him a peck on the cheek.

Harwyn smiled, "I offer you an invitation to visit our realm of trees with golden leaves, building of silver birch and lakes that sparkle like the jewelled pearls of one thousand moonbeams."

He stood, "prepare the fallen to be returned to Elfield."

"Agish called the Skeltonians brothers, was he born of the dark elves?" asked Sylviana.

"That explains his obsessive campaign to catch you, he was infuriated after he was outwitted by those false trails Flora had set all those years ago," said Roheck.

Taking Sylviana's arm, "sister, why do you and Flora want to live with these uncultivated humans?" admonished Roheck.

Shaking away from his grip, "you are wrong, Laura, show my brother your rope."

Laura shrugged, "here," as she tossed it to Roheck.

"You have made a fine, strong and intricate elf strand sister."

"No, Morgan, made it."

"Did he?" Roheck's mouth twitched.

"They are not all barbarians—Laura, tell Roheck what you see," spreading her arms across the landscape.

Lowering her eyebrows, "we are standing amongst couch grass and wood avens, a ladybird is crawling up a leaf of ryegrass . . ."

He relented, "enough, you have made your point sister. I will return to Elfield, you will be left in peace."

Flora intervened, "we will live across the river," sweeping her arm towards the Aswin river, "alongside the white wolves. We will be a bridge between man and elves."

As they prepared to leave, Roheck approached Gavin and Morgan, "take care of our kin, we will visit again—as friends."

Harwyn knelt before Flora, placing his hand on his heart, "you are, and always will be our princess."

The archers followed Harwyn's lead and vowed allegiance to Flora, then they made ready to leave.

Chapter 21

Return to the Forest.

The following day Sylviana treated Baron's wound, while Gavin and Morgan set about completing their new elf home.

Laura swam out to her rock, the yearning edge. She sat with her head resting on her hands, staring into the catacomb forest, with a distant look in her eyes. In her mind's eyes, she saw Clare, the bruised arm, the sadness she carried in her eyes. *She comes to me in my dreams, my nightmares. I told Clare I was her friend, yet I have abandoned her, and her sibling. Clare is suffering, struggling, entrapped in a downward fall, spiralling into a futile life. The problem is her father, the monster I must come to a decision, Ives is the key.*

Her mind went on a wild flight, searching for a solution. Like the ebbing tide, the solution always returned to the same answer. *They must be removed from Bryok.*

Gavin looked across at Laura, "Laura, she looks sad, upset."

Morgan replied, "leave her alone, she has had a lot to digest these last few weeks."

"No, something is troubling her, and she is keeping her distance from me," observed Sylviana.

Jayden stood next to his mother, carefully watching Laura. He had seen that look before. He knew what was causing her discomfort.

‡

Late afternoon, as they all made to return to the farmhouse, Jayden hung back. Returning to the river's edge, Jayden took Laura's hand and helped her up the river bank.

His words soft and understanding. "Something is troubling you," he touched her arm. "It's the Roth children."

She felt a bond with Jayden; they were both half elfling and had an affinity with each other. A reply wasn't necessary; she still nodded.

"I have the answer, I must sleep on it."

As they reached the farmhouse door, Jayden took Laura's hand, "keep away from my mother, she is concerned about your wellbeing."

Laura stopped, "will you tell Martha I'm tired, I'll have my supper in my room, away from prying questions."

"Go directly to your room, I'll bring your food."

☦

The next day Laura took Jayden outside, "can I ask you for a favour?"

He nodded his head.

Laura confided in Jayden, "I want to go to the garrison to talk to Ives about Bryok Roth, can you contact Storm?"

"Yes, I have a bone ocarina when I blow it, they will both come. You're not going alone, I will accompany you," insisted Jayden.

Laura smiled, "I was hoping you would accompany me."

"Are you telling your family?"

"No, they don't want me going through the Catacomb forest again, they will stop me. With Storm and Trinity's help, we can be there and back in five days."

"When do we leave?"

"We must leave without delay; I feel your mother is watching me."

"You're right, Sylviana knows you are troubled."

A look of urgency crossed Laura's face, "tomorrow, before dawn."

They went into the forest and found the track that Storm used to return them home. Jayden blew a few notes on his ocarina.

"Is that what your mother used when we were in Starfall?"

"Yes, the unicorns can hear the pitch anywhere in the forest."

They sat on a dead tree stump and waited. With a piece of ivy stem, some fallen bronzed heart-shaped leaves and one white daisy, Jayden sat making a head wreath. He placed it onto Laura's head; a gilt line of sunlight pierced the clearing and stung Laura's face.

Jayden smiled, "the forest has crowned you princess Laura. What's wrong; you look drained?"

"Last night I had a disturbing, strange dream; everything was framed in a bowl of rock crystal."

Jayden swallowed his smile and tensed up, "what did you see in the crystal?"

"I saw Clare walking down a path. With every step, her feet were sinking into the ground. She was getting older, without ageing. Anna was tugging my shoulders; Giselle was on her knees begging for help, her words caused my head to ache." She gulped, "I woke at midnight; I lay trying to unfold my dream, was it a dream; did it mean anything?"

"I don't think Flora realised how much she has implanted in you. It's a crystal dream, a forecast of what's to come. Only unique elves have this ability. She should know what she has done and explain the meaning."

"No, we can't, not yet, you know they will watch me, keep me indoors; can you decipher the dream?"

Jayden turned away.

"What does it mean?"

His voice hushed, she almost missed the words, "Clare's dying."

She gripped his arm, "we must get her away from the monster."

‡

It was early afternoon before both Storm and Trinity arrived. Laura explained that they wanted a lift to the moss garden, and back home after two days.

Trinity lowered her head, "we will rest here tonight, come to us before dawn, we will run as unicorns, and get you to your moss garden by nightfall, travel light."

It was early morning, and still dark when Laura tiptoed into the kitchen, Jayden followed a few moments later.

Laura said, "I will leave this note in Martha's apron, she'll find it as soon as she rises. We'd best not hang around; I hope Storm and Trinity are ready."

They filled their travelling bags with bread, Sylviana's cakes, pies and water, then slipped out to the farmyard. The animals were still asleep in their pens, they sneaked out of the farmyard, once clear they ran across the fields to meet the unicorns. Storm and Trinity stood waiting, they both knelt, Jayden on Storm, Laura mounted Trinity.

"Lower your head and hang on tight, if you want to stop, tap our neck," said Trinity.

They set off trotting, increasing their speed with each stride until they ran at full gallop, Laura hung on for dear life. After a while Laura relaxed, she noted that they were so light-footed at times, all four legs lifted off the ground. Flying unicorns, she observed, both the front and rear legs were fully extended.

At midday, they passed the wooden derelict cabin. Laura patted Trinity on the neck, she wanted to stretch her legs; the run came to a shuddering stop.

Trinity said, "have a few moment's rest, don't be too long if you want to complete your journey before nightfall."

Laura puffed, "I never realised riding was such hard work, I ache all over."

"This is the third time you have travelled through this place; I shall rename you Laura, queen of the forest."

"Come on, stop nattering, we'll reach the moss garden soon, you can rest there," said Storm.

Moments later they set off again, this time the unicorns sped up at a faster rate, they reached their destination as the sunset. Laura and Jayden dismounted and thanked Trinity and Storm. Laura put her arms around Storm and humbly asked another favour. Both the unicorns nodded and wandered off to eat and rest.

When they walked into the moss garden, they were both downhearted, everything had been trampled.

"It must have been those Skeltonians Agish had tracking us," said Jayden.

Laura yawned, "I'm so tired I'll sleep well tonight; we can eat in the morning. Do you think they have found my note?"

"Yes, they'll be livid and worrying about us. I agree I'm tired, let's make the best of it, the moss is still soft."

⸸

Zee was standing at her table mixing a new potion when Tad with his band of imps in tow scurried into the lair. With the remains of a squirrel dripping from his jaws, he tugs at Zee's ratty cloth she wore around her waist, draping down her twisted body.

194

"Mistress we saw Laura the witch riding through your realm."

Zee sprang round, lifted Tad onto her table, "where; what do mean riding?"

"She was with an elf boy; they were riding unicorns."

"Where are they?" She thundered.

"They stopped on a narrow path south of the forest, down past the wild boar's den, near a decaying cabin." Tads claws ground together, "the elf boy called the witch—queen of the forest."

Zee's orbs grew wild, about to burst from their sockets, "she teases, mocks me and wants my kingdom. She will die."

"Shall we go and attack her?"

She swept her arm across the table, knocking Tad to the floor. "No, you failed me three times, I will deal with this insignificant insect. Take me to this path, the place you last saw her."

She selected the sharpest knives from the chest of jewels and weapons and followed Tad out of the labyrinth. What was left of Zee's mind was focused on one aim; to kill Laura.

☦

Martha picked Laura's note up and shaking her head, went to Raoul and Morgan. Morgan read the note to himself before reading it aloud.

'Gone to the garrison to see Ives about Bryok Roth

Will be gone for five days

Unicorns will take us and bring us back

Do not worry we will be safe

Laura'

In between each word, Martha stood banging her rolling pin on the kitchen table, "stupid girl, stupid stupid stubborn girl, hasn't she put us through enough."

Her eyes flared, "Flora told her never to enter that forest again, hasn't she any sense!"

Sylviana arrived and said, "this time Jayden is with her, and Storm and Trinity. I could try to call Storm but they are well underway by now. If the unicorns are galloping, they won't stop, try not to worry."

Raoul said, "she must have decided to have that brute put into the garrison."

Morgan looked perplexed, "I'm surprised!"

Sylviana nodded her head, "that's what's been troubling Laura, she been worrying about those children she met."

‡

Next morning at dawn, after eating, they travelled to the edge of the forest, reaching the open fields, just as the sun rose.

"I'm glad you came with me," Laura said.

Jayden nodded his head.

Laura told Jayden, "when we get near, you wait between the village and the garrison. I will go to the garrison and tell Ives what I want, don't forget to keep your cloak on."

The journey was uneventful, they kept to a direct path using hedgerows and trees as cover. The sunset early now, they carried on by the moonlight, finding the dell they had slept in last time.

The next morning, a flock of dark-coloured, noisy birds murmuring under the dawn, woke them.

"Starlings," remarked Jayden.

196

Laura looked up and nodded.

Under the grey flat sky, they each ate a piece of bread, a small sip of water and set off towards the garrison. The ground felt hard, there was a chill in the air.

"Watch, when I leave with Ives, follow us to the place where Bryok Roth lives, you can join me there," said Laura.

Laura ran to the garrison excited that her plan was unfolding. She was pleased that the same two men, Pete and Ely were hanging around outside, in the same blue uniforms.

"Look, it's miss Laura," shouted Pete, as she entered the compound.

"What do you want? to see Ives I expect," said Ely.

"Yes, I would like to talk to him about Bryok Roth," replied Laura.

Ely asked Laura, "first, I want to know how you got out of Ives office? they think I let you out."

"I used magic," she replied flippantly.

With a sigh, Ely said, "you're a one for making jokes."

Pete gestured, "come through he will be pleased to see you, he's happy now our cells are full, thanks to you."

Pete pushed the big, decayed, old creaking door open. They all walked in; everything looked the same as it was last time Laura was there. She noted there were more biscuit crumbs on the floor. Laura stood opposite the desk facing Ives.

Ives eyeballs Laura, "it's nice to see you have you travelled here alone; do your parents know you're here?"

Laura took his stare, "I travelled here with a friend, yes my parents know I'm here." *Only because I left a note.* She glanced at his desk, noting the gouge. It hadn't been hidden or repaired.

197

Ives said, "that's a reminder for me to listen when people come in here, what do you want?"

Leaning right across the table, Laura whispered, "I have a favour to ask."

After telling him what she wanted, he leaned back in his chair, tipping it back so it was resting on the two back legs. He shut his eyes for a few moments, considering Laura's plan. Opening his eyes, he looked at Laura, stroked his chin and nodded his head in agreement.

"Ely, Pete fetch two prison wagons, another two soldiers, and bring them to the village, to Bryok Roth's hut. I'm going ahead so I can talk to Laura."

It was a short walk from the garrison to Drewcott village. The road was a straight and dusty lane with pebbles laid at each side. Laura told Ives that she had dispatched the Nash brothers to the Catacomb forest.

Ives said, "they are wanted throughout the land, they have been known to murder some of their victims!"

"Don't worry, I don't imagine we'll be seeing those two again," Laura answered, sauntering along the track. She gripped his wrist, "your badge, it's different?"

"I'm now captain of the garrison, in charge of the guards—and the soldiers, all thanks to you!"

They passed a group of children playing hoppers outside a merchant's store. Further on two men arguing over the price of a piglet. Laura watched women pawing over colourful material that was laid over a trestle.

"The Roth hut is on the edge of the village," said Ives, as they walked through the centre of the village.

"That one?" indicated Laura, pointing with an outstretched arm, for Jayden's reference.

As they neared Bryok Roth's hut, Ives stopped dead.

Turning to face Laura, "are you sure you know what you are doing? you can still change your mind."

"I'm sure, I've had a long time to think," replied Laura.

The news spread rapidly that the captain of the garrison was heading towards the Roth house, with a young girl. More villagers ambled out when they heard the two prison carts swaying and grating on the path, steered by Pete and Ely, with the two soldiers alongside. They had now reached Bryok Roth's hut, the piece of rotting timber had been replaced against the entrance.

Ives removed the timber telling Laura, "wait here until we bring Bryok out, then you can talk to the children."

Ives marched into the hut with authority, approached Walter, who was curled up in the corner.

"Where's your father?" Ives boomed.

Walter, with a shaking hand, pointed to the floor. He was lying in a semi-conscious state, oblivious to the commotion in his hut.

"Drag him out," commanded Ives.

Pete and Ely, with an arm each, heaved the listless body up and threw him outside.

"Now take him to the pig trough and throw him in, until he sobers up," turning to Laura he said, "If you are sure . . ."

"I'm sure."

She pushed herself through the door and entered a dingy room. Jayden stepped behind. The scene they saw saddened Laura. A makeshift kitchen hidden under a cloth next to a three-legged stool with an oil lamp on top cast a soft yellow glow. In one corner of the room, huddled together, were the three girls. Walter sat in the opposite corner; the twins sat in between. They were dressed in the same clothes they wore when they first met. Between the children, two rooms with doorless frames. Inside, Laura caught a glimpse of the old sacks they used to sleep on. The stench was unbearably pungent; she walked on rotting straw, stepping over an old flagon of foul ale. Jayden trod in a pool of vomit, his head was reeling, he staggered outside to take in a lungful of fresh air. Laura took in a deep breath to try to calm the feelings of heartbreak, disgust and sorrow. She moved to the centre of the room.

When jay returned, Laura, in a hushed voice said, "the animals on our farm have better living accommodation than this."

Clare, who had been staring at the floor, raised her face, briefly, to look at Laura. Through the dimness of the hut, Laura caught a glimpse of Anna's bruised arm. Any doubts were instantly dispelled.

Laura folded her arms and snapped out, "I want you all to come and live with me!"

The room was silent for the briefest of heartbeats.

Anna jumped up, gleefully throwing her arms around Laura, "Yes, yes take us away from here, please. I'll do anything to get away. I hate living here, please, take us all away."

Laura whispered in Anna's ear, "this afternoon you will be riding on a unicorn."

Giselle, with sadness in her eyes, lamented, "the monster—he won't let us leave."

"Yes, he will, my friend is asking him to let you all live with me," shouted Laura, "leave now and never see that brute again!"

Giselle looked at Clare, "please, let's leave this place?"

Clare didn't respond, she continued staring at the floor.

The twins looked at Walter who said, "do as you please, I'm stopping here, it's a trick, she's lying. She's a witch!" he voiced in a muffled tone.

Laura walked determinedly over to Walter and sat beside him, running her fingers over his swollen jaw.

"Who did this?"

"He did it, the monster," revealed Anna.

Laura continued to run her fingertips over his jaw, Walter's arms straightened up, he tried to fight the sensation Laura was having on him; his arms relaxed as the pain in his jaw eased. Laura shuddered; a strange sensation touched her mind.

"We are having a lift to the edge of the forest, where the unicorns are waiting, if I'm lying you can gloat to your sisters. Then you can leave us and be back here tonight."

Anna whispered in Giselle's ear, "why is Laura trying to get Walter to come with us?"

"I'm not sure, maybe because he is our brother."

‡

On his third dunking in the pig swill, Bryok, with green slime dripping from his face was sobering up.

"What have I done?" he burbled out.

Ives, asserting his authority, and using his most commanding voice, "you tried to murder two children by the Catacomb forest."

Bryok babbled, "don't know what you mean, it wasn't me."

"We know it was you if you don't want to go to Ecrind prison, listen to my demand," Ives boomed out in his forceful voice. "If you allow your youngsters to live with another family, I won't have you sent to gaol!"

Ives held Bryok by the throat, their faces only a hairs breath away. Bryok started twitching at the thought of going behind bars.

"Get rid of 'em, I don't care," whilst planning to make the villager return his skivvies.

Ives called Pete, "you heard that you'll be a witness if he tries to change his mind."

To the two soldiers, "take this man to the garrison, lock him up, don't release him until tomorrow morning, when he is sober." *Laura should be well away by the time he's released.*

Some villagers started clapping as Bryok was escorted away.

He marched back to Roth's hut, put his head inside and said, "Bryok Roth has given permission for his children to leave with you, Laura, your transport is ready."

Laura stood and holding Walters's hands pulled him to his feet, "come on, you've nothing to lose."

As they left the hut, Laura noticed that Giselle and Anna had to pull Clare to her feet, but didn't think any more of it.

Outside, Laura, speaking to Jayden said, "I will travel with the girls, you travel with the boys."

Turning to the siblings, offering reassurance "do not be afraid, they're not locking us in, the guards are taking us to the forest to meet my friends, we'll be there by midday."

As the children climbed into the prison carts, the village was buzzing, the commotion had caught the attention of everybody.

Before climbing into the cart, Laura shouted to Ives, "thank you."

He looked at Laura, winked and walked away.

The two prison carts rolled away from the village; the wooden wheels were creating a mini dust storm from the arid soil. As they passed, the villagers were muttering, 'poor mites wonder what will happen to them'.

Laura, sitting in the wagon, looking at the girls was a little confused. Giselle and Anna were both stroking Clare's hands, who was just staring at the floor.

Laura went over to Clare asking, "what's wrong?"

Giselle answered, "she's given up, the monster has beaten the will to live out of her."

She went on to tell Laura about the beating she received when the two strangers arrived. "Clare wouldn't go out, ashamed of the injury on her face. After a couple of days, he grabbed Clare's arm, dragged her across the room, threw her outside and told her to get him some food and money by begging."

Giselle's voice started to break up, "she just curled up outside, telling us she wants to die!"

A shudder of unease ran through Laura's body. *My dream.*

Giselle was finding it difficult to continue, "we made her come inside, but when he returned and saw Clare sitting, he pulled her up by her hair and slapped her around the face, over the bruises he had already inflicted to her. She was crying so much from the pain. We have never seen him so brutal."

Laura placed her hand onto Giselle's shoulder.

Giselle swallowed hard, "Anna ran over, putting her arms around his leg, begging him to stop. Ignoring her pleas, he swung his leg, sending Anna across the room."

"He finally let her fall to the floor, like dropping a scrag of meat. She lay still, barely breathing; unconscious."

"We have tried to force her to eat . . ."

Giselle faltered, not able to continue.

Clare muttered, "my life—it means nothing . . ."

Laura held Clare's chin and gently raised her face. She immediately wrapped her arms around Clare's neck and pulled her head, until it was resting on her shoulders, hiding her own tears from Clare. She didn't speak, just held Clare in her arms. Unbeknown to Laura, an indiscernible field of incandescence was radiating from her body, an elf aura. It was bringing comfort to Clare.

Laura spoke softly, "no, you will never see that monster again, you are going to live in a better place now. No one is ever going to hit you again, I promise you. Your sisters, they need you, I need you, you're my friend." Looking at Anna and Giselle, "you are all my friends."

Laura reached into her bag and pulled out one of Sylviana's cakes.

Cupping Clare's hands in her own, and guiding them to her mouth said, "this is the most delicious thing I have ever tasted—eat."

Laura encouraged Clare until she had eaten every crumb.

looking up, Clare, forcing a smile, "the person who made that is an exceptional cook."

Giselle and Anna both cuddled up to Clare.

"Your sisters love you with all their heart," observed Laura.

Laura again wrapped her arms around Clare reassuring and comforting her until the wagons reached their destination.

In the other wagon, the twins Dudley and Oake were watching the countryside, they had never been so far from the village. Walter and Jayden were watching Laura and the girls talking.

Jayden, who was the only one to see the aura between Laura and Clare said, "Laura is an exceptional person."

Walter replied, "he beats Clare because she looks like our mother."

They alighted the carts alongside the forest where Jayden had directed them to stop. The three girls shuddered with uncertainty, Laura placed her arms around them, offering reassurance.

"Are you sure miss Laura?" Pete asked.

Laura replied, "we'll be fine, my friends are meeting us, thanks."

She waved them goodbye as they disappeared over the horizon.

"Well," said Walter, "where are they?"

Jayden removed his ocarina from around his neck and blew. Trinity was the first to step out of the forest, followed by Storm, Hart and Gilda.

Anna took a long intake of breath, stumbled and fell backwards, sitting on the floor said, "oh look Clare they're real."

Laura put her hand on Walters' arm and said, "after riding a unicorn you will see inside an elf dwelling."

"Two will ride on each unicorn, Clare you first, Walter you sit behind, take care of your sister, she is very weak. Make sure she doesn't fall off," said Laura.

Clare gave Laura a look that would freeze the fires of hell.

Laura took Clare's hands into her own, "please, trust me."

"Can I ride with you, pleeease?" Anna asked Laura.

"Giselle with Jayden, Dudley and Oake, Anna will ride with me," Laura said, as she lifted Anna onto the back of Trinity.

Jayden on Storm led the way, with Laura and Trinity at the rear. The girls were consumed with curiosity, calling back and forth to each other, while the boys were silent and apprehensive.

At Starfall, Jayden took everyone in, Laura and Anna were the last to arrive. After dismounting, Laura whispered into Trinity's ear.

Trinity replied, "right Laura, at dawn tomorrow," and trotted away.

Anna stood with her arms draped and quivering said, "Laura she spoke, the unicorn spoke, she spoke your name, she talked."

Laura smiled, took Anna's hand, "this way."

They joined the others who were looking wide-eyed around the room, as she had done not so long ago. Laura and Jayden removed their cloaks. The children stared at Jayden's striking green hair and his sparkling greenish-brown eyes.

"Yes, he's an elf, now come with us," Laura said, leading everyone along the passage that led to the water grotto.

"I heard the unicorn talk," Anna excitedly told her sisters, "now I have seen an elf boy," as they followed Laura and Jayden.

Laura said, "you all need to bathe before we eat."

To Jayden, she said, "take the boys to the upper spring, and bring their clothes for washing."

The twins followed Jayden, but Walter stood arms folded, refusing to move.

Facing up to him, with forcefulness in her voice Laura said, "you will have a bath or I will rip your clothes off myself and throw you in. I'm doing this to help you, now follow your brothers—Now." Stamping her foot and clenching her hands.

Walter stood aghast, no girl had ever spoken so bluntly to him, he glanced at Tad bashed hanging inside Laura's tunic, turned and meekly followed the twins.

Jayden and Laura washed the clothes, they were threadbare, torn and had a musty smell about them.

"This won't do," bemoaned Laura, "did you notice they had nits in their hair."

"Yes, our mothers will sort that out, I'll see how many cloaks and fleeces we have. They will have to wear those on top of their clothes until we get home, I'll see what I can find."

After handing out the clothing, Jayden led the children into the round room where Laura had filled the table with most of the food they had bought.

Laura and Jayden stood to the side, guiding the Roth family to six seats. They had decided to skip meals until they returned home, giving their share to the children. The children all sat, staring at the table.

"Is something wrong?" Asked Laura.

"That's for us? We could live on that for a week," Giselle said, with wonder in her eyes.

Laura picked up one of Sylviana's creations, "yes; these are the finest cakes you will ever eat, tuck in."

Seeing Clare was just nibbling, Laura sat and wrapped her arm around Clare's body.

Pulling her in a close embrace, "dear friend please eat, the nightmare is over."

Laura gently ran her fingertips down Clare's face, Clare felt the warmth of Laura's friendship, she started to eat steadily. To the surprise of Clare, Walter pushed one of his cakes over.

Laura then stood next to Walter and put her hand onto his arm and said, "I'm glad you came, you will have a better life now. Did Bryok do that to your back?"

"Leave me alone, don't touch me," he replied looking around for somewhere to hide.

Laura, standing, placed both her hands onto Walters' shoulders. "I'm not a witch, just a girl who lives on a farm—no one will ever hurt you again." She looked at all the siblings, "I vow, no one will ever lay a finger of pain on any of you."

"Will they make us work?" asked Walter, gazing at the floor.

The children were quiet now, wondering and waiting for Laura to answer.

"No—my parents will take care of you."

The question had worried Laura, she realised that she had acted rashly.

After they had demolished the food and drink, Laura said, "at dawn tomorrow, the unicorns will take us to my farm. With each unicorn carrying two, they will only be able to canter. It will be two long and exhausting days; I want you to rest now."

Jayden led them along a corridor that led to two big rooms. The sisters were led to one room with one large bed to share, Anna and Giselle ran in rubbing their faces into the fleece. Clare flopped onto her back, with her arms and legs outstretched, a human cross.

"If I die tomorrow, I die happy," Giselle cried out.

Anna held Clare's arm, "you're not going to die, are you?"

Swallowing hard replied, "No."

The boys were taken to the room opposite the girl's, again one large bed for the three to share. Dudley and Oake seemed happy but looked for Walter's reaction.

Walter's apprehension was beginning to wane, he began to realise that maybe his life was going to change, for the better.

He put his arms around the twins, turned to Jayden and said, "thanks."

Jayden, re-joining Laura said, "the girls won't sleep tonight, they're too excited, Anna is telling Clare and Giselle she heard Trinity speaking."

Now they were alone Laura, looking at the floor and biting her bottom lip said, "have I made the right decision? Mother has got to feed another six, how will she cope now most of our crops are lost due to those robbers. A bully, the twins—they cannot do anything for themselves, and three girls, they're all uneducated. I'm going to get a scolding."

Feeling despondent she continued, "do you think Raoul and Morgan will take them away—to the big town?"

Jayden thoughtfully said, "perhaps, I don't know, maybe not. If you hadn't rescued them from that monster, Clare would have starved herself to death. You saved her life, so let's worry about the punishment when we get home."

"When I was in their hut and touched Walter's bruised jaw, I experienced his feelings—it frightened me."

"It's an elfin ability, I have it. When Flora gave you her healing powers, something else must have happened, she unwittingly gave you so much more."

‡

Cheerful sunlight shone through the canopy, waking everybody. Jayden collected the Roth siblings and led everyone to the kitchen where Laura was preparing a large pan of gruel from oatmeal she had taken from the larder. Laura instructed everyone to side at the kitchen table. Clare wandered over to watch Laura.

"Can I help? With Giselle I had to make the monsters meal every morning."

Laura smiled and handed over the ladle, "carry on, I hate cooking."

When the meal was ready, Clare tipped the gruel into a large bowl intending to carry it to the table.

Laura placed her hand on her shoulder, "we have individual bowls to pour portions in."

"At home, we would all eat from the same bowl, after the monster had finished."

"You had to eat after your pa had finished?"

"Yes, we had to share his leftovers."

Clare set out the bowls, Laura sat next to Jayden.

Anna's eyes, as wide as a lake, said "one bowl each?"

"Yes, now eat up the unicorns will be here soon," answered Laura.

Anna was the first, she dug her fingers deep into the hot food and shovelled her fingers dripping with the broth into her mouth. Soon they were all following Anna, scooping handfuls of the broth into their cupped hands.

Laura slid out of her chair, moved behind Clare and lightly held her arms still. Clare twisted her head back as Laura s hand moved over the back of Clare's left hand. She entwined their fingers and moved her hand to the side of the plate where a spoon lay. All the children had stopped eating and were watching Laura. She wrapped Clare's hand around the handle of the spoon and dipped the bowl of the spoon into the gruel, raising it to her lips.

Clare supped the food, and tearfully said, "we didn't know, we have never used such implements."

Laura replied, "you're going to learn lots of new things, and live a proper life." Laura gave Clare a cloth, "dab your face, from today, the only tears I want to see are tears of joy."

The meal was quickly consumed; they tidied up, stood and went outside, the four unicorns were waiting on the track.

Laura called Storm and Jayden over, in a hushed voice asked, "can you stop at the old wooden derelict cabin I saw on the trail? It should be ideal to rest there for the night."

Storm lowered his head in agreement.

They set off in the same formation as yesterday. In single file they ran with bounding strides, Storm leading the group with Trinity at the rear. The initial excitement started to wane as they went deeper into the forest. They saw beasts and ogres in the forest shadows, Giselle panicked when she saw a long-legged hairy red and yellow spider running up a tree.

Jayden held her tight, "shut your eyes, you're safe with me. Think about the smell and taste of those delicious cakes my mother makes."

Many strange and gruesome creatures scampered out of the way of the unicorns as they made their way along their path. A loud eerie squeal, kee-ah from high above made everyone stare into the trees.

"Hawks are flying overhead, he just seized his prey," said Jayden.

Anna tried her hardest to get Trinity to speak, she kept whispering in her ear, "my name is Anna, what's yours?" nothing worked.

By nightfall, they had reached the derelict cabin. They all dismounted, Jayden went in first to establish if it was safe.

He emerged saying, "Its dry and dusty inside, but it'll be warmer than sleeping outside on the path."

Laura had her arm around Anna, they were about to enter the cabin when Trinity neighed.

She quietly said to Laura, "we'll sleep further down the path where it's wider."

Anna just breathed wearily, "nobody heard!"

Inside, Laura and Jayden laid out the fleeces and Cloaks to sit on, the children consumed the remaining food.

Jayden whispered to Laura, "Trinity is having fun playing up Anna."

As they settled down for the night Laura said, "this time tomorrow we'll be at the farm, in a comfortable bed."

"Can I sleep next to you?" Anna asked Laura.

"Sleep alongside your sisters, I want to keep watch tonight."

The Roth children slept in a line along the back of the cabin. Laura and Jayden sat at the doorway, keeping watch all night. Apart from a group of fluorescent blue beetles scurrying along the path, they were undisturbed.

Next morning, they prepared to leave in the same formation as yesterday. The others had moved away as Laura was lifting Anna onto Trinity. Laura then mounted Trinity behind Anna.

A creaking branch above made both Laura and Anna look up, Zee, with a knife in each hand came crashing down, landing on Laura, Anna and Trinity.

Trinity reared up as Zee's body landed onto her back, throwing Laura and Anna off. Zee was trying to thrust her blades into Laura but missed as they fell to the floor. Laura landing on her back, Anna on her knees nearby. Jayden, hearing the commotion jumped off Storm and ran back to help.

Zee was now standing astride Laura, knife raised plunging towards Laura's heart. Without a second thought, Anna flung herself across Laura's body. Zee screeched, grabbed Anna's arm and tossed her aside like a piece of wet rag. With both hands raised, the knives were plunging towards Laura.

Laura by now had recovered and rolled over as the knives came towards her body, one sinking into the soil, the other caught Laura's leg. Laura jumped to her feet pulling Tad basher out. Staring past Zee, she saw Anna's twisted body dripping blood everywhere.

Laura's lower jaw clenched tight; her eyes were burning scarlet with rage. Every particle of her body shook with adrenaline. she ran at Zee, blindly swinging her weapon. Four five six swings, they all missed, Zee had dodged every swipe. Laura was now gripping her weapon that hard she cracked two fingernails; her rage was emotionally charged. She again assailed Zee, this time taking aim, on the third stroke she hit Zee on the arm, making her drop one knife.

Jayden was close by, but couldn't help. Laura was in a blind fury, swinging her weapon furiously towards Zee, again and again, she missed, another blow hit the side of Zee's body. Panic jarred through Zee. She was now backing away. Never had she encountered such ferocity. She glanced back intending to run. Laura in that instant had changed direction. Tad basher swung around and down, hitting Zee on the shoulder. As her body lurched forward, Laura now swung her weapon up, hitting Zee in the chin, knocking her backwards. Another blow on the head, Zee issued out a gasp as she fell forward. Laura, with one mighty blow to the face, sent her sprawling backwards towards the forest floor.

Zee lay on her back, her arms stretched out semi-conscious as Laura jumped onto her body. Zee was winded and broken, she looked up at Laura, for a brief moment Zee's black eyes met Laura's bloodshot eyes. At that moment Zee knew she was done as Laura had her arms raised high, Tad basher behind her back ready to strike her skull. Zee shut her eyes waiting for the final strike. Everyone heard the thud—as Laura's weapon slid from her hands

213

onto the forest floor behind her back. Laura turned her back on Zee and made her way to Anna.

Jayden ran between Zee and Laura, battered and bruised, unable to walk, Zee rolled over and dragged herself away on all fours.

The children were standing around Anna's body as Laura approached; they parted to let her pass. Laura cautiously picked up Anna's body from the pool of moist blackened soil and ran her shaking fingertips over her bloodstained body.

Clare was standing next to Laura, tears cascading down her cheeks when she heard a noise at her back. She turned to see Walter with his arm to his eyes, trying to hide his tears.

Jayden knelt beside Laura, agonisingly asked, "Is she—?"

"There's life, I can sense it."

"Is there—anything you can do?"

"I'm trying—nothing is happening—I don't know what I'm doing. I can't keep my fingers still."

Jayden jumped up decisively, "Storm, can you take Laura home without delay?"

Laura looked up pleadingly, "why; how?"

"Give me your cloaks," demanded Jayden.

He took Walters and Clare's cloaks, and with his own tied them together.

"Flora can tell you what to do, I'm making a cradle to tie around your body. Use it as a sling to carry Anna, your hands will be free to hold on to Storm."

Storm knelt, and with the help of Jayden and Walter, Laura sat with Anna wrapped around her in the sling.

"I still can't hold on," groaned Laura.

"Pass me your rope," motioned Jayden.

Holding Storms head, looking him in the eye, Jayden said, "will you permit me to wrap this rope around your neck so Laura has something to grip."

Storm bayed in annoyance.

Trinity, standing at his side said, "when I was caught, the man that lassoed me was able to hold on to me. Laura will be able to do the same if you allow Jayden to wrap the rope around your neck. That child is near death. I would take her but you are so much faster."

Reluctantly Storm agreed, Jayden wrapped the rope around his neck. Storm shuddered and pushed his front hooves into the ground as if suffering indescribable pain. Jayden looped it around Laura's back and twirled it around Laura's arms, pulling it taut.

Laura squeezed her eyes shut and whispered to Storm, "please, as fast as you can."

Storm started trotting as Laura felt more confident, he picked up speed until he was running at full gallop.

"I don't understand," choked Clare, "what does Laura think she can do for Anna; why didn't she kill that beast?"

"Laura has got special healing powers, but doesn't know how to use them, someone at the farm may be able to help, I will explain as we travel," replied Jayden.

‡

The journey back to the farmhouse was swift and subdued, Storm concentrating on the path, Laura resting her head on Anna's body whilst holding onto the reins.

Storm, on reaching the edge of the forest ran out directly to the farm, slowing to a stop just short of the farmhouse. Laura carefully untied herself leaving Storm to canter back to the forest.

Laura ran into the farmyard screaming from the depth of her heart, "help, someone help me I need Flora, help me—help."

Martha came running out of the kitchen, "What's the—"

Laura was almost on her knees holding Anna in her outstretched arms, "I need Flora."

Martha was staring at the bloodstained cloaks, "What have you . . ." saw Anna's arm flop out of the cloak. "Take her to your room, they are across the river, building their enclave."

Raoul, who had been working in the fields came running into the farmyard.

"Get the Elves, now!" cried out Martha.

Raoul promptly ran to the Aswin river where he saw Flora and Morgan by the river bank.

"Laura urgently needs your help."

"Fetch Sylviana," said Flora as she made her way to the farm.

Martha had removed Anna from the bloodied cloaks and laid her face down on Laura's bed. Then she cut Anna's clothing, so they could determine the extent of the stab wound. Martha gave a sigh of resignation when she beheld the injury.

As Laura placed her shaking hands over the wound, Flora came bursting into the room, she saw Laura holding a blood-soaked child. Laura's hands were shaking, one held over Anna's wound the other holding Anna's hand. Her lips were curled in, and her eyelids quivering as she tried to concentrate.

Martha moved out of the way as Flora moved towards Laura and the child.

"Put your fingertips around the wound this way," said Flora taking Laura's hand under her own and carefully spreading it around the wound.

"Calm yourself, you must be dispassionate while you use the healing powers within you."

Flora took Laura's other hand and wrapped it around Anna's wrist. Laura's whole body trembled as she looked at Anna's body, she couldn't control her hands.

Flora gripped Laura's shoulders and said, "you can't help her in this state you're too emotionally charged."

"She's my friend—she's only seven—I'm her only friend, please help me, I don't know what to do, I don't want her to die."

As Laura spoke Sylviana entered the room, "what can I do?" looking at the wound, "that's way beyond my capabilities."

"Can you calm Laura, she's deeply attached to the child, she can't focus on the healing powers."

Sylviana moved behind Laura and delicately placed her fingertips over Laura's face, with her thumbs below the ears.

Martha, who had her head resting on Raoul's shoulder said, "only a few days ago it was Laura lying there, now she's trying to save the life of that young child."

Sylviana moved her fifth fingers over Laura's eyelids, delicately pulling them down, shutting out the sight of Anna's physical suffering.

Flora looked at Sylviana mouthing the words, "this child's life is hanging on a thread."

Sylviana placed her head alongside Laura's, radiating her aura into Laura.

In a faint voice, "you're a healer, now concentrate. Look inside the child's body, stem the flow of blood, close the tear."

The shaking subsided, Laura's mind started drifting, her body her soul became peaceful.

Flora moved Laura's fingers closer together, relaxing, letting them spread out, then again bringing them together, action elves used to close a cut.

Flora spoke softly, "you have a great power within, the young girl won't be able to withstand a strong surge of your powers, you must trickle it slowly. Delicately cauterise the wound, a little at a time, it's a large gash to repair."

A flickering glow surrounded Laura's fingers.

"Laura, don't let go, concentrate your mind, you can do it," whispered Sylviana encouragingly.

A glimmer of light danced from Laura's fingertips into Anna.

The children watched Storm galloping down the track, now it was their turn to follow. The unicorns pace varied between a trot and a canter as they headed towards the farm. Clare had her head bowed the whole journey, watching the changes in the terrain. The twins chatted about how Anna worshipped Laura. Giselle asked Jayden what animals they kept on the farm. She asked about Laura's and Jayden's parents. Jayden kept her talking, realising it was taking her mind off Anna.

It was dusk when they arrived at the farm, stopping just inside the forest where Storm stood waiting. Jayden untethered Laura's rope she had left around his neck. With much trepidation, Jayden led the children towards the farmhouse, wondering what Laura had told her parents.

Martha Raoul and Morgan were sitting in the family room when Jayden walked in with the five children. Both Raoul and Morgan looked taken aback. Martha looked confused as she scrutinized all the children. Jayden realised Laura hadn't told them they were coming.

The first one to speak was Giselle, through trembling lips she asked, "our sister Anna, is she still—alive?"

Martha put her arms around Giselle and said to the children, "Laura is doing everything in her power to save Anna."

"Raoul, Morgan prepare the annexe," Martha said abruptly. "I will feed the children."

Gazing at the siblings she said, "you are all exhausted, sit and eat, then rest tonight."

Giselle asked, "can we see our sister?"

"You can peer by the doorway—don't disturb Laura, she is intent on healing your sister. You two girls come first, I will take you boys, after," taking Clare and Giselle by the hand.

Laura's bedroom was lit by a single candle in the corner by the bed. As they looked into the dim light, they saw two elves holding Laura, who herself was holding Anna. The only noise was a moth flickering around the flame of the candle. Martha now had her arms around the two girls who were watery-eyed. Walter and the twins, seeing their sister's reaction decided they would wait until tomorrow morning.

After a small meal of boiled eggs, the weary children were taken to the annexe to sleep.

Laura was now sitting controlled and serene.

Flora said to Sylviana, "go and join the others, I will sit with Laura tonight."

Raoul Morgan Gavin and Martha, followed by Jayden were heading towards the family room when Sylviana came out, Jayden looked up at his mother with imploring eyes.

"We don't know, the girl is still alive, but no improvement."

"What was Laura thinking, bringing six hungry mouths here, we haven't enough food for ourselves, and now winter is fast approaching," said Raoul, as they entered the family room.

Morgan said, "you're right, but what do we do?"

"Take them to Ecrind, they have a place for children," Raoul suggested.

"Their clothes, their bodies, hair, they're covered in fleas and nits, that's why I wanted them in the annexe. That room will need cleaning when they leave," complained Martha.

The conversation went back and forth for a few minutes, everyone agreed that Ecrind was the best place to send them.

Jayden had been sitting in the corner on a wobbly, chipped wooden stool listening to their views. With a frustrated groan, he jumps off the stool, picks it up slams it hard onto the floor. This grabs everyone's attention. he jumps onto the stool to reinforce the point he has something to say.

"Laura risked her life for you—her family. She befriended those children; she has been torn with emotion after hearing of their beatings. They call their father the monster, Walter is a punching bag. Has anyone wondered why Clare was hiding her face it's . . ."

"Jayden, you're a guest in this house sit down," shouted Gavin.

"No!"

"Let him speak," said Martha.

"Clare is the same age as your daughter, you raised Laura with love, whilst Clare only knew the pain of beatings. she had given up on life, she was starving herself—she wanted to die. I saw the tenderness in Laura as she coaxed her into eating and gave her hope and a reason to live."

Lowering his voice, "you have raised a compassionate daughter, you should be proud of what she has done. Her heart will break when she finds out you have sent them away."

Sylviana looked at Gavin, "I have never seen Jayden so emotional, must be his human side."

Martha, with a guilt-ridden face, said, "It's decided, for Laura's sake they stay—for the time being, we will discuss it in thirty days, with Laura."

Morgan, speaking to Jayden said, "before we go to bed, tell us what happened at the village."

He let everything pour out, the disgusting conditions they were living in, the filth over their bodies, begging for food in the village.

"There's something else," perceived Sylviana.

"It's Laura, she's got more than Flora's healing ability, she's had a crystal dream and felt Walters feelings. Riding to the forest she was emotional talking to Clare, she took her into her arms and held her tight; I saw an aura circle the two girls."

"Tomorrow, we must talk to Flora," replied Sylviana.

‡

Zee was crawling in circles, lost, crushed, and desolate, she fell into a divot curled up and went to sleep. A shard of sunlight shimmered through the trees as a burning pain woke Zee. A pair of shrews were nibbling at her leg, her hands flew into their bodies, piercing them; with one in each claw, she swallowed them whole. With a barbed grin, she sat there looking at her new claws; they were so suitable for killing. Without a supply of human essence, she was transforming into imp form. With blood dripping from the corners of her mouth, she rolled onto all four limbs and scurried back to her den. Close to the labyrinth, she came across one of her imps.

Gripping the imp, she muttered, "that witch child, she is the same as the others that tormented me, calling me names, now pretending to kill me. I will get my revenge on her!"

Turning to Tad, "find the rest of my snivelling sheep, and bring them back—now!"

Scraping along the floor she finds a flint rock which she uses to sharpen her claw-like nails. When Tad returned with ten imps, she gingerly picks one up by the neck and runs her claw into its body, killing it instantly.

With a crazed sounding cackle, she crowed, "the next person to feel my pincers will be that witch!"

Tossing the dead imp into the undergrowth, with the nine imps in tow she headed towards the Lovet farm, with Tad by her side.

Chapter 22

The cook, carpenter, livestock custodian and the farmhand.

"Where are the children?" asked Morgan.

Martha said, "they had an exhausting two-day journey, let them rest, we can prepare their treatment when they wake."

Giselle and Clare were the first to come out, followed by Walter, a few moments later the twins arrived.

Sylviana approached Clare, who was walking with her head drooping. She held her shoulders, "Clare, raise your face. Look at me."

Clare reluctantly lifted her head a touch. Sylviana knelt and brushed her hair aside, like opening a curtain. In the clear daylight, the injuries on her face became clear. The colour drained from Sylviana's face. She swallowed hard and gently ran her fingertips around her face. Clare took in a deep breath as she immediately felt the soothing effect of Sylviana's touch.

Sylviana glided her hands over Clare's shoulder and pulled her head close, she whispered into her ear, "that man will never strike you again. Raise your face and don't be ashamed. I have a little healing power, but I need to collect healing herbs and some willow bark and prepare the potions. From tomorrow morning I will treat you every morning and evening. Now go and join your sister."

Her mouth curled up, Clare tried to raise a smile; she turned and went to join her siblings.

Sylviana gripped Gavin's hand and started sobbing uncontrollably, "what's happening to me? My emotions, I've lost control."

Gavin dropped his hands onto her shoulders and pulled her close, "that poor child has suffered immensely, I'm not surprised you were affected. I'm glad Jayden accompanied Laura and saved that poor girls life."

"I was proud of him last night, defending Laura," Sylviana answered through her tears.

Martha stood watching Sylviana, called the children together said, "before you eat, we need to tidy you up—follow me."

Giselle took Clare's hand, "you have tears in your eyes, what did the elf woman want?"

"She wants to help; she ran her fingers over my face and brushed my heart with solace and kindness. These are tears of relief and happiness."

Martha led them out into the farmyard. They followed like a parade of marching ants into the bathhouse.

"We had a bath two days ago," complained Walter meekly.

"Well, today you're going to have a haircut, hair cleanse and a bath, and new clothes, I want you looking fresh and clean for Laura—and Anna."

"No," cried Giselle, "My long hair, I don't want it cut!"

"Every one of you has nits in your hair, I'm not having those creatures in my house," said Martha sternly. "Look," she said grabbing a tuft of Giselle's hair, "see those, they're nits, biting your scalp."

Martha started on Giselle first, she sat crying, every cut felt as if a dagger had pierced her heart. Next, she was passed to Flora who bathed her, then treated her hair with a potion made from the sea buckthorn plant. Finally, Sylviana dried her off, then dressed her in Laura's spare clothes, that Sylviana had adjusted.

"Laura has spare clothes?" said Giselle in amazement.

All the siblings went through this routine, with Raoul and Morgan bathing the boys.

Clare had a set of Laura's clothes, they fitted her well. The boys were given Raoul's and Morgan's clothes. Sylviana had worked from dawn to alter them.

While she was waiting for the others, Giselle wandered around the farm looking at the goat, the pigs, the flocks of chickens, and the brood of hens.

Martha called the children to the farmyard, "where have you been?" she snapped at Giselle.

"I've been stroking Nanny."

"Nanny?"

"Nanny the goat."

Martha raised her eyes and puffed.

"Before we go to the farmhouse, there's one more job to be done," said Morgan.

Their old clothes had been put into a stack, with their cut hair on top, then Morgan set fire to it.

"That's the last reminder of your former life, let's go inside and eat," beckoned Raoul.

It was late afternoon before anyone ate.

Early evening, all the children had drooping eyes. Martha suggested they retire early; she let them to their prepared rooms. Morgan and Raoul had constructed six makeshift cots from spare timber they used for fencing. For bed covering, Martha used some fleece and cotton. Two spare rooms on the first floor had been cleared and used as the bedrooms.

Laura was now in control of her healing power, she had been sitting with Anna all day, there was no improvement.

‡

Their second day at the farm, the children rose at sunrise. Giselle now sported short, flaxen tousled hair.

Clare running her fingers through it said, "your hair is soft and glossy, I have never seen it looking so good. We must thank Martha. Laura was right, perhaps this is the start of a new life, we have never been so clean."

On the way to the family room, the boys joined them, Clare smiled at Walter, who like his brothers now had a short-cropped haircut. Walter made a quick nod of the head. After eating porridge, Giselle went into the farmyard, looking inside all the farm buildings, all the animals fascinated Giselle. The boys played together in the fields and around the river. Martha stood at the door glaring at the children as they aimlessly wandered around the farm.

Sylviana took Clare's hand and led her into a bedroom. "Drink this herbal mix it will ease the pain, then lie on the bed, I'm going to repair your broken nose first. After I have to realign your nose, I will apply my potion over your face, you will feel a tingling sensation as my fingertips stimulate your skin. Now shut your eyes and try to relax."

Clare lay on her back, her eyes closed, floating on a wave of wonderment. She felt Sylviana's fingers tweak her nose; the pain was a good pain. Stroking and applying the cooling balm over her face, she drifted into a peaceful state. When she had finished Sylviana gave Clare a long tight hug, flooding Clare's body with a warm glow.

Clare opened her mouth; Sylviana placed a finger on her lips, "don't say anything. Go outside to your sister."

226

The rest of Martha's day was filled with preparing food. The children explored the countryside. That night in the family room Martha frowned, "I have never scolded Laura before, now she has gone too far."

Anna showed no sign of improvement.

‡

In the kitchen, Martha was preparing more bread dough. Her mood was surly. *Now that the robbers were gone things should be easier, but not now, thanks to Laura bringing all those children to the farm.*

On entering the kitchen, Clare asked, "where's Raoul?"

"He's feeding the animals," replied Martha, grouchily.

"Can I watch, please?" Giselle excitably asked.

"Don't be long," warned Martha, mixing her bread dough and trying to make porridge at the same time.

Giselle rushed out and sat in the barn, captivated by Raoul mixing the feed for the different animals. She followed him as he gave hay and grain to the goat, vegetables, grit and eggshells to the hens. Then he went into the pens, collecting the eggs. He continued feeding the rest of the animals, with Giselle at his heels.

Giselle was the last to sit at the table, excitably talking about the animals, in-between mouthfuls of porridge.

"Don't talk with your mouth full," Martha said glaring at Giselle.

She nodded her head, gulped the last drop of porridge from her spoon, jumped up and ran outside to the animal pens. The boys followed, running down the meadow and played by the Aswin river. During the afternoon, they wandered to the fields and watched Morgan repairing the fences.

227

When Sylviana had finished treating Clare, she sat in the family room, digesting everything Martha was doing in the kitchen, kneading her bread dough, and preparing the meals.

"Can I help?" Clare asked Martha.

"No, sit at the table."

"Why are you pressing the bread dough; what are the ingredients?"

Martha, irritated by Clare's constant questions about cooking, sent her outside. She walked down the meadow, drawn to the river that sparkled like a flint. She sat on the bank bored, contemplating. *This idyllic life isn't for the likes of us, we're in the way. Sylviana is so kind, perhaps she will show us how to live off the land, maybe we could build a shelter nearby.*

Laura hadn't shown herself since coming home, the children always looked in but they never had any response from Laura. Sylviana often sat holding Laura, enabling her to get a little rest, while still holding Anna, who hadn't shown any response to Laura's nursing.

‡

On their fourth day, as the children passed the kitchen, they saw Martha once again preparing her bread dough. With the extra mouths to feed, Martha was having to bake bread twice a day.

Clare leaned against the door jab, watching Martha, fascinated by the process of bread making. When Martha slipped into the pantry for a cup of salt, Claire Instead of asking permission found a bowl and picked the ingredients Martha has discarded. She threw them all into a bowl and mixed them together, trying to make a bread dough. Martha returned, eyed Clare and grimaced,

Clare sidled beside Martha, "I've prepared a bread mix, will you show me how to cook it?"

Martha agreed to bake Clare's dough in the bread oven. she dismissively said, "It will be ready for tonight's meal."

After eating, Giselle took Clare to the animal enclosures and told Clare Where Raoul kept the animal feed. How to mix the various ingredients, what the different animals ate and how much to give each animal.

Walter and the twins wandered around the farm observing Morgan cutting fence posts, and Raoul in the toolshed, cleaning the farm implements.

At supper, Clare sat fidgeting, drumming her fingers impatiently on the table, waiting for her bread to be served. Martha gave her the first slice. Clare took one bite and tried to eat it, but it was gooey, sticking to her teeth, it was tasteless.

With a sigh, Clare groaned, "what did I do wrong?" She had a tear of disappointment in her eyes.

Martha, touched by her desire to bake a loaf, said, "be in the kitchen at dawn, I will show you."

Sylviana broke Laura's concentration, "go to your mother's room and get a night's sleep, I'll stop with Anna."

"No! Anna is my responsibility, it's my fault . . ."

"It's not your fault, but I will stop with you tonight. Lie on the bed and wrap your arms around Anna; shut your eyes and rest. I will drape my arms around you both."

‡

On their fifth day at the farm, both sisters were up at dawn, Giselle ran outside to help Raoul who was feeding the pigs. She entered the chicken coop with the egg basket. Raoul raised his eyes a degree and carried on feeding the animals.

Giselle came skipping out with a beaming smile, "look, Snowball has laid two eggs!"

With a smile, Raoul asked, "who's Snowball?"

"There, sitting next to Dolly—silly."

In the kitchen, Martha was standing behind Clare with both pairs of hands in the bowl, showing her how to knead the dough.

"Now it's ready to bake, find your sister it's time to have our first meal of the day," said Martha.

While they were eating Raoul said, "I'm going to make a start digging over the top field for next year's crops, shouldn't take more than three to four days."

When they were outside, Walter tried to open the tool shed. The door was jammed; he pushed against it and entered. He came out with two shovels, giving one each to the twins, Dudley and Oake.

"Our sisters are starting to make themselves useful we should do the same. Go to Morgan in the top field, tell him you have come to help, don't come back until he does—understand?"

The twins nodded their heads, swaggered away, using the shovels as walking sticks, made their way to join Raoul.

Walter returned to the tool shed, picked a mallet, chisel, rip saw, and marking knife and joined Morgan, who was repairing fencing that the Nash gang had wilfully destroyed.

Early afternoon, Clare called Giselle and told her she had heard Martha talking to Raoul about their food shortage.

"Down the lane that leads to the main highway, growing in the hedgerow there are hawthorn berries, chestnuts and rosehips, there are still plenty of edible blackberries. Let's go and gather some," suggested Clare.

Giselle agreed, "I'll get the egg baskets."

Late afternoon Martha was in the kitchen preparing the supper when Clare and Giselle walked in with two baskets laden full of assorted berries they had picked.

"Will these be useful? They could be used to make pies and preserves," suggested Clare.

Martha turned; a look of warmth drifted across her face. Nodding her head and smiling brightly said, "that's a wonderful idea, thank you."

At supper, Martha asked Raoul, "how far have you got digging the field?"

"It's done!"

"What!" exclaimed Martha and Morgan together.

"Oake and Dudley came and helped me, four days' work done in one," looking at the twins, Raoul continued, "thanks!"

"Well Walter helped me, he's a fast learner and a natural carpenter," Morgan said.

Clare came out of the kitchen carrying her bread, cut it into slices and gave the first one to Martha.

She spread a portion of butter over the warm slice and nibbled a corner, "It's good."

The bread was quickly devoured.

Before they had finished their supper, there was a squeal from Laura's room. Everyone looked at each other, Clare buried her head deep into her folded arms resting on the table.

As everybody started to rise, Flora raised her hands, "let me go in first."

Flora slowly opened Laura's door, the candle had burned itself out, Flora, through the dimness of the room saw Laura's hands

231

trembling, she had lost her composure she had held for five days. The only noise was the soft sounds of teardrops littering the floor.

Flora took a gulp of air, quietly asked, "Laura, what is it?"

"Her eyes, they opened, she spoke, she spoke my name, Flora I've done it, she spoke."

She turned to face Flora, "she's alive, I can feel her heart beating stronger!" tears of joy streaming down her cheeks like a meandering river.

That night's supper turned into a party, Sylviana had made her famous cakes that afternoon, she fetched those out. Everybody retired to bed happy.

Martha said to Raoul, "that was nice of Clare and Giselle."

Raoul agreed.

Laura regained her composure and continued to sit with Anna.

‡

The next morning, Giselle was up before dawn, she skipped outside to prepare the animal feed. By the time Raoul arrived, she had fed the animals, collected the eggs, and placed them in the pantry.

"I've given nanny a brush, tomorrow I will change the chickens bedding," Giselle informed Raoul.

Raoul, in awe just nodded, and returned to the farmhouse for his food. In the kitchen, Clare had finished kneading the dough and placed it into the wall oven. She was now helping Martha prepare the porridge for everyone. In the family room, when Raoul entered, the twins Dudley and Oake asked if they could help him again. Walter was enthusiastically repairing the fencing when Morgan got there.

Raoul returned mid-afternoon, Martha said, "if the children are stopping for another twenty-four days, they should have a bedroom each, I have tidied five rooms upstairs."

Raoul looked out of the corner of his eye and nodded.

After they had eaten supper, Martha called all the children together. They were taken up a flight of creaking stairs along a short landing.

Martha said, "we have decided to give you a bedroom each. You can choose whichever one you want, no arguing, they are all the same."

Opening the doors, they looked inside each room. The wooden walls were chipped. A raggedy chair rested in one corner, a three-legged chair opposite, a small table beside the bed and a chest for storage.

Martha said, "they're not much but you have your own private rooms, for the time being. I'll leave you to settle in."

The children were as quiet as a mouse. Martha returned to the kitchen to clean the bowls when she heard the stairs groaning under running feet.

Clare ran into the kitchen throwing her arms around Martha, "we were overwhelmed, we didn't know what to say, no one has ever shown us kindness. We were a broken family only Anna bore any optimism. Saying thank you doesn't tell you how happy, grateful we all are."

Martha gave Clare a tender hug and kissed her forehead.

Anna was getting stronger by the hour.

‡

A week had passed since the siblings had arrived at the farm, Clare and Giselle decided to share a bedroom, as did the twins. They were both up long before the dawn broke the sky, Giselle heading for the animal pens, Clare entered the kitchen.

When Martha entered the kitchen, the day's bread was cooking in the wall oven, the first meal of the day, porridge was cooked to perfection. Everything was ready for the residents of the Lovet farm.

"Sit," commanded. "you have done so much for us, today I'm doing all the cooking."

Martha, without a word, sat. A few moments later everybody came in, Raoul and Morgan looked at Martha who raised her head, and with her eyes pointed at Clare in the kitchen.

Sylviana, looking at Martha mystified, "I don't understand, Clare has had nought education, yet after six days she is cooking—for everyone, how?"

"She's got a natural talent, I'm sure she would sleep in the kitchen if I put a bed in there," beamed Martha.

Clare insisted on carrying all the bowls and laid them on the table, each one decorated with blackberries.

Martha folded her arms, "what's this?"

"The blackberries add a little flavour to the porridge, try it," replies Clare.

Jayden was the first to try a spoonful, "mother, it's tasty."

Raoul hesitantly eyed Martha, "it's as good as yours."

Stop being tactful, "it's better than mine!"

Sylviana ran her teeth along her lemon tongue, "you've also put a pinch of cinnamon in the mix." She kissed Clare on the cheek, "thank you for a delicious meal."

Clare felt a thud of achievement when everyone nodded their approval.

Raoul lifted himself up to dig over the middle field; the twins followed. Walter walked out with Morgan to help to repair the fences.

That night, when the children were in bed, Martha took hold of Raoul's hand, and in a dreamlike voice said, "it's nice to have the farm brimming with activity."

Raoul smiled.

‡

The following evening everybody was in the great room. Walter and the twins were playing a dice game. Giselle was drawing pictures of the hens, Clare was still in the pantry, inspecting and smelling all the herbs and spices.

Martha called Clare, and said to all the siblings, "you have settled in remarkably well, and we appreciate your help around the farm. From today you will stop working, I am not having children working as slaves! You can do as you please, go out and play."

"But I want to learn how to cook!" protested Clare.

"No, you're only a child, do as you are told!"

"Please, the monster always threw me out, please I want to cook, please."

"You can help once a week, no more; that applies to you Giselle and the boys."

Giselle ran to Clare, "Snowball and Dolly will miss me."

Clare, her eyes wide and tearful, looked at Martha.

"Don't look at me like that, you will do what I tell you."

"Please," she cried, "I can't read or write, I never will, I can learn to cook—please."

"You're in my house, don't argue with me."

"But . . ."

"No, I already have one stubborn dau . . ."

There was an awkward silence, Martha was breathing rapidly, all eyes turned towards her.

The silence was broken by Giselle, who innocently asked, "do you want to be our mother?"

Martha half turned and stumbled to leave the family room.

Raoul caught Martha's arm and said, "answer Giselle."

Martha just stared at the floor like a naughty child.

Raoul stood and took Martha in his arms, whispered into her ear, "me too."

Martha, looking at the bewildered faces, swallowed hard and whispered, "yes."

Giselle took Martha's hand and placed her head on it, with a warmth in her voice said, "mother."

The twins, without consulting Walter made their way to Martha.

Raoul approached Walter and placed his hand on his shoulder, "we want to be your parents—if you agree?"

Walter nodded his head, looking at Clare replied, "She is speaking for all of us, our life, it has a purpose now."

Martha freed herself from Giselle and the twins and went over to Clare, who was still standing alone—crying.

Martha took both of Clare's hands, "Clare are you . . ."

Clare looked up, her eyes begging forgiveness, "I'm sorry—I'm so sorry I argued with you, you have taken us in, done everything for us, I'm so ashamed. Laura dragged us from the gutter, you have given us a taste of heaven."

Martha ran her hands through Clare's hair "you are like Laura in many ways if you hadn't argued, I may never have let my feelings for you show."

"I never had the chance to learn, just thrown out at dawn, now I have this ache. I want to learn, to create something with my hands, I love cooking." Looking up, biting her bottom lip, she asked, "did you mean it?"

Martha knelt, hugged and reassured Clare, "more than anything else in this world. If you want to learn, then I will teach you everything I know, all day long if that's what you want."

Giselle hugged Martha, "what shall I call you?"

"I don't know, I'm not your birth mother, perhaps Martha."

Giselle said, "I would like to call you mother!"

The other children crowded around Martha, who was glowing.

Gavin turned to Sylviana, "you don't look surprised, did you know how Martha felt?"

"Yes, and I didn't need my elf perception to see how Martha started caring for the children. She was trying so hard to distance herself from them and not get attached. Teaching Clare, she finally let go. I was watching when she was helping Clare to mix bread dough. As Martha spoke, Clare looked up at her with a sparkle in her eyes, Martha returned the look. Standing behind Clare mixing the ingredients, they were almost in an embrace, Martha stood that way much longer than needed. After that, she would often touch the children on the shoulder as they passed, or ushering them to bed."

Speaking in a louder voice said, "She supposes they are working through a sense of duty; she cannot see they are beginning a more fulfilling life. Yesterday I was watching Giselle cleaning out the pigsty—she was enjoying it!"

Martha, looking at Sylviana relented, "if working gives you pleasure, then you can all carry on!"

Anna could now sit up and looked forward to visits from her siblings. Flora restricted the visits to twice a day.

‡

After nine days, Anna was improving enough for Laura to leave her for long periods. The smell of bread and porridge drifted into her room, so Laura decided to get something to eat. She walked into the family room and looked puzzled at seeing her mother sitting at the table. Her head tilted sideward when Clare came from the kitchen carrying food for everyone.

Clare, smiled warmly at Laura, cast aside the food she was carrying onto the table and rushed over to greet her.

Martha leapt to her feet, caught Clare's arm and whispered in her ear, "I must speak to Laura."

Taking Laura's hand, Martha said, "before you eat, come outside, I need to tell you something."

Martha motioned to Flora and Sylviana to give them a few minutes, then join them at the outdoor bench.

Martha sat Laura on the blackened and flaking bench they had in the farmyard. She told her that Clare was learning to cook and Walter woodworking. Giselle caring for the animals, and the twins working as farmhands. As Martha told her this, Laura was having trouble taking it in, she sat there, tongue-tied.

"Now I have something important to tell you," taking Laura's hands, and a deep breath, "I told the children, that—I will be their—mother."

Laura looked wide-eyed at her mother and gushed, "I have three brothers and three sisters?"

". . . Yes."

Sylviana and Flora joined them as Martha and Laura were hugging each other.

Sylviana, sitting next to Laura asked, "why didn't you bring your weapon down on that creature Zee when she was defeated?"

Laura half closed her eyes, looking at the floor said, "as I jumped onto her, our eyes crossed, I saw—I saw so much in that instant. Who she was, a girl a few years older than me. She used to be tormented for her beauty. Something inside her happened, now she hates every child my age, I saw—I felt her pain, I felt everything. It startled me; it was so scary."

Sylviana cast a glance at Flora, which didn't go unnoticed by Martha.

"What is it; What's wrong?" asked Martha.

Flora's eyes flashed wide, "Laura has not only taken my healing ability but has absorbed elves perception." Flora looked at her fingers. "I feel naked without my healing ability but I'm glad you learn to harness the power; I couldn't have done any more than what you accomplished."

Sylviana placed a hand on Flora's shoulder, "Jayden told me Laura experienced a crystal dream about Clare walking to her grave." She looked at Laura said, "you will never again be like others, you are special. Jayden my son is half-elf by birth, Laura is truly half-elf by transference," remarked Sylviana.

They all sat silent, allowing Laura to absorb Flora's and Sylviana's words.

"I'll be glad when everything is back to normal, I miss my lessons with Morgan."

"Morgan won't be teaching you again, he has taught you everything he can." Flora, taking Laura's hand continued, "I will take your class from now on, I will be teaching you—and Jayden. You did a remarkable act in saving Anna's life, but you need more instruction on using the healing power. Your elfin perception came to you when you were emotional, you also need guidance. I will continue teaching you wolf language. Jayden also has magic running through his veins; he needs to learn how to harness his ability."

Laura puffed her cheeks out, "that sounds like a lot."

"Yes, but you're both intelligent and quick learners, you will no doubt bounce work off each other."

As they turned to return to the farmhouse Walter and Morgan came by.

Laura waved and shouted, "hello brother."

Walter came over to Laura, hugged her and said, "thank you."

During the following days, Clare would prepare food for Anna, and hand feed her three times every day until she was well enough to eat unaided.

Chapter 23

The green-eyed Elf.

In the great room, Martha, sitting by Clare, said, "two weeks, and not only have you learnt everything I know but started to improve my recipes by adding a little extra ingredient turning them into your own creations." Wrapping her arm around Clare's waist, she continued, "maybe Sylviana will show you some of her recipes for you to learn."

Sylviana, who was making outfits for Anna and Giselle asked Clare, "Is there anything particular you want to learn?"

"Yes, your special cakes, everyone loves them."

Sylviana looked into the air, "that is the most difficult recipe I know, let's try something easier."

"No, it's your cakes I want to learn first."

"But they're too difficult for you, try something else."

"Please, cakes first."

Martha mumbles under her breath but loud enough for everyone to hear, "stubborn, just like her sister!"

Both Clare and Sylviana smiled, Laura who was helping Sylviana exhaled a sigh.

"All right, tomorrow afternoon, be prepared to struggle," said Sylviana.

Next afternoon, far from struggling, Clare's first cakes were palatable. With the ingredients and recipe in her head, Clare persisted at every opportunity. Over the next ten days the fresh smell of cakes cooking wrapped around the farmhouse. Every day they all enjoyed tasting a new flavoured cake.

Now all the fields were prepared for next year's crops, Walter and Morgan had started to repair the damage that the robbers had done to the farmhouse. They had carved their initials into every piece of wood, all the chairs and tables around the farmhouse. All the doors, wood panels and beams had knife incisions. Slowly, one by one every door was replaced. Mingled in with the fragrant smell of Clare's cooking was the aroma of freshly cut wood creeping into everyone's noses.

"Why can't I get it right," complained Clare to Sylviana.

"Clare, your cakes are excellent, I cheat I use my elf gift for the final touch."

"That's not fair."

Clare stomped back into the kitchen to try again.

‡

It was early evening, twenty-seven days since the children had arrived at the farm. The daylight had faded; Raoul, Martha, Laura with the six children were sitting in the great room. It was roasting warm with the sounds of the crackling fire. Laura was showing Clare simplified ideas for keeping records of her recipes, using drawings and a single letter.

Laura said, "by illustrating your ingredients with this method you could learn your letters."

"Do you truly believe I could?"

"Yes . . ."

They were interrupted by an unexpected rap-a-tap-tap on the main door, Laura jumped to her feet with a worried look.

Martha gave Raoul an anguished look saying, "it was robbers last time we had visitors this late."

"Laura, go to the passage, if it's trouble, fetch the elves."

Raoul slid open the peephole on the door, "Its captain Ives," he announces.

Opening the door, he observed Ely and Pete behind Ives. Martha with Laura, Clare and Giselle came out to greet them.

"I have important news; is there anywhere we can stable our horses?" asked Ives.

"I'll take them," interrupted Giselle, reaching out to take the reins.

"I don't think so," said Ives, pulling the reins away from Giselle.

Laura said, "I'll take those."

Ives gladly handed the reins to Laura, who promptly passed them to Giselle; she confidently led the three horses to the shed.

Ives' eyes narrowed, "what do you think you are doing, giving our horses—to her."

Laura, with a cheeky smile, shouted after Giselle, "don't forget to feed and water them!"

Giselle looked back, and in an indignant tone replied, "I know what I'm doing."

The three guards stood staring after Giselle.

Martha said, "Giselle looks after all the animals on the farm, come in."

As they entered, Ives paused and stood running his fingers around the door's ornate lines, while trying to gauge the thickness of the two sliding iron bars running across and the one that sunk into the lintel.

"I see you have replaced your door since those robbers broke in. It's a solidly built. I like the reinforced iron grating, that peephole is a clever extra, did you design and build it?" Ives asked Raoul.

"Walter made it; he has a natural talent with wood. I design and mark the measurements, tell him what needs doing, he makes it."

"That is remarkable," replied Ives as he followed Pete and Ely into the family room.

Martha moved into the kitchen, "sit down, I'll fetch you some food, then you can tell us why you're here?"

Pete responded, "thanks we haven't eaten since this morning."

Martha returned with bread, homemade jam, cakes biscuits and raspberry flavoured water.

"That looks mouth-wateringly good," said Ives licking his lips.

"This is good," said Pete wiping his mouth with his dirty bandana.

"I have tasted nothing like this in my life," Ely gasped in glee, snatching the last cake.

"Everything here is outstanding, you are the best cook I have ever met," said Ives.

Martha replied, "Clare made everything you ate."

Ives threw his head back and started laughing, "that was so funny."

"Remember your desk," said Laura pointedly.

Ives, speechless stood pointed at Clare said, "she, did this," waving his hand over the now empty table.

"Yes," everyone shouted.

Ives sat down with a jolt.

Giselle walked in saying, "I have fed Mr Ted, Ben and Mary. Gave them water and brushed them."

Frowning at the three guards continued, "It would be nice if you brushed them occasionally!""

Ives plonked his elbows on the table, put his head in his hands and scratched his hair. After composing himself he looked around and counted the children.

Standing up, in his official voice said, "now all the Roth children are here, I am sorry to tell you—your father is dead. He drowned in the river Ner eight days ago!"

Ives paused, rubbing the back of his hand, waiting for a reaction, the children stared blankly at him. "He came out of the tavern, staggered the wrong way home, and fell in. The hut you lived in, is now yours, you can return to the village to claim your property, and live there."

Anna threw herself at Laura screaming, "nooooooo don't send me away, please."

Clare and Giselle were each gripping Martha's arms shivering, Walter began edging along the wall, while the twins with the palms of their hands pressed against the wall looked pleadingly at Raoul.

Martha gave Ives a daggering scowl, "how dare you come in here upsetting my children."

"I am duty bound to tell you . . ."

"Don't you use that tone of voice here, look at the poor souls, does that answer your question?"

Laura walked over and stood in front of Ives, hands on hips, "choose your next words with care."

Ives' gulped, his voice softened, childlike, reassuring the children, "I have not come here to take you away."

Glancing across at Martha he continued, "you will stop here for as long as you wish."

Raoul spoke, "did you hear—you are not going anywhere—ever, now it's time for you to go to bed."

Anna wrapped herself around Raoul's leg and sighed, "thank you—daddy."

Clare pulled at Martha's sleeve and whispered into her ear.

"Yes, that's a wonderful idea, now go to bed."

After all the children had gone to their rooms, Ives said, "you have done a wonderful thing, adopting those youngsters; would you like to make it legal?"

Martha's face paled, "I thought, without parents, we could take them in?"

"Yes, that happens in many rural villages, but, if you wish, if they wish it, they could legally take your name. I'm going to see the carpenter in Ecrind, I would be happy to see the adoption agency, confirm their father is dead, I can arrange everything."

"We must speak to the children tomorrow morning."

Ives grinned, "from what I just witnessed, their hearts are full of love for you."

"Thanks, Laura has made you three beds in our annexe, it's basic but clean and warm, Laura will show you the way," Martha replied.

Next morning the aroma of freshly baked bread and sweet apple pie awakened the three guards, the scent floated around the farmhouse. They were drawn to the kitchen where Clare presented them with three steaming hot bowls of porridge decorated with slices of quince.

Ives, putting his hand onto the back of Clare's hand said, "they are lucky to have you and your siblings here."

246

Clare hesitated, lost in thoughts of what she had left behind and what life in the future held. "No—we are the lucky ones. Each day is the best day of my life. Thanks to Laura."

Later, in the family room, Ives turned to Raoul, "we were travelling on to see the carpenter in Ecrind to commission four new doors for the garrison. Would you be interested in making four for us? I will pay you seven silver coins if you and Walter are interested."

Martha, gripping Raoul's arm said, "that's amazing just think what we could . . ."

Clare came briskly into the room saying, "thirteen coins, my brother will make them for thirteen coins each."

Ives caught off guard looked left, right?

Clare continued, "I heard you talking to Pete, you said his work was poor quality, Walters work is superior."

Martha went to speak, Laura pulled hard at her sleeve and put a finger to her lips.

Ives, somewhat flustered said, "eight."

"Do you want good strong doors with the iron grating? Twelve coins."

Ives turned and looked at Martha, who flipped her hands out pointing towards the ceiling.

"Shall we say nine silver coins," retorted Ives.

"Do you want that secret peephole with those tiny bars? Eleven coins."

"Can we agree on ten silver coins for each door?" asked Ives.

"Agreed," said Clare, folding her arms.

Clare stepped across the room to Raoul and asked, "how long will it take to make the doors?"

Raoul, tapping his fingers on the table said, "it will take about twenty days."

Clare turned to Ives, "to be sure they're completed, send someone to collect the doors in twenty-two days.

Clare and Martha enter the kitchen and returned with two sacks containing freshly cooked cakes, biscuits and apple pies.

"Could you give these sacks of food to the villagers? Last night Clare asked me if she could cook an assortment of cakes and biscuits for the villagers, in appreciation of the food they used to give them," disclosed Martha. "Clare was up and cooking well before sunrise, and don't worry, here's another three travelling bags—one each."

On his way out, Ives again run his hands over the door, admiring the craftsmanship. He gave Raoul the measurements for the garrison doors.

Giselle led the three horses across the farmyard and said, "they have been fed, had a drink and I gave them a brush this morning."

Ives, smiling said, "thanks, we promise to brush them every week."

As they prepared to leave, Ives informed Raoul, "in twenty-two days I will send a guard, with the forty silver coins for the doors."

Ives and Pete had the village food, Ives hung the three bags around his neck, so the aroma will follow me on the way home he said.

After the guards had gone, Clare, chewing her nails asked, "is ten silver coins for each door a good deal?"

"Every year we sell our excess crops in Ecrind, we make four silver coins a year," Martha replied.

Seeing Clare's puzzled look Martha continued, "it would take us ten years to earn what those four doors will make. How did you learn to barter so well? Which was remarkable considering you had no idea how much the coins were worth."

"I watched the men barter in the village square, one would start low the other high, they always met in the middle, both thinking they had outwitted the other."

‡

When the guards reached the village of Drewcott, Ives told Pete and Ely to ride up the main track and call the villagers out to the main square. When Ives was certain most of the villagers were present, he sliced open the sacks of cakes, pies and biscuits and told everybody to help themselves.

"What's this about?" queried Farrar the blacksmith, the first one to bite into one of the cakes. "That is the most succulent cake I have ever tasted," he declared.

Soon hands were flying into the bags snatching at the contents, they were all empty within minutes.

"Where did you get them from; Why us?" exclaimed the villagers.

Ives revealed that Clare Roth had cooked everything in appreciation of their help.

"The children have been adopted and are now living at the Lovet farm. That ragamuffin girl you knew, made them herself—I saw it with my own eyes," insisted Ives. "Clare has scrubbed up well and looks a different person."

‡

The children had been at the farm for thirty-six days.

Clare's cooking was growing from strength to strength. She was refining her tastes and instinctively knew what proportions to use

249

in her recipes. They could hear her stamping her feet when a new recipe wasn't as flavoursome as expected.

Giselle was now caretaker of the animals on the farm, she had given every animal its own name. Raoul had overseen Giselle for a few days but realised she had an uncanny ability.

Anna was growing a collection of flowers in two long boxes that Walter had constructed and placed either side of the farmhouse door. When she wasn't gardening, she was often seen riding her friend Trinity.

Morgan and Gavin, with the help of Dudley and Oake, were building a bridge across the Aswin River using the yearning edge rock as a centre support. When completed the unicorns would live near the elves enclave, providing the wolves agreed not to use them as a new food supply.

‡

It was the first week of December, the first snowfall, everything had a dusting of white powder. Everybody was gathered for the midday meal; Clare entered the room with a bowl of small ring-shaped rolls of bread.

"What's this?" said Sylviana, who prided herself as a cook.

Martha replied, "Its Clare's idea, individual bread portions, no need to cut, just help yourselves to a piece."

Clare then presented a bowl of cakes, offering the first to Sylviana.

Sylviana took a bite, her eyes shut tight, with crumbs dropping from her mouth said, "How?"

"They're as good as yours," said Gavin.

"Told you she was stubborn," said Martha enjoying her cake.

The second week of December, everybody was sitting in the family room when Clare came in and presented another bowl of her creations.

Sylviana, after eating one of Clare's cakes thumped the table making everyone jump, "stop it!" she cried out, "bettering an elf at cooking is unacceptable."

Everybody laughed, then applauded Clare, Morgan stamped his feet in appreciation.

Sylviana put her arms around Clare, smiled and gave her a loving hug said, "perhaps you could teach me some of your new recipes."

Martha chipped in, "tomorrow you can teach both of us."

Clare, her face flushed and anxious ran over to Laura, tried to talk but was speechless.

Laura, resting her forehead onto Clare's whispered, "you can do it, just tell them to watch as you prepare your dish. I have watched you cooking, you are extremely fast, just do everything slow. It's a great honour for a human to teach an elf."

Clare shook her head with a soft smile.

Laura looked up and said, "she would be delighted to teach you."

"The guards will arrive in two days to collect their doors," said Martha chomping on one of Clare's cakes. "are they finished?"

"We finished them this morning, come and see for yourselves," answered Raoul.

Everybody entered the shed which had been converted to a workshop for the doors.

"They're better than ours," complained Martha.

Two days later, late afternoon a tapping on the door, it was Ely with a horse and cart, and Pete on his horse.

Ely placed forty silver coins on the table, "payment for the doors." He then lay seven scrolls next to the coins, "the adoption papers, one for each child, and a master copy for yourself. Once signed you are their legal parents. Ives told me to take the papers to the agency in Ecrind if you sign them."

Raoul sat at the table and immediately signed each scroll; Martha lay a cross next to Raoul's signature.

Clare ran her arm across her eyes, looked at Laura, "tears of joy, they're tears of joy."

Pete surprised everybody by slapping twenty bronze coins on the table, with a roll of cloth.

"What's that for?" exclaimed Martha, examining the cloth.

"The villagers want Clare to send more cakes and biscuits, they send this money and goods as payment," explained Pete.

"I don't know," a stunned Martha said.

"Yes, I'll do it, two sacks, one of fruit pies, the other full of rings of heaven by tomorrow morning," said Clare, pushing the coins towards Martha.

Martha scratched the side of her head, "what are rings of heaven?"

"I decided it's time to name my creations, these cakes, my latest are named after; my family, my home."

Martha, tears brimmed on her bottom eyelid, placing both her hands onto Clare's shoulder said, "I will help you this time, and don't you argue."

Next morning, they loaded the ornate and heavy doors onto the cart.

Pete took the sacks of cakes, saying, "I must ride ahead, the villagers told me to make haste."

Back in the farmhouse, Raoul gave ten silver coins to Walter, Martha gave the bronze coins to Clare. Walter, with a look of disquiet, grabbed Clare's arm and yanked her to a corner in the room. Martha, Raoul and Laura watched in wonder as Walter and Clare spoke in hushed voices, Walter had his hands on his head, Clare stood with her arms folded. After a few moments of discussion, Clare, with Walter following behind walked determinedly back and slammed the coins onto the table.

"We want none of this money, it's yours," insisted Clare.

Raoul said, "you did the . . ."

"No," snapped Clare, "we don't want it—any of it, we just want to live here—forever."

Martha opened her mouth to talk, Laura grabbed her hand and shook her head.

"Let's sit and talk," suggested Laura, pulling out a chair and sitting.

"We want you to have the money, it means nothing to us, if it wasn't for you," looking at Laura, "I would be . . . it's like waking up in heaven, every day," Clare blurted out as soon as she sat.

"I can travel to Ecrind to buy goods we need," said Raoul, "while I'm there I will buy you new clothes."

Clare shaking with clenched fists sobbed, "no, it's for you."

Laura put her arm around Clare and pressed their cheeks soothingly together. "sister . . ."

"No, we don't want anything."

Laura placed two fingers over Clare's mouth, "sister, where did the clothes you and I wear come from; your sibling clothes, our parent's clothes?

"Martha made most of them, sometimes Sylviana helped."

"And how hard does mother work to keep us all clothed?"

Clare looked a little confused, "she works every night sewing." A flicker of ruth danced across her eyes, "the money . . ."

"What if mother and father travel to Ecrind to buy you, me and everybody new clothes?"

Clare put her arms around Laura and nodded her head. "Then she wouldn't have to work every night; yes."

"Peas in a pod, both stubborn," observed Martha.

"That's settled, you both go to Ecrind, buy your goods and clothes for everyone," said Laura.

"It's a long walk to Ecrind, Raoul goes alone," replied Martha.

Laura rubbed her mouth with her hand, raising her eyes, "have you enough money to buy a horse and cart?"

Raoul pondered, "the cost is around eighteen silver coins."

"That's settled, tomorrow we'll walk to Ecrind and ride back in style, we have always wanted a horse and cart," said Martha.

Next morning Clare gave Raoul a basket full of pies, bread, cakes, biscuits and raspberry flavoured water.

Martha smiling said, "we won't starve, that's for sure."

"Don't forget Morgan and Jayden will be stopping here whilst we are away, they should be here soon, the elves are only across the . . ."

"Stop worrying," said Laura.

"Don't forget to buy yourselves nice clothes," yelled Clare as they walked across the farmyard to the dirt track.

Chapter 24

The Returning Enemy.

Inside the farmhouse, Laura told Clare. "I'm going to the bathhouse before Morgan and Jayden arrive."

High in the treetops of the Catacomb forest, Zee was watching with renewed interest of the goings on at the farm. For forty-nine days Zee had been waiting for an opportunity to attack her mortal enemy, Laura. She had been grinding hers, and the claws of the imps every day, watching and waiting. Arriving at the edge of the forest she had ordered the imps to spy on the farm and watch the elves across the river.

"The elders have walked away leaving those succulent children alone. The elves are far away on the other side of the river; we will surround the house and you will feast on their flesh and bones. I will drink their blood and take their spirits," laughed Zee.

Stroking Tad, "you were cunning finding out that the wolf-beast had gone to the mountains looking for a mate. You're the only one to hold your name, my strong and favourite imp."

"Look, mistress, that witch girl is going to that washroom—alone," shouted one of the excited imps.

As Laura walked across the farmyard, to take a bath, Zee's black eyes glistened, her mouth parted into a grin exposing a set of barbed fangs.

"The wait is over; the witch is trapped inside that building without a weapon." Saliva dribbled out of her mouth, "we kill that witch girl first, follow me," snarled Zee.

Laura entered the bathhouse, undressed and lay soaking in the bath.

Zee, like a widow spider, crawled down the tree head first, her gangling limbs, fanlike spread around the trunk. Her body like a crustacean creaked with every movement. The different elixirs she filled her body with neither helped nor improved the likelihood of her former beauty been restored.

She called to the imps, "follow me."

On the ground Zee crawled along like a predator after its prey, unable to stand up straight. She stealthfully weaved a passage across the farmyard, scratching her claws on the cobbles as she made her way to the bathhouse, with her ten imps following.

Laura feeling exhilarated and tingly clean sat on the stool tying her boots. Zee quietly pushed the door open and crept into the bathhouse.

Turning to two imps, "keep that door shut, and keep guard," she hissed.

As the door swung shut, it grated on the stone floor, Laura turned and saw Zee. She jumped backwards knocking the stool over, her rope dropped into a coiled heap. Zee was advancing rapidly towards Laura, on all fours, surrounded by her imps. Laura looked around for a weapon, nothing, she stepped back. With a high-toned cackle, Zee sprang, with her clawed hands reaching out for Laura's neck.

Laura was caught off guard, she swung her hands up, grabbing Zee's wrists moments before the claws struck her neck. Zee's feet landed on Laura's stomach, where she tried to force her claws closer. Laura gulped air; she felt the needle-like pins nicking into her neck.

Laura was losing, Zee the stronger was forcing Laura's hands back. Laura, putting every ounce of strength into her right hand forced the clawed hand away. When it was away from her neck she let go, and, with the free hand grabbed Zee's other hands claws.

Zee's free claw struck Laura in the right cheek, sinking into the skin, then dragging it down tearing the flesh. Laura screamed out in agony as she grips two of Zee's fingers pulling them back, hoping to break her fingers, instead, the bony fingers snapped off.

Laura fell onto her back with another cry of pain, holding her cheek to stem the flow of blood. Zee fell backwards with a hideous squeal, staring at her hand with only one claw and blood spouting out where two used to be.

Morgan and Jayden had just arrived at the farm, ran towards the bathhouse when they heard the ear-splitting cries.

They both sat up, their feet nearly touching, gazing at each other, Laura with two of Zee's fingers, still wearing the blueberry rings.

"Kill her now," cried out Zee.

One imp took a running dive at Laura, imitating Zees' lunge.

Laura passed one of Zee's fingers over to the other hand. As the imp landed on her, she stabbed it in the side of the neck, both sides. It gave one gasp and collapsed onto the floor with the fingers sticking out of its neck.

More imps were surrounding Laura, one approached from the side. Laura grabbed the stool leg and swung the stool at the imp sending it crashing into the wall.

The two imps standing guard by the door had moved towards Laura as Morgan burst through the door. His eyes dart around, surveying the scene, like a theatre of battle with Laura the centre of attention. He grabs one imp by the legs and swings it into the door frame as Jayden came running in.

Morgan ran towards Laura and swung his foot at Zee's face. She moved sideward, dodging the boot and lashed out her claws gashing his leg, from above his knee to his ankle, he cried out as he slumps to his knees. Zee rolled onto her side and tried to dig her claws into his face.

Before the claws hit its target, she felt her body jerk away. Shooting her eyes back, she saw Jayden had gripped her foot and was pulling her. Zee turned on her side brought her free leg up, and smashed it into Jayden's face, smashing it into his nose. He rolled over with a squeal, holding his nose.

Two imps dived at him, and stuck their claws into his body, he rolled himself into a ball as the two imps danced over his body slicing their claws into his back.

Zee on all fours snaked towards Laura, Morgan grabs her legs, Zee distracted, turns to swing her lethal claws at Morgan.

Laura, grabbing her rope in each hand leaps onto Zee's back and wrapped it around Zee's neck, hauling her away from Morgan.

An excruciating pain in her shoulders. An imp had impaled itself on Laura's back. She howls out from the pain; the imp dragged his claws down her back. Blood poured out of the wounds, beads of sweat ran down her face. Still holding the rope as she slides backwards onto the imp, killing it.

Two imps jump on top of Morgan, seizing the arm of one he used it as a staff to buffer the other one, killing both.

The children hearing the commotion, arrive at the door.

"Help them," Clare shouts to the boys. Grabbing Giselle and Anna's hands, she pulled them away; telling her sisters, "go to the river and call the elves."

The twins grabbed the legs of the pair of imps attacking Jayden and looked at each other, they swung the imps around cracking the heads of the imps together.

Zee, on her back, was trying to free herself using her claws to sever the rope. Laura on her back, had her feet locked on Zee's shoulders. She looked around for the stool, the only possible weapon.

A strand of the rope broke, Laura and Morgan looked at each other, Laura's eyes darted towards the stool as another strand was severed.

Zee followed Laura's eyes, "you won't get to it in time. I'm going to rip your heart out, take your soul and feed your bones to my imps."

Laura, blood flowing from her cheeks and seeping from her back was drained and panting.

She cries out, "Morgan, she's right, I won't get to the stool in time."

Walter grabbed the legs of the imp attacking Morgan, swung it into the air and smashed it into the ground.

The rope splits, sending Laura crashing backwards, the back of her head hits the floor with a bump, causing her eyes to flash. She shuts them, blindly reaching out for the stool.

Laura hears a gasp as Zee's limp body falls across her own. Forcing her sticky eyes open saw that Clare was straddled across Zee, holding a bread knife she had thrust into her heart.

Gavin arrived first, and helped Morgan to his feet, Sylviana next entered and went over to Jayden. Flora followed, rushed past everybody towards Laura, who was still lying under part of Zee's body.

Laura put her blood-soaked hand up and pointed a bleeding finger at Clare. She was still lying across Zee's body, taking in long deep gasps of air through her nose. As injured as everyone was, Laura realised the distress of what she had done would affect her mental state more than the physical wounds of everyone else.

Flora one by one removed Clare's fingers from the knife, slid her hands under Clare through a pool of blood and tenderly lifted her away from Zee's body.

Clare instinctively wrapped her arms around Flora's neck, Flora took Laura's hand and pulled her to her feet. limping away from Zee's body a single teardrop rolled down Laura's cheek.

When everyone had left the bathhouse, one imp silently sneaks out the door and creeps into the forest back to the labyrinth. It had two dimples on the top of its head.

Back in the farmhouse, Sylviana directs everybody towards the great room, where the injured could be treated.

"Burn it to the ground—now, we'll build a new one when we are well," Morgan gasped to Gavin.

Gavin, with Walter, and the twins dug a trench around the bathhouse; their hands were stinging with the chilly weather.

When it was set alight, the sounds of crackling woods and sparks flying were heard in the farmhouse. Gavin, Walter and the twins warmed their hands against the dancing flames that lit up the gloomy skies. It took all day to burn to the ground; it smouldered throughout the night.

Next morning nothing remained of the bathhouse and its contents, except for ashes and bones. Gavin and Walter took the remains to the Aswin river where they were washed away.

Although in pain herself, Laura sat with Clare most of the day. Laura was at hand to put her arms around her whenever her head dropped and tears fell. She helped Sylviana tending Morgan's gash and Jayden's broken nose.

After supper, Laura pulled Clare close, and softly whispered, "sister, sleep in my room tonight?"

Clare shut her eyes and nodded her head; Laura's healing power was helping Clare come to terms with her act.

Gavin called everybody together after the children had gone to bed.

Gavin said to Sylviana, "there's a small brook running by the crop fields, we divert it towards the annexe. We then convert it into an indoor bathhouse, you could create a range of elfin warming rocks."

"Yes, with three, maybe four private rooms, now Martha and Raoul have an extended family."

Next morning Clare came into the kitchen looking refreshed and ready to cook.

Sylviana, placing her hands on her shoulders said, "no cooking today, I'm doing it—no arguments, go and spend the day with Laura."

Dropping her head, "Laura is too intelligent to want to spend time with me."

Sylviana replied, "Laura doesn't think like that, you are sisters, she loves you and your brothers and sisters with all her heart."

Flora took Laura into the family room, "you look terrible is it your injuries?"

"No, I'm controlling the healing and pain, its . . . last night Clare was having a nightmare—I took it—it kept recurring. She goes into the kitchen, selects the sharpest knife and runs to the bathhouse. Dashing through the door towards Zee takes a flying leap onto her body and plunges the knife into her heart. Over and over."

"Is this healing ability a blessing or a curse?"

Taking Laura into her arms, "It's both, you helped Clare recover, she's not as strong as you." Stroking her hair, "removing a nightmare is something I have never done."

Clare came running into the family room, "no cooking today, I'm having a day off!"

Laura's eyes lit up, grabbing Clare's hand, "come sister I will show you where the wolves live."

As they ran past the kitchen, Sylviana caught Clare's eyes and smiled.

Chapter 25

Epilogue.

Today, the twenty-first of March Laura is twelve years old.
Laura walked out of the new bathhouse warm and bearing a
Smile; she pauses to take in the smell of new wood mingling
with the aroma of freshly baked bread.

She casts her mind back to the time Martha and Raoul returned
from Ecrind, on their new horse and cart. They gave everyone
three sets of clothes. When Martha told Clare, she had a special
present and pulled a large chest off the cart, Laura with a half-
moon smile remembered Clare's scowling face morphing to elation
when she saw all the cooking utensils, spices and herb plants.
Martha saying Anna can grow the plants in her flower garden. She
had tears streaming down her face. She looked at everyone, I'm
crying tears of joy.

Then the news, they had an order for a large table with twelve
chairs worth thirty-five silver coins. The same merchant also
wanted two new doors. Ives had been to Ecrind boasting about his
new doors, and the master craftsman, Walter.

Smiling she continues to the great room where everyone is waiting.

Running her fingers along their new table announcing, "this is the
best birthday ever. Summer is approaching we should cross the
new bridge and spend one day every week having a picnic."

Everybody nods in approval.

"Can my friend Trinity come?" asked Anna.

"They can all come, along with Kylo his mate and parents."

263

"This year you told us not to give you any birthday gifts," Martha said, looking over at Sylviana.

"You have got one present," said Sylviana. "When my brother last visited, he told me the Elvin council wanted to give you a gift for your part in preventing bloodshed between elves; he's waiting outside with it."

Jayden took Laura's hand, "you will like this."

They all followed behind Laura and Jayden, Gavin muttered, "all his life Jayden has longed for a friend."

Flora whispered back, "we all know where that friendship is going, three, four years they won't be holding hands as friends."

Laura opened the door. With arms raised, palms pointing out, lips opening and shutting in a hushed voice, "that's for me?"

Stood there was one of the finest white yearlings from the stables of Elfield.

Laura dropping her arms said, "do I have to learn horse language now?"

Printed in Poland
by Amazon Fulfillment
Poland Sp. z o.o., Wrocław

59555474R00152